ELSIE AND ELSA

Books by Ronn Perea

How I Got My Kicks on Route 66
(aka Smiles Giggles and Laughs)

Email Tango

ELSIE AND ELSA

Ronn Perea

SPEAKING VOLUMES, LLC
NAPLES, FLORIDA
2019

ELSIE AND ELSA

ISBN 978-1-62815-744-4

With love to
Julian, Elsie and Rose

Who else? They would never guess that the life experiences, inspiration and stories they told me as a snot-nose kid would end up in black-and-white. It is as if this novel was meant to be written before I could even write my name.

Acknowledgments

Peggy Herrington, my editor, also offered motivation, guidance, and literary services during the years it took me to craft the storyline. I am especially grateful for her assistance in linking the varied unrelated historical events in the story.

Melinda Barlass was there for me during the early years of initial storyline development. She kicked me in the butt where necessary.

Royeal Dee Jones, what can I say about this literary sharpshooter? She pulled edits out that caused me amazement.

SouthWest Writers provided an amazing variety of professional techniques.

Foreword

Historical events recorded in this novel actually took place during the 20th Century within the geographic epicenter of the American southwest. Many impacted internationally on human history. They are woven together in a fictional story about the lives of two teenage girls as they mature.

History reveals that the greatest and ugliest confrontation Mother Earth undertook during that time was WWII. Its earliest battles were in the South Pacific. Our enemies, the Japanese, gave up few prisoners. Concurrently, on the other side of the world, the American theatre of battle was engaged in North Africa and Sicily. Other enemy combatants that surrendered soldiers in droves were the Italians. Their POWs had to be placed somewhere. So, they were brought to America. One place they were sent was to Camp Albuquerque, which already had a large Italian immigrant population dating back to 1880 when the Atchison, Topeka and Santa Fe Railroad spurred the great American expansion westward. Then, during the 1930s Depression, the Civilian Conservation Corp. (CCC) offered jobs to strong, young American men. In New Mexico, these men built the camp in Albuquerque next to the city zoo. When the CCC ended in 1940, that camp was abandoned. The empty barracks found new use by housing WWII Italian prisoners where the local American Italian populace could keep these half-hearted enemies pacified.

The Camp Albuquerque Italian POW internee period lasted for nine months before being rotated out. Soon thereafter, Nazi POWs were brought in.

Walking distance away, other international WWII era developments were already in progress. Several independent espionage efforts contributed to the transfer of Atomic Bomb secrets to the Soviet Union. One of them occurred at 209 N. High Street in Albuquerque. Five years later, FBI interrogation found the male occupant at that location was a twenty-year-old corporal technician at Los Alamos. The other was his nineteen-year-old bride. They provided testimony that would convict their own sister and brother-in-law, internationally labeled as the Atomic Bomb Spies. Despite pleas from world leaders which included the Pope, these Atomic Bomb Spies were sent to the electric chair at the Sing Sing Prison in 1952. He went first; she required a second jolt. To this day, where our world experienced its first incident of nuclear proliferation, a placard is fixed onto the front of that High St. address that reads, Spy House.'

Again, only walking distance away, readers of this tale learn about a few days in the life of a local boy's success story. Key players, the scientists of Trinity, mere hours after that famous first test blast, stopped in Albuquerque for lunch. Little did they realize that they walked by a man—their host—who would become the most famous American hotelier in the world.

During WWII, most American men were in uniform, which enabled the female workforce to come into their own. Women took over jobs that previously went to men. An industry that employed many women was Southern California airplane factories. Women from all around the country migrated there to become Rosie The Riveters.

We Won the War! Women reluctantly went home so the returning men could resume their previous role in American society. Like their women, most men were stronger because of their war experience. Tragically, some came home never to heal from the horrors they endured.

It took a year or two for many men to return. Some came home broken. Others, in good health, returned to their families and sweethearts. One veteran did not make it back to Albuquerque. Forgotten by those after his generation, despite having coined the phrase GI JOE, he became the most internationally famous correspondent in the English-speaking world of WWII.

Throughout history, wars have produced countless atrocities. Many are forgotten. but one atrocity should always be remembered. Despite life itself reducing chorus of voices who made it home, their experiences should be kept alive. History books until now have preferred to sweep the event under the rug. Why? Because in all the wars America has fought, never have so many American soldiers been forced to surrender in one evil swoop as they did in the first four months of WWII at a place called Bataan.

All Americans know what happened on the morning of December 7, 1941 at Pearl Harbor. But few realize that on that same afternoon, our bases in the Philippines were also attacked. American and Pilipino troops over the next four months became known as the Battling Bastards of Bataan. They knew the American naval fleet had been wiped out and could not help or resupply them. As their food and ammunition ran low, they knew they were on their own. In early April 1942, 70,000 starving American and Pilipino troops surrendered to the helpless motto No Mama No Papa, No Uncle Sam. Few would realize the magnitude of the horror that was yet to come. It became known as the Bataan Death March. When it was over, a mere fraction of survivors came home. Only then did America learn of the years of depravity in Jap slave labor camps that these men endured.

Time moved on. Other events occurred to help memories heal—including an incident that may or may not have happened in southeastern New Mexico in early July 1947. Since then it continues to become internationally famous. It's introduced UFO to the lexicon due to what happened north of the town called Roswell.

Not known then as the Greatest Generation, society would give birth to a generation called the Baby Boomers. New developments in society were introduced, such as rock 'n roll music, which fashioned its own icons. Another was our competition with the Soviet Union called the Space Race. This undertaking too would bring another term into the lexicon: Astronauts.

Despite competition from television's westerns, variety show hosts, space adventures and detective stories, as always, motion pictures created their own icons. From the late fifties to the early sixties, the highest American political icons merged with their Hollywood counterparts. They all had their famous playgrounds, some of which were little known and since forgotten. Yet still, some of the highest profiled events occurred in that little-known, out of the way place, as they still do to this day.

As the sixties advanced, American tragedies shook the world. How American reacted to assassinations of our top political leaders are remembered to this day. The events that changed generations at a place called Vietnam would cause the worst upheaval in our history by ripping apart the fabric of American society. Fortunately, the sixties closed with momentous events. World population became unified like never before and since with pride as we all witnessed the greatest accomplishment in human history: "Houston, the Eagle has landed." For the younger generation and its counter societies, a new way of life began and demonstrated in a motion picture that would cause social upheaval when it was released in 1971: Easy Rider.

Then came the early 70's. A series of rock n' roll icons succumbed to drug overdoses, a social problem would grow to epidemic proportions. But this constant plague was considered miniscule compared to ongoing problem of Vietnam.

War was ripping America apart. Some of The Greatest Generation found their kids, the Baby Boomers, splintering away from mainstream society. Every family in the country was impacted by knowing someone who was killed or wounded in Southeast Asia, which caused growing revolts for those being drafted into military service in record numbers. This was best demonstrated by LSD, long-hair, tied-dyed, counter cultures, many of whom asked if they would consider dodging the draft by skipping to Canada or other friendly countries. More did exactly that than in any other American war. So, in early June 1971, away from the eyes of the national media, the growing national hemorrhage caused the largest antiwar riot west of the Mississippi on the campus of the University of New Mexico, along America's Mother Road, Route 66. National Guard troops with fixed bayonets swept over UNM campus through clouds of tear gas, forcing the thousand now joined by the mainstream, onto Route 66. Many businesses along the way fell victim to fire bombing and looting. The entire state, city, and sheriff police forces were on full time duty for the entire week that followed. It was the first time the heart of the American southwest came under martial law!

Finally, disguised as a negotiated settlement, the Vietnam war came to an end. The military pulled out, handing the American psyche its first war loss in history.

But few cared that the ten-year nightmare was over.

It did, however, move America's attention to its government. Countless Americans watched their country's first presidential impeachment proceedings in almost 110 years. While forcing a sitting president to quit the Oval Office, every minute was examined as he left Washington D.C. on his homeward trek.

America wanted to move on. Time-tested diversions such as TV, music, motion pictures, sports, beer and wines commanded American lifestyles. We would see this as current generations introduced the American thirst for technological innovation. A hundred years earlier, invention of Edison's light bulb in Menlo Park, New Jersey, foreshadowed in a birth in Albuquerque, New Mexico, that would take over the world: the desktop computer. It would entice migration to this southwestern city by two Harvard dropouts. No one would realize its importance then, especially the financiers who blatantly rejected their financial needs. These guys already had a working company, but were forced to move to the American northwest where, soon enough, they make its owners the richest men in the world.

These historical events of the middle thirty years of the 20th Century were of national and international importance. Few of us would remember that their origins were in the geographical epicenter of the American southwest. All are woven into the fabric of this novel.

This author thought you'd like to know.

Chapter One

Teenage boys clad in plaid shirts tucked into blue jeans dash into Albuquerque High School when the bell rings. They are joined by girls in oversized shirts, their jeans rolled up to the calf. Teachers and teens swarm the stairways. Students carry books held together with straps and hall lockers clank open and shut. Although they scramble in different directions, they all have one thing in common—they move under hallway banners proclaiming: WELCOME BACK CLASS OF 1944.

Students walk into a classroom where two girls occupy desks next to each other. Both chewing gum with gusto. The raven-haired girl extends her hand.

"Hello," she says with a light Italian accent. "My name is Elsa Santoni."

The other—a brunette—snaps her gum. "Elsie Lovato here."

They share a smile as they shake hands.

"Going to the welcome back dance tonight?" asks Elsa.

Elsie nods, watching the teacher arrive. Looking about the age of her students, Mrs. Sanchez stops at the front of the class. The girls unobtrusively stick their gum under the tops of their desks.

When she stands under a photograph of Franklin Delano Roosevelt, the students notice their teacher's bloodshot eyes. They watch as she spreads out the American flag hanging nearby.

"Attention, please," she says, turning to her class. "I'm sorry to start our first day back by reporting sad war news. But..." she clears her throat.

"We learned today that last year's class president, Bobby Ortega, was killed in action several weeks ago, in Sicily." Elsa's attention is riveted—before the war, her family emigrated from Sicily.

"I remember Bobby as a solid student and a brave soldier," says Mrs. Sanchez. "Let's honor him with a moment of silence."

During this uncomfortable pause, the students glance at each other in sad wonderment. In their years at Albuquerque High, they've never seen Mrs. Sanchez teary-eyed. Several girls brush away their own tears at this unexpected news.

A boy pounds his desk with a fist and shouts, "Damn! Damn it!"

Elsie mouths to her new classmate, "Did you know him?"

Elsa shrugs. Both bow their heads.

"Please open your history books to page one, The American Revolution," says the teacher. She pauses, evidently changing her mind. "No, close your books. Let's talk about our present worldwide calamity. Go ahead and ask questions."

Several students raise their hands. The teacher notices two girls in the middle of the room, both waving furiously.

"Okay, you first," she says to Elsa, directing her to stand. "Tell us about yourself and how your family is coping with the war."

With a nervous Italian accent, Elsa says, "I am Elsa Santoni. My family came here from Palermo, Sicily to escape *Il Duce*."

"That would be the Italian dictator, Mussolini—Hitler's ally," Mrs. Sanchez explains.

"*Si, si.* We now have the bakery on Gold Street. I see some of your families in the shop sometimes."

"You have great cannolis!" another boy calls from the back of the room.

"*Graze*, thank you," Elsa says. "My question is… what is done with the Italian soldiers when they lose these battles?"

The same voice from the back says loudly, "I hope they shoot them."

"That would be a crime, Mr. Pervis," says Mrs. Sanchez. "The Geneva Convention requires prisoners to be detained in prisoner of war facilities."

She nods toward the student next to Elsa.

"My name is Elsie Lovato," Elsie says, coming to her feet. "My family has been here forever. Ma says we are direct descendants of the Conquistadors from Spain."

Elsa senses a one-up challenge to her immigrant status and decides not to wait for Elsie to finish. "As the war continues," she says, "more and more regular items get harder to come by at the bakery. Why is that? Papa has to find interesting ways to bake without sugar."

Elsie decides to use the same tactic. "And another thing, yesterday I noticed the neighbors on both sides of our house have blue stars in their front windows."

"Elsa and Elsie, hold your horses," says Mrs. Sanchez. "First, Elsa, your father must find other ingredients because most likely they are war-rationed. I am afraid that number will only increase. And Elsie, those are Mother's Stars in your neighbors' windows. They mean a household member is in the service."

Before Elsa can interrupt again, Elsie adds, "Yeah, my neighbor Jimmy is in the Marines and another neighbor, Pancho, is in the Army. Mom says she went to school with their moms."

Mrs. Sanchez continues to dab at her eyes. "And, at Bobby Ortega's house, I am afraid that blue star will change to gold."

Elsie suddenly realizes that the two neighbor boys are in harm's way. A worried silence overcomes her as she listens to questions from the other students.

***

The high school gym is decorated with streamers hanging over the students' heads. Bleachers are fully rolled back. A banner over the gym stage reads WELCOME BACK CLASS OF '44. This reminds the seniors that they have eight months before they finish high school. American flags and banners drape all four walls.

Five gray-haired men wearing tuxedos walk onto the stage. They move to the waiting piano, drums, and bass fiddle. Another carries a clarinet, and the last steps up to the microphone. Without introduction, they start playing warm-up music familiar to all: Benny Goodman's "Swinging at the Savoy."

The mirror ball dangling from the middle of the gym roof begins sprinkling light reflections throughout the room.

Predominantly in pink, teenage girls in chiffon sweaters and slacks fill the room – tall, short, lean, plump, blondes, brunettes and redheads. Only a third are teenage boys. At first and second glance, they all appear to be shorter and younger. A few teacher chaperones are visible.

As the night progresses, wanting to dance, some of the girls resign themselves to asking the closest shy boy while others, with no boys available, dance with each other. The chaperones smile at the sight of the taller senior girls dancing with their shorter male classmates and some girls who dance with others.

Elsa Santoni notices Elsie Lovato at the other end of the refreshment table evaluating the room. They walk over to each other. A few inches taller than Elsie, Elsa sips her punch. The two seventeen-year-olds wear knee high, rose print dresses with no collars. Elsie is dressed in yellow and Elsa in pink. Elsie's long crimson-tinged hair and Elsa's long jet black hair fall around their shoulders.

Breaking the ice, Elsie says, "Look around. Damn war," as couples dance past in front of them. "He's in 10th grade and she's due to graduate with us in June."

The band plays the next tune: Artie Shaw's "Begin the Beguine."

"The guy on the clarinet is half bald—and so is the piano fellow," adds Elsa.

"They're all too old or too young," says Elsie.

Several fellow female students dance by in couples.

"I want to dance," says Elsa.

"Let's go."

Elsie walks out onto the floor as Elsa follows.

Chapter Two

A month passes and Santoni Bakery is doing well. Even extra help is necessary. Elsa suggests they hire her new friend. Papa and mama agree that it would be good for business to have two fresh faces out front selling their baked goods.

The front door bell clangs as another customer exits, cake box in hand. Dressed in her lavender flower dress, Elsa smiles through her red lipstick and pushes the cash register drawer closed. After tightening her little frilly, lacy apron she immediately carries a coffee pot to her regular Saturday morning customers seated at their usual corner table.

Hot coffee steams from their cups as a young couple holds hands across the table while they talk. He's in his civvies now, but Elsa remembers how he sometimes wears his army uniform, also because this patron has the first New York accent her Italian/New Mexican ears have ever heard. As she walks away, she hears her customer comment.

"...they even put chili in the cream cheese here," he says in amazement.

Elsa wipes down the counter allowing her mind to float through the store's front window. Her smile widens as she watches a few model T's sputter by and folks on their Saturday noon stroll.

The doors from the back kitchen swing open. Elsie carries out a tray of baked goods into the showroom then slides them beneath the glass showcase counter. Her face is lightly powdered with white as she adjusts the hairnet around her brownish red hair that is also lightly grayed with flour.

"This is the last batch of cannolis for today. Your dad said to add a couple more pennies to these sales. We're out of flour till Monday," she says.

Elsa quickly replies. "Papa knows how to squeeze every cent that he can."

Elsie tightens her oversized, stained cotton apron that drapes around her neck and shoulders down to her ankles. She swats excess powder off her lap as the front door bell jingles. Both girls perk up as two army uniforms enter—

both new customers. Two privates remove their caps as they approach Elsa at the counter. Elsie smiles at the sight of the two cute boys, about her age.

"Welcome to Santoni's Bakery, fellows," greets Elsa.

One private says to the other, "Looks like we came to the right place, Jimmy."

Winking at Elsa, he adds, "Didn't I tell ya there was an Italian beauty behind the cash register," Private Jimmy responds.

With caps in hand, both privates crowd closer to Elsa.

"My name is Jake and this is my buddy, Jimmy."

"Hello there, and again welcome to Santoni's."

Jimmy moves in. "You gotta understand, miss, we're new in from Kansas and we've never seen an Italian girl before."

The radio in the background plays Glen Miller's big band trombone sound of Tuxedo Junction.

"Well, my friend here..." directing attention to Elsie. "...and me are from here. And we don't see many boys from Kansas," Elsa quips.

Both soldiers acknowledge Elsie's presence. They choose to focus on Elsa whose smile absorbs their attention. Elsie rearranges the baked goods under the glass case that she had arranged only seconds before.

"What can I get you two soldiers?"

The taller of the two asks, "How about your name?"

"My name is Elsa and this is my friend Elsie."

Elsie shyly smiles, unaware of her smudged, white flowered complexion.

The soldiers remain focused on Elsa. Through a jealous frown and without saying a word, Elsie carries an empty tray back through the swinging doors into the kitchen.

Still frowning, she carries the tray to the sink, pours water over it, washes it down, and dries it off. Then she takes it across the kitchen to a table top, on the end of which sits a container with a spout. With an attentive effort, Elsie spreads five carefully measured pours of olive oil over the pan. Standing behind her is Elsa's mother, Abra, who watches her well-trained employee.

"This oil is very precious thing," she tells Elsie. "It comes from our homeland. If the rationing board heard of this, I don't know what would happen."

Elsie has heard her say this several times. "Yes, Mrs. Santoni." She then carries the oiled tray to a table covered with assorted baking flours.

Abra Santori watches her daughter's friend flour the oiled tray then stack it with the other floured trays, all with a sad frown. Abra wishes that her own daughter could be as good a worker as her friend, Elsie.

"Ah, *bambina*, why the frown?"

"Mrs. Santoni, Elsa is so beautiful," Elsie says.

"Ah, *grazi, bambina*," Mrs. Abra Santori says. She also wears a stained cotton apron. "You are a crazy girl. Come." Abra nods across the kitchen, pointing to a mirror over the sink. "Wash your face, then take a good look. Crazy girl."

At the sight of her flour-coated complexion, Elsie does not notice Abra Santori being hurriedly diverted away. Soon, she closes her eyes while feeling like she is using a pound of soap. She feels around and finds a towel. No sooner does she bring down the towel when she catches her friend's reflection behind her, feeling slightly jolted by the Santori women's switch.

"That shows the difference between your luck and mine. Yesterday, it was your hair netted and washing this stuff off," Elsie tells her amiga.

Then Elsa waves two tickets, "Tonight you, my Albuquerque friend, and me, Elsa Santoni, are going to the USO Club on those two soldier boys."

Both girls immediately jump up and down with happy screams. They don't want the parents to hear as Mrs. Abra Santoni is in the back of the kitchen behind the cooler watching her husband knead dough repeatedly. He lays rolls of dough over oiled trays. Without noticing his wife, Giovani Santoni turns away to pull a tray of bread from the oven then replaces it with a fresh tray of dough. Abra Santoni feels the wave of heat reach her.

"I will wait till they cool before I slice them," she says matter-of-factly.

Giovani wipes away the sweat using his stained apron around his waist. "Do not bother. The slicer is broken." He frowns at the latest disappointment while still kneading the dough.

His wife of twenty years asks, "So, what do we do?" She carefully walks up behind him.

In his broken English, he said, "With the war, replacement parts are no no illegal. So, we just sell no sliced bread."

As his wife reaches for the unsliced loaves, he suddenly spins around with a smile. Giovani sweeps his nicely proportioned wife into in his well-developed arms.

She coos with a laugh. "You will hurt yourself you..."

She is muted when his flour covered lips meet hers. With her palm, she wipes away his powdered sweat as he carries her into their back office and closes the door. She giggles.

Chapter Three

Rose carries the bowl of rice and chicken to the table and puts a spoon in it.

"Ah, que chicos. We must say grace and thank the lord for this Aroz con Pojo. Think of all the starving girls your age in Europe right now."

"Oh, mama, you're so dramatic," says Esther as she puts one, two, three spoonsful onto her plate. Long brown hair falls over of her face.

"Tie your hair back. We're eating supper here," orders the brother sitting next to her.

"Johnny, you have no room to talk," says his mother standing over the wood burning stove. "You didn't even shave." As she pulls biscuits from the oven she shouts into the other room. "Elsie, we're waiting for you at the table. Come now, *chica*."

Johnny doesn't wait. He digs into the bowl of rice with chicken with hunger written across his face. But he stops cold when he feels his mother's stare as she carries a bowl of red chili to the table. She has been carrying food to dining tables long before she met and married her departed husband. He was a traveling salesman and she was a Harvey Girl at the Alvarado train station, but that was decades ago. Now she is the matriarch of her family.

She says, "We all wait for Elsie, this is our family."

"Hey sis, hurry. We're hungry," Johnny shouts from the table.

"Okay, okay, hold your horses," says Elsie as she walks in, dressed in a blue dress, and her special dancing shoes. She smiles.

"I thought the high school dance was weeks ago. Sit, sit down girl," directing her youngest to sit next to her. "Shall we?" Instinctively, they all bow their heads. "Dear Lord, *gracias por la comida y mis ninos Johnny, Esther y Elsie, gracias*. Especially take care of our fighting boys overseas." They all draw a sign of the cross over their chests.

Instantly Johnny digs into the food by filling a plate and handing it to his mother. *"Gracias madre por la comeda."* Then he fills another plate and passes it to Esther. Then another for his baby sister.

"Gracias O Johnny, O Johnny, O Johnny O," Elsie sings.

Esther says, "I'll be taking off in a couple of days. Tia Della wrote that she is looking forward to having me." She wants a clean conscience from her mom.

Rose says again, "The only reason I will let you go to Los Angeles, California without supervision is that my sister already got that job waiting for you in the airplane factory."

"Aunt Della is great." Elsie says.

Esther still feels the need to add ammunition. "I'll send money home. Working in an airplane factory will be great for me and the family."

Johnny wants to help his sis. "You'll still have Elsie and me here, mom." Then he adds, "Aunt Della needs family out there, too. Especially since Uncle Bob is overseas. You know that to be true."

Rose wonders if her husband were alive today would this be as difficult. So, she reluctantly nods at all the solid logic. "Like you, Esther, my older sister was also the first to leave the household." She grabs hold of her oldest daughter's hand, "You and Della will be good for each other."

Smiles fill their faces except for Rose.

***

The enormous El Rey Theatre ballroom filled with Sandia airfield base personnel is known on the weekends as the USO. Air Corp, Navy, Army, Marine, even Merchant Marine insignias adorn the walls from the entrance at one end of the stage to the other.

Live big band swing music bounces off these walls. Two soldiers walk in proud with the underage Elsa and Elsie on their arms. Both ladies wear red lipstick to match their dancing shoes. Their wide-eyed mood seems to become energized from the first moment that they glance around.

"So, this is what this place looks like inside after all the times I've passed by," amazes Elsie.

"Come on, ladies, let's find a table," leads one of the soldiers.

No sooner do they find seats, the high-energy swing music sparks all their youthful exuberance. Elsa's soldier grabs her hand and tugs her onto the dance floor. His buddy does likewise with Elsie.

After a couple of dances, both couples laugh as they rush back to their table.

"What would you like to drink, Elsie?"

"A Shirley Temple please."

Elsa also speak up, "Me, too!"

"Wouldn't you want a beer or a whiskey," encourages Elsie's red-headed private.

"Yeah, doesn't a beer sound good?" encourages Elsa's date.

"I've never had a beer before," answers Elsa.

"Come on ladies, let loose," encourages Elsie's date.

Both ladies look at each other, then nod their heads in unison.

Elsa's wide eyes show her thinking. "I've always been curious about a drink called a Singapore Sling."

Elsie likes that idea. "Me, too. I'll try a Singapore um, um..." She looks at her friend Elsa, "...Sling." As the waitress walks away, she tells her dates, "You guys know we are too young to be in here, don't you?"

The red-headed soldier replies. "Just kick back and enjoy. We'll be dancing shortly anyway."

Soon the two high school girls have fancy drinks in front of them. Both drink slowly. After several more dances, the second drink goes down faster.

"So, what do you guys do at the base?" asks Elsie.

"We're not at the base," says the red-headed private. "Actually, we're stationed at the zoo."

The girls show surprise. "Zoo?" Both say at once.

One private glances at the other for approval. He gives a go-ahead nod.

"We're preparing an addition to your zoo—a prisoner of war installation," the red-head says.

"Prisoners of War? Here in Albuquerque?" Elsie shares Elsa's surprise.

Elsa asks, "Japs or Nazis?"

The blonde private says, "Italian."

"I'm Italian," she says.

"And we're going to stay on to be guards," he adds.

Elsa shows her misgivings. "But I'm Italian."

"That's one of the reasons Albuquerque was selected," says the red-headed private.

The band kicks in with Benny Goodman's Swinging at the Savoy. The dance floor immediately fills up.

Both privates bottom up their beers.

Elsie needs to satisfy her curiosity, "Why Albuquerque?"

A blonde-haired gal carrying a tray approaches their table.

"Here you go, folks."

"To answer your question," says Elsa's date, "The Army explains that it is Article 22 of the Geneva Convention..."

His buddy throws in, "Don't forget Article 25!"

"Anyway, it dictates that POWs are to be held in environments similar to where they were captured."

Defensively, Elsa pushes for more information. "What's that got to do with Albuquerque?"

"Albuquerque had hundreds of left over barracks from your 30's Civilian Conservation Corp. They were filled with dirt and cob webs. But we cleaned them up."

The other private says, "These jerks were captured in North Africa and now Sicily."

The other adds, "And apparently, the climate here is similar plus you have a large Italian population."

Elsie recalls their classroom lesson to Elsa. "Sicily? Isn't that where Bobby Ortega was killed?"

Not liking the news, Elsa asks, "When is this all going to happen?"

"The Itie scum trains start getting here soon is what our Sergeant said today." The blonde private downs his beer in a single gulp.

"So, these Italian soldiers are scum to you?" Elsa says. The other private responds by downing his beer. "I want to go home," she says.

"Ah, come on girls. Let's dance," insists the blonde soldier, reaching for Elsa's hand.

She jerks it away.

"Elsie, let's hit the floor," the other private urges.

Siding with her friend, "We better go," adds Elsie.

The red-headed private shows signs of feeling insulted. "You can't walk out on us!"

Elsa snaps, "Watch us." She faces her friend, "Let's leave."

Elsie nods her stupor-filled head as she stands.

The blonde private breathes beer breath on Elsie, then tries to pull her back. "Ah, come on. Sit down," he demands.

"You, sir, cannot tell me what to do," Elsie snaps back.

As Elsa stands up, her date also tries to jerk her down. Elsa pulls her hand back. And as the band plays a crescendo, Elsa slaps his face.

"Do not even think about coming into the bakery. Good bye."

In support of her friend, Elsie instinctively throws her drink into her date's face. Then both high school girls stand and walk toward the USO exit.

The privates look at each other and wonder what in the hell just happened?

Elsie, too, wonders what's bothering her amiga. But she still feels the rhythms and beats as she follows through with some dance steps.

Elsie asks Elsa, "Hey girl! what gives? They were cute."

Elsa wants for her friend to catch up.

"Italian prisoners are coming here!" Elsa responds.

"So?" She starts to feel the room spin and feels the need to grab hold of the railing that leads to the exit.

"I'm Italian!"

"You're American! Don't forget you got your citizenship last year," Elsie corrects as she tries to steady herself.

"I wonder if mom and dad know," Elsa asks as she pushes open the front doors. As the fresh air hits her face, she too must correct her balance.

***

Morning sunshine splashes through the bedroom window onto her Elsa's face. Quickly sitting up, her head starts to throb. The familiar surroundings of her bedroom begin to sink in. She tries to remember how she got home. She's still wearing last night's clothes. Then she remembers. Her legs were so heavy after walking home she strained to sneak through the store, upstairs, and past momma and poppi's room. It was easier just to lay down.

The Sunday morning church bells of Saint Mary's call in the distance. Her head aches with each ring. Gotta go to church, gotta go to church is her instinct.

The clock beside her reads 8:15—she overslept a rare hour. A quick wash, change of clothes and she'll be okay to tell the folks the news before they leave for church, if she could only get out of bed.

But then she begins to wonder why mom didn't wake her up. Only then does she feel the wood floor below her vibrate. It's coming from out front. She rushes to stare out her second floor bedroom window to see one, two, three, and more ugly green-covered army trucks roll by.

Barefoot, she flies down the stairs into the bakery store. Her mom and dad are staring out the window trembling as they hold each other. Elsa runs into their embrace.

As the trucks roll by, Abra sees their occupants, particularly what they are wearing, green khakis with PW written on the backs of their shirts.

"Ah, *mamma mia*. What is this PW?"

Her husband answers. "They are war prisoners, mama."

"Popa, mama, they are Italian prisoners of war."

Abra embraces her family, *"Mai in vita mia."*

"Never in my life either mamma," Elsa says.

An angry father murmurs under his breath, *"Andare all'enferno Il Duce!"*

His daughter shares his emotions. "Mussolini will burn in hell, poppi. He must."

Chapter Four

A bicyclist peddles along the residential street tossing evening newspapers at Victorian styled houses. He whistles at two young ladies as he rolls by. Carrying their books, Elsa and Elsie giggle and wave as he passes them.

Elsie opens a white picket fence gate. The girls climb the front steps, go past the front screen door, across the screened porch and through the front door.

"I'm home," Elsie calls out.

No one answers. They walk through the house and into the kitchen. Elsie notices an open envelope laying there and reads the return address.

"Hey, a letter from Esther."

"Read what she has to say," Elsa suggests.

"Looks like mama's read it already." She pulls out a thin sheet of paper and starts to read.

"She met an air corps flyer from New Mexico who was on leave. Apparently, he was injured in the Pacific... and her job at the airplane factory is okay."

"Hopefully she'll be able to get us jobs there after we graduate next summer."

"Getting the jobs will not be the problem, my Aunt Della says. Finding a place to live will be."

Elsie steps over to the stove. A pot is simmering on the back burner. Lifting its lid, she stirs the stew.

"Mom must be at work."

Using wrought iron tongs hanging over her head, she opens the potbelly stove's hatch to toss in a small piece of wood. A noisy ruckus announces the entrance of Johnny and a buddy through the back door.

"They put up that place quick," he says.

"It's amazing how they turned those barracks around. It's *bueno* that the animals can't complain about their neighbors," says his buddy.

Both laugh out loud. Johnny wears a jacket over blue jeans and t-shirt. His jet black hair is greased back. He carries a paper bag with a few groceries. His friend has pimples face and wears an Albuquerque High baseball cap.

He notices his sister, "*Como esta*, sis?"

"Hi, Johnny, Carlos"

"How's it today for you Elsa?"

"Hi, Johnny."

"You know, *mi amigo,* Carlos, don't you?"

Elsa nods while Elsie continues stirring the stew.

Carlos smiles, "Hello, Elsa."

In an attempt to ignore this, Carlos adds, "Let me stir that stew, Elsie."

Elsie smiles at her friend's mature snub. "I'll get the bread."

"Speaking of bread, how's the bakery, Elsa?" asks Carlos.

"We are doing fine since we got a contract from that new Army base."

"Don't you mean that new POW camp?" says Carlos. "It's only correct. Italian bread for Italian prisoners," he smirks.

Elsa drops the spoon into the boiling pot.

"*Cochino*," Elsie says to Carlos.

"What did I say?" he asks.

Elsie glares at her brother.

Johnny shoves his buddy's shoulder. "Think, Tonto. Elsa's Italian. Show some sensitivity." He pulls a loaf of bread from the bag and tosses it to his sister. She catches it as Johnny produces a bottle of Jack Daniels from the paper bag. "*Ven aqui*, Carlos," he tells his friend while walking off into the living room. The door closes behind them.

"Good riddance to those four efers," as far as I'm concerned," says Elsa. Seduced by the aroma, she leans closer to the simmering pot.

Breaking off a piece of bread, Elsie naturally defends her brother.

"Johnny's not that bad. He's been trying to get into all of the services and cannot help that he's turned down. He's checking out the Navy this time."

"If that whiskey is boot camp training, they're a shoe-in." She takes a taste from the spoon.

"Johnny can't help it if he's flat footed."

Showing her comfort in her friend's home, Elsa pulls a couple of bowls from the overhead cabinet. She pours a ladle full into one and passes it to Elsie.

"Elsie, face it, they're not military types. I heard your mom say, you can put a boot in the oven, but you still won't get a brisket out of it."

"Johnny is my brother and I love him. Flat feet or not."

Elsie blows over her steaming bowl while smiling widely at the taste of her mother's broth.

Elsa eagerly digs in, too. "mmm...Your mama is a great cook."

***

Outside the high school gym, cardboard signs lean against the brick walls. Written on them with colors of red, white and blue is SCRAP METAL DRIVE. Recycle for the war effort. Nearby is a growing pile of broken tractor tools, rakes, shovels, dull axes, old car bumpers, and doors. A tinge of gold graces the autumn leaves of the campus trees.

With red, white and blue ribbons draped over their forearms, Elsie and Elsa thank each contributor through their red lipstick smiles. A light breeze bounces off the gym wall making them both shiver. They button up their jackets.

"Some girls write to anonymous soldiers overseas," says Elsa. "But no, we do this."

"I've always been interested in writing some lonely soldier in a fox hole. But for now we're doing this." says Elsie as she visually calculates, "I say we're looking at half of a ton here."

"Wasn't the record last summer half of a ton?" asks Elsa. "We've got an hour to beat that."

"Y mi amiga, it looks like we got the new record," Elsie points to the far side of the plaza that spreads out before them. Walking across toward them are two groups of boys carrying lengthy, obviously heavy strips of metal. Each wears freshmen letterman jackets with As on them.

"They're coming through for us, putting us over the top!" rejoices Elsa. "You know what that means?"

Elsie nods as they pull out their lipsticks and apply on a heavy coat. Then they shake each other's hands as they prepare for the lettermen who place on the pile two ten-foot strips of rails from the nearby abandoned railroad tracks.

"As the head of the Albuquerque High Lettermen's club," one of them says, "we are proud to make our contribution."

"Oh, you are so cute. You are going to kill 'em again this year. Guys, thank you," Elsie says while handing out ribbons. She then kisses several of them on the cheek, leaving her lipstick mark.

Elsa throws in the come-down comment, "It's as if you are my own little brothers." She gives each of the rest of the smiling six a light sisterly peck on the cheek, purposely leaving her lipstick mark.

Chapter Five

New Town Albuquerque's Saturday morning bustles as Elsie quickly steps across Route 66 Avenue. She's late for work at the bakery. The sun is already bright over the top of the 11,000-foot crest of the easterly Sandia Mountains. She remembers not long ago when this main street was just called Railroad Street because of the active trolleys on it. But since wartime cut backs, the electric trolley company abandoned their tracks a couple of years back. Now, as the road cuts through the middle of town, the few gas-rationed cars and trucks sputter then thump over the abandoned tracks.

The corner of Route 66 and 2nd Street features the Sunshine Movie Theater, hotels, and bars. Elsie's history teacher's husband owns the corner café, the only business that is open. A sign in their front window reads, `Toast & Coffee, 2 Eggs and Sausage, pancakes, 25 cents.' Elsie recognizes some of the folk inside as she walks by.

In front of her, a couple of storefronts ahead, a gray-haired man is sliding a key into the front door of a men's clothing shop.

"Good morning Mr. Stromberg," Elsie smiles as she stops.

"Good morning, Elsie. Isn't this a beautiful October morning?" The haberdasher inhales a deep breath of fresh air. "This is why me and the Mrs. came out here from back east. I'll be in shortly for my meet up with my *amigo* Elfego for our usual coffee, bagel and newspaper."

She smiles at how he pronounces Spanish words through his eastern accent.

"We love your green chili smear," he adds, as he walks into his store, "If only New York knew of this green chili!"

Elsie waves and resumes her walk, thinking that Mr. Stromberg is right. The sun does fill her with cheer. When she turns onto Gold Street the first thing she notices is the SANTONI BAKERY sign, all of the second level windows of home above the bakery are wide open, venting the rising bakery heat. But then she stops in her tracks. American soldiers with rifles watch over five or six khaki dressed `P's as they sweep the sidewalks and wash store front windows. She's hesitant as she approaches the front of the bakery. A prisoner is washing the front window. Anxious to slip inside, she stops cold at the sight of a cute Italian prisoner. He looks up at her and smiles. She can't help but notice his deep blue eyes and jet black hair. Surprisingly, he jumps to open the door for her.

"Good morning, *signorina*," he says.

She steps through, "Gracias, senor," she responds in Spanish. The door closes behind her.

"He's Italian, not Spanish," Elsa teases while waiting for her buddy. She's already wrapped in a hairnet and large dirty apron. "It's your turn to handle the front."

"No argument from me."

Walking around the front counter Elsie again thinks that Mr. Stromberg is right. It is a beautiful morning. She watches the cute prisoner dry off the front window before he moves next door to Mr. Stein's law office.

Without thinking about it, the first thing she does is turn the knob on the radio. Glen Miller's `A Nightingale Sang in Berkeley Square' plays while she ties the small lacy belt of her yellow doily apron. Elsa carries out a tray of cinnamon rolls then places them in the glass show case.

"Did you see that cute prisoner?" asks Elsie.

"Cute? Cute? Do you call Mussolini cute?" she snaps.

The radio moves into another Glen Miller swing tune. "...Pardon me, boy, is that the Chattanooga Choo Choo..."

"Well, excuuuse me," Elsie says as she kicks into a solo swing step behind the counter. Only then does she notice her regular Saturday morning customers sitting at their usual tables.

First there is the ancient, heavy-set man at a table next to the front window awaiting his friend, Mr. Stromberg. But she prefers to remember this older gentleman as her youthful, much thinner elementary school principal, Mr. Elfego Baca. She can't help but remember his history. In his day, he was a prominent fellow. Born right after the Civil War, he would later become a famous gunslinger. He reputedly shot it out with thirty banditos once and he was the one to walk away. Then he became a prominent lawyer. Shortly before World War I he was defending one of Pancho Villa's generals who was jailed here in Albuquerque. But authorities found it strange that Baca claimed not to know anything about his client's midnight shootout back in Mexico. He then became an educator. With a high regard for this man, Elsie respectfully pours his coffee.

Then there are her other weekly regulars. A young couple barely older than her. He's a barrel-chested fellow who wears his Army uniform, raising his empty coffee cup with a smile. Elsie carries the coffee pot over, but not before taking a quick swing step to the right then to her left in time with the music from the radio.

"This is why we like coming here, we like the service," the barrel-chested soldier says.

"David likes his caffeine," his lady adds.

"My wife Ruth would know," he squeezes her hand.

Elsie takes notice of their New York accent. "I can't keep up with you folks," she remarks. "Are you coming or going this time?"

"He just got in. But had no sleep so its coffee time," volunteers Ruth as she stares in her man's eyes.

Elsie laughs. "Thanks for coming in folks." She eases her step into spinning around in a dance step.

The front door bell jingles as Mr. Stromberg carries a newspaper as he steps over to his waiting friend. Elsie's face turns bright red as she stops.

"Oh, do not let me stop you, little one," he smiles as he finds his chair at the table next to his amigo, Elfego.

"I love Glen Miller," she says to her customers.

With a practiced routine, Elsie pulls a bagel from under the showcase and slides it into a toaster. Moments later, with butter knife in hand, she spreads on his smear. She pours the coffee and carries the tray to the gentlemen's table.

"Looks particularly delicious this morning," Mr. Stromberg says.

Through the front window, Elsie watches the prisoners walk across the street. Both Mr. Stromberg's and Mr. Baca's faces sadden as they watch a GI prison guard shove a prisoner with his rifle butt. Both girls are shocked when the prisoner wipes blood from his face.

Elsie's dancing suddenly dissipates. Her beautiful day has turned gut wrenching.

***

Mr. Santoni adjusts the BUY WAR BONDS HERE sign in his front window. He watches as a light breeze blows golden leaves down the sidewalk.

"Yesterday was a warm October day, and today she blows. This Indian Summer Albuquerque weather..." he says, shaking his head.

"All four seasons you and I see here, *amori mio*," Abra approaches and kisses her oven-warmed husband.

He puts his muscular arms around his wife's waist. "If we can see the four seasons together, that is all I care about," he says.

The door upstairs closes loudly before Elsa walks down the steps. "I need a cup of coffee and breakfast, and I will be ready to start work," she says as she catches her parents end their kiss. She rolls her eyes.

"It is time to pull the breads from the oven," Papa says. He walks back into the kitchen while his wife tightens her apron.

With a smile, Elsa says, "Maybe I should have come down a moment later, mama."

"It is 8 o'clock in the morning. Your papa and me been working since 5. I talk, you do not." The mother hands the daughter an apron as a loud crash emanates from the kitchen.

Both ladies rush there to see Mr. Santoni laying on his back on the floor surrounded by broken dishes and baking pans.

"*Dios mio!*" cries Elsa.

Abra rushes to her husband's side. "*Ah, amori mio.*"

His Italian accent speaks English, "I slip on pastry on floor, a *stupido*," he mutters to himself.

He tries to sit up but falls back. Pain captures his face.

Abra quickly orders her daughter, "We help your father upstairs so he can lay down."

"I will survive family," he winces with pain as the women help him to his feet. "Let me try..." He falls against a baking table but is caught by the two ladies.

"You must lie down," Abra tells her husband. When he says nothing, she adds, "Elsa, we carry him upstairs."

As they reach the thin staircase, mama changes her mind. "Take care of the counter."

A feeling of helplessness almost overwhelms Elsa as she watches her hurting papa. But as the customers start to walk in, she dons her apron and a smile.

Her mother soon comes back down the steps. Her worried expression vanishes when she sees her daughter expertly serving a customer. And as if all is well, she too snaps on a smile and joins her daughter at the counter, taking over the cash register while her daughter serves cinnamon rolls, cookies, and assorted pastries.

Then it happens, an hour later. Silence. The bakery is empty. For a moment, the ladies look at each other with expressions of satisfaction.

"We are almost out of everything," Elsa observes.

Her mother nods and says, "Your papa and me are now happy that you learned to drive the bakery truck. He and me decided you must now make deliveries to prisoner camp."

A startled expression appears on Elsa's face. "You mean the Prisoner of War camp? No mama. I don't want to go to that horrible place. Please don't make me. Please."

"Your papa must rest and he cannot make today's deliveries. I do not drive. So you must. There is no other way."

"I can't! I can't, mama. Please do not make me!"

A lady customer with child in hand enters, jingling the doorbell. Abra snaps on her smile to attend to them. She immediately takes a cookie from a counter basket and hands it to the child.

"Good morning, signora. Welcome to Santoni's Bakery."

Elsa still stands there in horror at what she must do today. A slight feeling of relief passes over her as her best friend walks through the front door ready for another day of work.

Elsie cannot help but notice her friend's ashen expression.

"What's wrong?" she asks.

"You're not going to believe what you and I are going to do today," Elsa replies.

Judging from the look on her friend's face, Elsie has an ominous feeling.

"What, what?" she demands.

Chapter Six

The girls are tense and silent as the Santoni Bakery truck rolls to a stop at the wooden gate. Over its portal, a sign reads: CAMP ALBUQUERQUE.

Hastily erected ten foot wooden posts stand every five feet and stretch out for several military-leased city blocks. They are connected by ten strands of barbed wire. The top is tied to endless circular razor-blade concertina wire. Attached to each post along the way are more signs: WARNING HIGH VOLTAGE.

They glance down the line practically next door and see another portal with a sign that reads Albuquerque Zoo. On the other side of the zoo, they can see the multi-level Tingley Baseball Field. Across the street behind them, majestically laid out is the half dirt and half green golf course of the Albuquerque Country Club.

Elsa points behind them, then beyond. "What a place to put this camp. Only in America."

Not thinking, Elsie nods and smiles.

A soldier wearing a white helmet approaches the truck from a shed at the gate. He wears an arm band with MP on it and carries a rifle at the ready.

"Papers, please," he tells Elsa.

"Yes, sir," she responds nervously.

"You are not the usual delivery person," he comments as he glances at Elsie.

"Papa fell and hurt his back so I am making the deliveries today. My friend is helping me."

Elsie gives a little wave.

The guard continues looking at her as he says, "The mess is the third building on the left," he points. "Towards the back."

"Does this third building need cleaning?" asks Elsa.

"The mess hall is the kitchen," he says. As Elsa nods, the guard signals to open the gates. "Take notice of the interior grounds. It is filled with guards covering the prisoners. But, still, be on your feet," he warns.

Then he evidently changes his mind. "I better show you ladies in. These guys haven't seen dishes like you in a while." He jumps onto the truck's running board. "Let's go."

As the truck moves through the gate, the Italian POWs stop in their tracks to ogle the girls. The guard jumps off as they pull up to the camp's mess.

Elsa and Elsie maintain nervous smiles. The mess guard approaches. Another white helmeted MP private sees the girls and anxiously joins him.

As they step out of the truck, the girls suddenly become aware of ten or fifteen POWs sitting outside, peeling potatoes. Apparently stunned at the sight before them, all the men stand up. Both girls move back.

"Don't be worried," the guard says. He points to other nearby prisoners, "You! Unload the truck," he barks at the front four prisoners.

One of them catches Elsa's eye. He smiles, then winks. She turns red and innocently smiles back. Elsie offers the guard a clipboard, which he signs.

In no time, the truck is unloaded, and they are again on their way. The guards smile and wave as they exit through the front gate.

Grinning, Elsie says, "Did you see how cute they were?"

"Those military guards? I didn't notice."

"Maybe, but I meant the POWs."

The gate guards hear the girls giggle as they drive away.

Chapter Seven

The kitchen staff at The Hilton Hotel hustle and bustle. The lead chef, wearing his trademark tall white cap, walks out of the kitchen cooler with clipboard in hand. While glancing around at his five busy staff, he closes the door behind him. Donning her white cap and apron, Rose Lovato stands next to her preparation table covered with her tools of the trade.

"Rose," he says, "it's time to prepare the cake mix."

Rose nods acknowledgment, and begins to crack open a dozen eggs into her special wooden bowl. With her own wooden whisk, she proceeds to whip them.

"I like the feel of wooden bowls better," she tells her coworker. "Fluffier egg whites come easier from them."

"Talk to the army, they use metal bowls and whisks," her coworker naturally replies.

"Well our boys do deserve a fluffier egg, that's for sure."

She adds in a full cup of sugar into the egg whites. Satisfied with the mixture of precisely measured war rationed ingredients, she adds it to the large mixing bowl already filled with flower. A fleeting question passes through her mind. How many war-short commodities has she just mixed together? This wedding cake will be her best, she tells herself.

A female co-worker walks up to her, "Your daughter is at the alley door asking for ya, Rosey."

Counting ten more seconds on the blender, she replies in her habit of using her Spanglish, "*Gracias*, deary." She turns off the machine before walking away.

A light chill captures the late October afternoon. Pacing out back in the hotel alley, Elsie waits out in the cold. She steps up to the bottom half door as her mom opens the top half.

"Hi, mom," exhaling breath puffs into the cold air.

Steam escapes from the warm kitchen. "Como esta baby."

"Well guess where I was today?"

"At the POW camp," Rose replies.

Surprised, "How did you know?"

"Elsa's mother called to tell me."

"And they were cute too. Elsa was dreading going. But she changed her tune, that's for sure."

Rose smiles. "I'm in the middle of making a wedding cake. We'll talk about that when I get home."

"But, but we got a letter from Esther." She produces it out of her skirt pocket and hands it to her mom. "She got married."

Rose stands there, numb. "My baby got married? A que chica!" She grasps at the letter and hungrily examines every word. "She married that injured fly boy." Reading further, "Apparently he wasn't so injured."

Trying to uplift her depressed mother, "She sent twenty dollars." Rose just reads. Elsie continues, "So I used it to pay this month's and next month's light and heat bills." Rose still has her face in the letter.

"That's a good decision Elsie." She folds the letter and tucks it into her apron pocket. "Get home, chica. We'll talk about your sister then. Now skedaddle."

"Yes, mama."

Rose watches her youngest turn and walk away down the dim hotel alley.

Elsie shivers then pulls over her coat hood while thinking to herself, `I got a brother-in-law. And the letter says he's apparently from New Mexico..."

Rose watches till her baby walks around the corner. But it's her oldest that just got married far, far away. Her first born ripped her apart when she was born. And twenty one years later, she's doing it again. She's jolted back when she feels the frozen tears down her ice cold cheeks. She hurries inside trying to hide her tears.

***

Giovani Santoni lies nervously in his bed staring at the trees swaying in the wind outside his second floor window. Heat from the ovens below radiates upstairs, creating a cozy atmosphere. His nervousness intensifies because he hasn't bounced back quick enough after his fall. He can still only work a half of a day before back pain stops him cold. This has cut his production and store hours in half. He hasn't heard any complaints from the women in his life on that matter, though. His sign in the window simply blames the half store hours on war time supply shortages.

Suddenly he hears quick steps up the stairs. He pushes up when the door swings open. There stands his beautiful wife with a smile and a newspaper in hand.

Abra Santoni gleefully tells her husband, "Italia has captured the *bastardo Il Duce*. He runs no more!" she says.

Instant happiness overcomes him at the sudden news. He quickly sits up further, and winces at the pain. Yet his face is stretched with the largest smile that he's had in years. Abra sits down next to her husband, embracing him intensely as tears roll down her face.

Elsa steps out of her room curious about the ruckus to see her mama's tears along with her papa's unusual smile.

"What's the matter, popi, mama?"

Her mother holds out the newspaper for her. So Elsa sits down next to them, reading. She quickly embraces her parents.

***

The next morning is crisp and cloudless as Elsa and Elsie pull up to the prison camp. They hear the elephant's roar vibrate from the zoo next door. The gate MP has a smile on his face as he approaches the bakery truck.

"Good morning, ladies."

"Hello Sergeant Jim." Elsa giggles back.

With her naturally sweet smile, Elsie waves hello by wiggling her hand's fingers.

"I guess your dad still isn't feeling better." With a frown, Elsa simply shakes her head. "You've been here every day. Your dad must be working hard just to feed all of us." He signals the other gate guard to open the gates.

"So is mama. Papa is still hurting and so he can't work like he used to," responds Elsa.

"And we have an extra-large delivery today," adds Elsie.

"Maybe your dad should take advantage of the new work release program with these prisoners," he suggests. He waves them through. "Well ladies, you know the routine." He helps close the gate behind them.

As the ladies drive through the camp compound, the prisoners stop in their tracks to watch them slowly pass.

"This part is always spooky, no matter how many times we've already passed through."

"And it's why I always need you to come with me," responds Elsa.

She pulls the delivery truck up to the camp mess and is immediately surrounded by smiling prisoners, wanting to help unload. Military police rush to the ladies' assistance to put a barrier between the girls and the POWs. Yet both ladies seem unfazed and smiling. It helps that they hear shouts from the Italian soldiers, "*Ah, belle ragazza! Bellissima!*"

The guards, as per their routine, direct the prisoners to unload the truck which is done in no time. As the girls prepare to leave, one of the prisoners works his way to the front of the truck with a note in hand. He manages to place it in Elsa's hand. She uneasily, but instantly notices the handsome, shaved, blue eyed man. A MP pushes him away before she can say anything. Both ladies get into the truck. As the Italians are pushed away, the truck begins to roll out of the camp. Elsie and Elsa giggle with the high of the experience.

"One of them gave me this," Elsa says.

"I saw him before when he was cleaning the front window of the bakery," says Elsie.

She keeps an eye on the wheel while handing a note to Elsie, who instantly opens it and begins to read.

"Out loud, if you don't mind."

Dear *Bellisima Senorina*. My name is Jenoa Domenici. I speak and write English. I want you to know that I think you are as beautiful as is your American movie stars. I look forward to your daily deliveries of bread and sweets. The vision of you is the bread for my soul. And I am sure you must be as sweet. Even as our stomachs are full I remain hungry for such beauty of you and your friend.

Elsie slips it back into her friend's pocket, "He writes English well, don't he? At least he mentioned me."

"The place is not so spooky any more, is it?" answers Elsa.

Both laugh as they turn north onto 2nd Street toward downtown.

Chapter Eight

Having gone through the back-porch screen door into the kitchen, Elsie inadvertently catches her mother sitting at the table dabbing at tears.

"Momma, what's wrong?"

Rose just shakes her head as Johnny walks into the room. He tosses a bulging satchel onto the table.

"Como esta, hermana?" he greets his sister.

"What did you do, Johnny?" Elsa asks suspiciously, looking at her mother.

Rose hands her a letter with an embossed seal and engraved lettering: United States Navy. Johnny slips his arm around her shoulders.

"They've accepted me, sis. I'm in the Navy. Congratulate me."

Elsie is lost for words as Rose stands and reaches for her grown son. He obliges his mother's need to drown him in her embrace.

Elsie must ask, "Why are you packed now, Johnny?"

"He's leaving." Rose squeezes her son harder.

"Now? So quick?" she asks them.

"Ma, I need some time on my own to see the road before I report in San Diego."

"Hitchhiking? Do you need to hitchhike to San Diego?"

"Ma, I want to hitchhike. I need to get adjusted mentally, and I might as well see what I can along the way."

Elsie says in shock, "You're leaving now, today? Just like that? No notice?" She glares at him. "Can't you even be with family for Thanksgiving next week?"

He shakes his head.

The realization slams at her. Her brother is going off to war. And he may not return. Oh, God! Tears well up in her eyes. She's compelled to join her mother and brother in their final hug. They all know it may be the last hug they share for a long, long time.

***

Elsie turns onto Gold Street where a bitter wind cuts through her. She covers her face and pulls at the front door of Santoni's Bakery. But it's locked tight. Amazed, she tries again before she notices the handwritten sign in the window: Closed Due to Family Medical Concern.

Worried, she rushes to the alley entrance. She's relieved when the rear door opens. The kitchen is like she's never seen before, idle and cold. Her concern deepens as she walks through the building to the front of the store. A knot grows in her stomach at the sight of empty glass display cabinets. She hears rumbling. Halfway upstairs she meets Elsa coming out of her parents' bedroom. Her eyes bloodshot, she is obviously distressed.

"Papa's asleep," she whispers to Elsie.

"What's wrong? Why is the shop closed?"

They step down into the shop and back through the kitchen.

"Papa is making himself worse by trying to keep the bakery going. He can't even sit up anymore. And mama is too worried about him to manage the store."

"I'll help—whatever you need," offers Elsie.

"Remember you said that," says Elsa, while glancing around the lonely kitchen. "I am thinking about skipping school to work."

"I'll come in before and after school." Elsie says. Then, as a light goes off in her head, she adds, "Remember when the camp guard said we could get help from the exchange program?"

"Maybe, but I don't know how papa and mama will like having those Mussolinis in our place."

"Do they have a choice?"

Elsa just looks at her.

***

Four Italian prisoners of war stand stiffly, shoulder to shoulder in the kitchen for review. Chains bind them together at the ankles while an armed MP watches. Elsa and Elsie stand behind Mr. and Mrs. Santoni. Giovani tries to hide the pain as he strains to bear his weight on walking canes, one in each hand.

"Please remove their chains," Mr. Santoni says through his thick Italian accent. "No need for chains among Italians."

"I don't know about that, sir," says the MP.

"The men cannot work in kitchen if they are chained to each other," Giovani insists.

With obvious reluctance, the guard complies.

The men rub their ankles.

"*Lei ha lavorata in una panattereria prima?*" Mr. Santoni asks.

Elsa whispers to Elsie, "He's asking if they have done this kind of work before."

No one responds, causing Mr. Santoni to glance at his wife and shake his head. She shrugs in response.

"*Como circa una cucina?*" he asks again.

One prisoner raises his hand. Those in the room suddenly focus attention on the lone prisoner.

"That's the one who slipped me that note at the camp," Elsa whispers.

Through a sly smile, Elsa's attention becomes focused on the handsome man with blue eyes. She watches as her papa walks up to him.

"*Che e'il suo soldato di nome?*"

"Captain Jenoa Dominici, il Signori."

"Did he say he was a captain?" asks Elsie.

"Ah, captain." A sudden respect envelops Mr. Santoni.

"*Si, il Signori.* And I speak English."

Mr. and Mrs. Santoni are set back in surprise as the girls' excitement about the handsome stranger grows.

"*Per favore,* Signori Santoni. I speak for my men when I say we will work hard for you. Thank you for this opportunity to work for your American business."

34

Mr. Santoni smiles at his wife, then shakes the hand of each prisoner in welcome.

Only Elsie notices the glances bouncing between Jenoa Domenici and Elsa Santoni.

Chapter Nine

It has been weeks since the kitchen has been so hot, what with both full-burning stoves and intense kitchen activity.

Giovani Santoni stands at the front of his kitchen. Having rid himself of a walking cane, he leans heavily on the one left.

An MP guard stands at alert beside him.

Giovani watches each man carry out the instructions he personally conveyed to them. One of the men pulls a steel tray off a top shelf and carries it across the kitchen to the sink. After washing it, he carries it back to form the basis for a stack of clean trays. He repeats this routine until all the trays are clean. Meanwhile another prisoner pulls loaves of bread from an oven and places them side-by-side on the work table to cool. Jenoa Domenici blends ingredients in a large mixing bowl for the next batch of bread.

Giovani clears his throat. "Where do your people live, soldier?" he asks the guard standing next to him.

"I'm from Memphis, Tennessee, sir," he responds proudly.

Giovani tries to think of something to else to say, "I do not think you see so many Italians in Memphis, Tennessee?"

Keeping his full attention on his prisoners, the guard replies, "This is correct sir." Without thinking about it, he rests his right palm over the baton synched to his belt.

Giovani keeps his eyes on his domain, "Mmm... mmm." He watches a prisoner walk to the rear and return with a sack of flour thrown over his shoulder.

"No, no, no..." Giovani shouts at the POW in English. "Carry a quart at a time." Realizing who he's shouting at, he says, *"Porta un litro alla volta!"*

The shout from the boss jolts the prisoner. He loses concentration as he tosses the sack on the table. The sack slides across a ragged table corner, ripping it, causing it to spill precious government monitored flour on the floor. Fine flour mist billows into the air.

The guard immediately pulls out his baton. Another prisoner steps back, but Jenoa Domenici holds out both hands to slow the charging military policeman who jabs the captain in the gut. The Italian captain doubles over and falls to the floor. The MP swings full force at the white-faced prisoner's belly, also knocking him to the floor. The MP swings a second subduing blow to his prisoner's mid-section.

"Stay back!" he shouts at the third prisoner while threatening him with his baton.

Mr. Santoni reacts. "No, no, no. This is not necessary. Stop!" He hobbles over to the guard. "Please let him up."

Suddenly Abra Santoni rushes through the swinging door to see what her husband is shouting about. "*Ah, mama mia!*"

She scurries to the aid of Jenoa Domenici while her husband helps the other prisoner.

"Let him up, soldier," Mr. Santoni orders again.

Suddenly, Elsa appears through the doors. The MP carefully stands away from his charge as Giovani Santoni helps him stand.

Abra Santoni directs her daughter: "Bring two chairs."

Elsa nods.

To the idle standing prisoner, Mr. Santoni points at a broom, then the mop and bucket in the back corner. "Prende lo e puliseer favore, per favore."

The prisoner grabs the broom and starts sweeping—initially moving in circles as far away from the MP as possible.

As Mrs. Santoni helps Jenoa Domenici to his feet, she signals to her daughter for a chair, and she turns her attention to her husband and the MP, purposely stepping between them.

Elsa tells Domenici, "*Qui sedere...* you sit here."

Elsa and Jenoa's eyes meet for one, two, then three seconds. He smiles. She blushes.

Chapter Ten

Still in her work clothes, Elsie sits at her kitchen table reading a letter from her brother in San Diego. He writes about finishing boot camp, sounding more mature than she remembers him to be. He writes about being mentally ready to go out on his ship, the USS Samuel B. Roberts. It's apparently a Fletcher class battleship.

"Whatever that is," Elsie says out loud.

Half of the letter seems to mention more, but large portions are blacked out by military sensors. But any letter from him is better than no letter at all. She places it on the table for her mom.

Rose has stopped leaving food simmering on the stove ever since he left home. She knows that her youngest can cook for herself, if she's hungry. Fortunately, Rose is working more hours due to the hotel's busy Christmas season and she has less time to dwell on her son or daughter.

With the house emptier this Christmas, Elsie stares at the small Christmas tree on the end of the kitchen table. Neither she nor her mom have any motivation to decorate it.

From movie theatre newsreels, she's seen dreadful news from Europe. And from the radio, she imagines our allies pushing those dreadful Nazis back into Germany from that awful place called Sicily. This week she met with a schoolmate who lost a brother at Palermo. This causes her to worry more about Johnny in the Pacific. Because she senses that the Japs are even worse. She must get to the movie theatre tomorrow for the latest news. It's the only place to learn more about these things.

She continues to stare at the naked Christmas tree on the table, she pushes it out of the way. And it'll stay there until she or her mom can get in the mood to decorate it.

***

The Santoni Bakery Christmas tree stands proud and tall in the corner of the bakery showroom in front of the picture window. Elsa looks forward to decorating it. But first she pours more coffee into the cups of her faithful Saturday morning New York customers.

"Dave," she says, "because you're wearing your civvies, I guess you came back last night."

"Very observant of you," he smiles back to Elsa. "This is our one year anniversary."

His wife Ruth grips her husband's hand across the table, "I miss him so during the week. I can't wait for the weekends."

Elsa carries the coffee pot back which enables her to hide her eyes rolling at the New York couple. She turns up the radio a little. She hears that new song she likes called 'When There Are Such Things.' It's sung by Frankie. She remembers him because he's Italian, too.

From behind the counter she retrieves a box of family Christmas decorations. Her anticipation builds to decorate the tree.

In the kitchen, Mr. Santoni shoots the bull with the MP guard.

"Since Italy is now ally of America, you now watch Allied prisoners."

In an unusually relaxed manner, "Orders are orders, sir."

Sweeping the floors around the doors, Jenoa Domenici peeks through the windows in the door to the show room where Elsa is decorating the tree.

He turns to Mr. Santoni, "Per favore signore, may I assist in decorating your tree?"

Not giving it a second thought, he nods. "*Si, Si.*"

In no time, Jenoa is through the swinging door.

"Your father said I am to help you, Miss Santoni."

He pulls over a chair and takes the decoration a surprised Elsa hands him. Jenoa stands on top of the chair and hooks it high up on the tree.

She studies him. "Why is your English so good, Captain Jenoa Domenici?" She hands him another decoration while pointing to a spot near the top of the tree.

"I studied at Oxford for two years."

"Oxford? Where is that?"

"England, of course."

"England?" She stops and focuses on him. "Then how did you become a prisoner of war?"

"*Il Duce* called all loyal Italians to serve. I arrived in Tripoli. The next day your army attacked. I was captured, and I have been the property of your country ever since." He steps down from the chair.

"*Il Duce*, a horrible beast."

"He did bring greatness back to Italy."

"Greatness? Look at yourself, an Oxford student who now is a prisoner of war. And, who is now forced to work in a bakery."

"*Si*. But I am in an American bakery with you. I have Mussolini to thank for that."

She notices empty coffee cups on her New York customers' table. She puts down the decorations and turns away.

Jenoa watches Elsa's sudden sway as she walks. He watches her pick up the coffee pot to pour her customers more java. The New York lovers do not give the man with the grey shirt with a P on the back, a second look. Elsa returns to take a step up on the chair. Jenoa examines her curves as she moves the ornaments higher up the tree. He smiles.

"I have always been a lucky man," he says. "There are much worse things that could happen to a soldier in war than the adventure to travel around the world to meet such a *bella regazza*." He cautiously loses himself in her beauty, "For me, a prisoner of war, I am lucky."

Elsa blushes as she walks around the counter to pour herself a cup of coffee. "*Il caffe,* captain?"

"*Grazi, si, si*. The coffee at the camp is toilet water. I would like to taste good American coffee."

She pours him a cup, which he gratefully accepts.

"Ah, *magnifico*," he sips the steaming cup as if it is pure ambrosia.

"Captain Domenici, or should I call you just Captain?"

"*Per favore,* call me Jenoa."

"Where in Italy does your family live? We are from Sicily."

His demeanor saddens. "I miss *mi familia* in Firenze. Do you know where that is, Firenze?"

She shakes her head, "We escaped five years ago."

"Firenze, which is north of Roma. Leonardo Da Vinci was from my home town."

Elsa notices his sudden subdued expression.

"But why does that sadden you?"

He hooks a glass bulb on a tree branch. "I have not seen my family in many years. They do not know what has happened to me since the North Africa desert. I miss them."

The doorbell tinkles as the young New York couple head out the door. They smile and wave at Elsa. "See you next time."

As they leave, a young mother ushers her two toddlers into the bakery, all shivering from the cold outside. Right away she notices the man with a large P on his back, placing ornaments on the tree. Instinctively, she pulls her children in close. Elsa notices her customer's concern.

"Merry Christmas, welcome to Santoni's Bakery," she says.

She pulls a tray from the counter and offers cookies to the kids. The mother scrutinizes the POW carefully as he places another decoration on the tree. "Care for some hot chocolate?" Elsa asks her.

She shivers, then nods. "We came in for holiday treats." She still maintains her guard from the unexpected stranger.

"You came to the right place," Elsa says to the children. "We have all the sweetness you'd like."

One of the children, through wide eyes and pointing fingers, asks, "Mommy, mommy can we have that and that and that?"

Elsa hands the young mother a steamy cup of cocoa which, as she'd hopes, draws the mom's focus away from Jenoa.

"It has been a long time since we've had hot cocoa," the mother says, smiling.

But after hurriedly picking out her items, and carefully counting coins into Elsa's hand, she rushes her kids out the door.

Elsa laughs, giving Jenoa permission to do likewise.

Chapter Eleven

The high school bleachers are half empty, but several students cheer for their Bulldogs. A player races down the basketball court, jumps to push the ball through the air and into the hoop. Three cheerleaders, dressed in their red and black neck to ankle uniforms, jump up and down to entice cheers out of their fans. Both three member teams run back down to the visiting team's side of the court.

Elsa comments to Elsie as they sit at the absolute top of the bleachers. "Look at them. Not one is over fifteen."

She points at a player. "There's David, number eleven. He is cute."

"Didn't we give him a fifteenth birthday card last week?" Elsa reminds her friend.

"He's still cute." She grins.

"You're almost eighteen, aim higher."

Both girls yell and jump to their feet as one of Albuquerque High players blocks a shot. They sit down together.

"Where?" asks Elsie.

"Well, it won't be here at school, that's for sure." Again, they both jump and yell as number eleven makes another basket.

***

Elsie shivers as she opens the back door to her house and the lonesome kitchen. Once in, she leaves winter behind her. She walks to the cast iron stove, opens its hatch, stuffs in some newspaper, and tosses a couple pieces of wood on top before putting a match to the paper. She guards the precious lit match across the kitchen to light the Christmas candle on the table.

As soon as her mom comes home from work, they are expected to the Santoni's for Christmas Eve. Then they are all going to St. Mary's for midnight mass. Elsie wants to take a bath and change before mom gets there.

She pulls a stack of mail from her coat pocket to thumb through. A thin letter from the U.S. Navy catches her eye, especially since it's addressed to mom. She tosses the rest on the kitchen table. Unable to resist temptation, her hands shake as she rips open the envelope to find a letter half blacked out by the military sensors. Elsie resigns herself to reading between the lines.

11/43

Dear Mom & Sis;

I'm doing great! Life in the =========== is unusual for this desert guy. Being from the desert, humidity is my main enemy right now. But everything is so green. You've never seen so much green ========== or so much blue ====== in your life! But the only green I miss is your green chili with your Thanksgiving turkey. I miss home. I now see what is for a desert boy, a once in a lifetime chance. It's great. I met a buddy from Arizona. I call him Boomer. When he talks, he's loud. A whisper for him is at normal voice level. He has the bunk below mine.

We were on shore leave in ============== last week. We did things that we could never do in Albuquerque. Believe me there is a big world outside of there, I promise you.

I got a tattoo on my right forearm. I know this will upset you, mom, but I am in the Navy now. I miss you mom and sis. Ship food is good and I am in better shape than when you last saw me.

I know it's a cold Christmas season there, but it's ======== here. Till I write again, I love you both.

Johnny

Elsie ponders his letter and decides that it will let mom have an easier Christmas.

Chapter Twelve

February 1944

An Army captain walks into the bakery and finds Elsa and Abra behind the counter. As he approaches, he takes off his cap. "Hello, Mrs. Santoni? I am Captain Ridges from the camp. I was hoping to meet with Mr. Santoni."

Abra nods, "Is there something wrong?"

"No. No. Just the opposite." He smiles.

"He's in the kitchen," Abra says. "I'll bring him out." The kitchen doors are swinging.

"Have a seat, sir. Care for a cup of coffee?" asks Elsa.

"Thanks. That's nice of you."

As Mr. Santoni enters, he notices the waiting captain and he tells his daughter, "The loaves are ready. Pull them out." Mr. and Mrs. Santoni join him at the table.

An hour passes before her parents come back into the kitchen.

Mr. Santoni tells his waiting daughter, "The Army feels that you and your friend have done a good job in making deliveries to the camp. They want me to make some emergency deliveries. And we need the money they offer."

Abra adds, "But your papa is not ready to drive the trip."

Elsa looks puzzled. It's only a couple of miles round trip.

"You are going to make a big delivery to Santa Fe," Mr. Santoni says.

"Santa Fe? I've never been to Santa Fe."

***

Elsa, sitting in the driver's seat, accompanied by her sidekick Elsie, can feel the strain on the delivery truck's engine as they start up extremely steep La Bajada Hill. Concern shows on both of their faces as their momentum is reduced to half of what it was moments before.

As they cut through the hills over the two-lane road, "This was once Route 66 up to nine years ago," Elsie says. She tightens her grip on the door handle.

"The weight of the load is not helping." Elsa shifts into lower gear. "Those people are short on supplies," she says.

"Why couldn't the Army deliver them?"

"Papa says their trucks are all busy with camps down south."

They pass a truck stalled on the side of the road, steam pouring out of its engine compartment. As their speedometer slows to ten miles an hour, Elsie glances at Elsa.

"We can't stop now to help. I don't know if we'd ever get going again."

Elsie grips the handle tighter but says nothing. As soon as the hill starts to level off and the truck's speed grows again, she releases it.

"I hope this trip is worth it."

A foot of snow covers the terrain as far as they can see, making them shiver. Elsie turns up the heater and turns on the radio. They both love Glen Miller's music and are amazed at the coincidence when *On The Road To Santa Fe* plays.

"Papa says we can use the money. Besides, he says the people are hungry and short on supplies."

"But we have Italian food and they are Japs." Says Elsie, remembering her own brother who is fighting on the other side of the Pacific. "I hate them!"

Elsa says nothing so Elsie turns to the map she was given. "Look for Saint Francis Road, then turn left through town till we see the national cemetery."

After many town signs and road markers, up and down snowy hills, Elsie notices a street sign they pass. "Hey, that sign said it's the El Camino Real!"

"So?"

"Don't you remember? In school they said that was the oldest and longest highway on this side of the world. It starts in Mexico City!"

Elsa looks unimpressed. The Italian delivery truck passes countless, beautifully aligned white grave stones of the national veterans' cemetery on their right.

Elsie studies her map. "Our instructions are if we pass the cemetery, we've gone too far. Turn around."

"They also say soldiers buried here date back to the Civil War."

They take another right which leads them up and over, then down another hill. Leaving the cemetery far, far behind. Finally, to the right are endless chamisa laden plains. To the left are multilevel lands filled with seemingly unlimited barracks and adobe structures, too many to count, surrounded by countless miles of multi-strand barbed wire fence of a concentration camp.

From the top of a hill Elsie observes, "Dios Mio, this place is much bigger than the Italian."

They finally arrive, stopping at the front gate.

Two soldiers step up to the truck, their faces soon show surprise to see the two serious-looking young ladies in it.

After they double read the sign on the truck's side, Santoni's Bakery, they check their manifest and wave them through an opening in the barbed-wire gates.

The truck is swarmed by the camp's angular eyed occupants.

In her high, excited voice Elsie says, "They're women and children!"

Elsa adds, "And babies! And they're shouting in perfect English!"

"You came at an inconvenient time," says one of the guards. "We have a special VIP guest here today."

Both girls glance around the compound. All they can see further inside is a large collection of government vehicles.

"You'll have to wait a bit," says the guard. He points to a side of the road that is seemingly out of the way. "Park there."

Elsa pulls over and turns off the engine. Their focus is naturally on the cluster of government cars. Before long they watch a cluster of uniformed guards surround a solo military-dressed old lady. As she barks commands, the military types around her seem to be kowtowing.

"That old lady looks familiar."

"That can't be... can it?" asks Elsa.

They watch the old lady command her surroundings.

They notice her sour and stern expression disappear as several American-Japanese children approach her. Suddenly smiling, she gathers a small oriental girl into her arms. She passes her warm gloved hand over the child's cheek as several other children gather around her legs. When an officer moves to chase them away, she places her hand out to stop him. When she places the child back down, she hugs all of them in a group.

"Look how all those Army guys jump at whatever she says to them."

Elsa wonders out loud, "Could that be Eleanor?"

Elsie focuses more closely. "Sure looks like her, doesn't she?"

"Naw. It couldn't be. What would Eleanor be doing here?"

Soon enough, they watch the old lady gently release the children and then shake hands with an obviously high ranking Army officer.

Elsie says, "That must be the camp's commander."

They watch the old lady get into a chauffeured military vehicle with Army officers jumping all around it. The car melts into the center of the cluster of military vehicles as they begin to exit the camp.

Then an Army green vehicle in the center passes and they get a closer view of the rear seat occupant. Their jaws drop.

Both state in unison, "That is Eleanor!"

Elsie excitedly tells her friend, "We just saw the great lady!"

The convoy of army green vehicles exits through the front gate. Both girls snap back to reality when the front gate guard blows his whistle at them. Elsa turns on the truck's engine to follow the directions given them by the other American guard as they slowly maneuver through the compound.

After driving through the camp, the Santoni truck finally pulls up to the mess. They can see small American flags on the occupants' barracks' frosted windows.

An Army soldier barks, "Stay in the truck!" American dressed Japanese men open the truck's back doors and start unloading the supplies. A soldier starts checking off the ladies' manifest. When the doors close, the Army sergeant again barks out, "You can leave."

When the truck heads back the same way they came, they pass female occupants bowing to them in gratitude. As they approach the exit gate, both girls notice groups of shivering children as they wave little hands and fingers goodbye.

Elsie says, "They're all American!"

Both girls wipe tears from their eyes.

***

Mr. Santoni rests at a table in his café while he enjoys a cup of coffee. While the kitchen bustles, he inadvertently watches people walk by his store window under a sunny February afternoon. Although constant, his back pain is reducing daily. He knows his restlessness has pushed him back to work, up to half days now. And since the prisoners arrived, bakery production has fortunately returned in full swing. Because of Abra's guidance in the kitchen and now behind the glass showcase, store hours are back to normal. He hasn't heard any comments from the women in his life who've been carrying the load, and smiles as he watches his beautiful wife sell another Valentine chocolate cake.

A Month Later

He stares out his second-floor bedroom window. Spring wind firmly shakes the barren tree outside. For some reason, he finds himself yearning for his home and familia back in Palermo. Someday, someday he hopes he will see them again.

Reluctantly, he gives Il Dulce a few kudos. *Il fascista* forced him to seek his family's fortune in America.

But today, an Irish holiday, will be his first full day back at work. As he closes the apartment door behind him, he smiles at the walking cane left in the corner. He still carefully walks down the steps unaided. His mind prepares to bake everything green.

***

Later in the day and a half of a mile away, Elsie studies her history book using the afternoon light shining through the kitchen window. Unable to focus, she marks the page with a wilted four leaf clover, as her attention snaps back when her mother enters the room. Rose's hair is neatly tied back as she wears her Hilton Hotel uniform.

"What time will you be home, ma?"

"It depends when the St. Patrick dance is over," she explains while she puts on her coat. "I pulled the short straw this week to prep for the late-night crowd. Finish your homework?" She makes sure her keys are in her pocket.

Having had her fill with schoolwork, Elsie closes the book.

"Yes, mom. I'm finished."

"You graduate in a couple of months. So I want you to pack in as much learning as possible." She stands there for a silent moment to stare at her daughter. Then, unable to hold herself back, she crosses the kitchen to place a kiss her daughter's cheek. "I am so proud of my high school graduate."

As Elsie blushes, she enjoys her mother's hug. Rose glances at the wall clock, 4:30, then checks again for the keys and leaves through the back door, her daughter a few steps behind.

"We are taking class photos next week. Then we must go get measurements for caps and gowns," Elsie tells her mom.

Leaving through the back alley is a shortcut for everyone. Soon they are walking south on the Third Street sidewalk.

"The warm early spring air is forcing buds on the trees already," Rose says as she pulls a bud from an overhanging branch.

Her daughter does the same, then studies what is in her grasp.

"So, mama, do you want to go with me to take my class photo?"

"I have already shifted my schedule at work. I only have one hour that day before I must return." She stops in her tracks and takes her daughter in her embrace. "But I want to be with my baby girl."

Contentment overwhelms Elsie. Within a couple more blocks they embrace again before Rose turns left on Tijeras Avenue, and Elsie continues south on Third Street to visit Elsa.

Chapter Thirteen

The April sun rises earlier each day through their bedroom window. With government-issued kitchen help, he can afford the luxury of strength building sleep later each day.

Giovani takes advantage by smiling at the sight of the tree outside the window, which is sprouting new leaves. He hears quick steps up the stairs. He sits on the bed and waits as the door swings open. There stands his beautiful wife wearing a smile with newspaper in hand.

"They are attacking Anzio," she tells him, opening the front page to the headline: Allies Land at Anzio. "And the bastard *Il Duce* is on the run!"

Instant glee overcomes him. He ignores the tinge of back pain as he stands and displays the largest smile he's had all month. Abra melts into her husband's arms as tears roll down both of their faces.

***

Elsa looks again at the clock over the front counter. It has been more than an hour since mommi went upstairs to check on poppi. Business is slow. She glances through the window in the door to the kitchen where she sees Elsie washing trays while the crew goes through their routines. It's time to find the newspaper but she remembers that mommi took it up to poppi. Since no one is in the café, she heads upstairs.

She swings open her parents' bedroom door.

"What's the matter, Papa, Mama?" The sight provides ultimate embarrassment. "MOMMI! POPPI!"

They are naked across the bed on top of each other. In that instant, Elsa grabs the newspaper to block her view before escaping downstairs. Despite her embarrassment, she's relieved to know that poppi is feeling better.

Composing herself, she puts the newspaper in the side pocket of her apron as her regular customers, the young New York couple, walk in.

"Welcome to Santoni's," says Elsa.

No sooner do they find their usual table, Elsa is ready to pour Joe in their cups.

When the front door bell rings again, Elsie steps from the back with her best smile, and kicks in to assist Elsa with the flock of customers around the front counter. Within minutes, the stock of bread in the glass case dwindles to only a few loaves.

"We need more bread," Elsa says.

As Elsie is about to go through the swinging doors, Elsa adds, "It's okay. I'll get them."

Elsie nods as Elsa disappears into the kitchen.

Capitan Domenici guides his two men around the kitchen in their well-practiced routines. The MP is standing outside the rear open door, smoking a cigarette. The cool spring air brings relief to the sweaty bakery kitchen.

Elsa goes directly to the rack of freshly baked bread where she sees the twenty-year-old Italian captain, Jenoa Domenici, cleaning a baking table.

When their eyes meet, he disappears nonchalantly behind the cooler. She follows while carrying an empty pastry rack. Momentarily out sight, they fall into each other's arms. Their lips seductively meet and stay joined in passion. His hands slowly glide down her back. As planned, he pulls the newspaper from her apron pocket.

"Don't read it here," she whispers.

"Ringraziarla, la ringrazi il mio amore," he says, kissing her passionately again, then whispers in his perfect English, "News is as important to us as food." She lets her lips meet his. He speaks as low as he can, "I yearn for you."

"I want to save myself for my husband," she whispers with a hungry smile.

He nibbles the side of her throat. "Will you save yourself for me?"

Trying to strengthen her weakening knees, she says, "We need more bread up front."

He releases her reluctantly, knowing the guard is only a few steps away. Her smile widens as she walks away carrying a tray of bread loaves back through the swinging doors where she places them in the glass case.

Elsie hands coins to a customer. "Thank you for your business," and does a double-take at the smile on Elsa's face. As she wipes her hands on her apron, she says, "I suppose he was grateful again."

Elsa, still smiling, nods.

Elsie shakes her head as she changes the coffee pot. The front doorbell chimes as new customers enter.

"Welcome to Santoni's," the girls say simultaneously. Both tighten their aprons.

Chapter Fourteen

Crisp, humidity-free May Day air covers the high desert climate. Yet the ten-foot-high barbed wire fences that surround Camp Albuquerque retain tension far beyond their electrified voltage.

U.S. Army troop trucks pour through from the gate to park in the middle of the compound. As they exit the trucks, all automatically line up to face toward the front gate. Fully armed contingents of soldiers with MP on their helmets, jump out and line up at attention. Their commanding officer parades up and down in front of his men.

"...apparently, some prisoners do not like how the war is going for the *Il Dulce*. Others like what is happening. In this situation, we do not give a damn who is who. This is no place for the two factions to fight it out. We are here to prevent fights from turning into full-fledged riots."

He continues to pace up and down in front of his line. "Fix bayonets. If necessary use force, but only if necessary," he orders. "Find the cause of this insurrection while securing each of the barracks. Move out!"

The wooden barracks are soon surrounded—and then invaded. Some Italian prisoners innocently open their doors allowing easy access inside. Other show angry men who resist, and are ordered to vacate.

"Fall out, outside," the troops shout at them. "Now!"

Italians who do not understand shouted English do not react instantly and are forcibly pulled out. Those who resist are knocked down to the ground with butts of bayoneted rifles. The message soon becomes clear. POWs quickly exit and line up outside their barrack doors.

An hour passes as platoon sergeants report back to their captain with the evidence. The Army captain, in full battle gear, reports to his commanding officer with a salute. His left hand grips evidence: several newspapers.

"Colonel, the POW camp is locked down and secured without a shot being fired, sir."

The colonel returns the salute, "Good." He glances at his watch. "And in less than an hour, very good."

The captain hands him the newspapers. "Here are samples of the contraband that we found. Undoubtedly, they incited the disturbances, sir."

The commander glances at the small stack of newspapers. He picks up the top paper, Allies Bomb Monte Cassino.

"This is months old," he says. He picks up the next front page. It reads, Il Duce Hunted. The next reads, Allies Land at Anzio. "Bring me the perpetrators of this contraband."

"Yes, sir." The captain salutes.

The colonel returns the salute. "Carry on."

***

Through the small window of the swinging door, wife and daughter watch their husband and father back at work in the kitchen.

"I am happy he is able to work again, but I wish he did not have to," Elsa whispers to her mother.

They smile watching him sing opera while he works. Suddenly, he winces with pain and grabs at his lower back. Abra moves to assist her husband but Elsa holds her back as her father is once again singing and slowly lifting a rack of fresh bread. Relief overcomes them both.

"I wish we still had the extra help," says Elsa.

"Until Camp Albuquerque tensions ends, we must not even think about that."

When the clock reads six a.m. Abra tightens her apron and hands one to her daughter. She opens the front door and turns the sign to Open. Elsa changes her smile to a frown, wondering when she'll see Jenoa again. She tightens her apron.

"Still, I wish we had the help."

"Si, si. I do not know how much longer your papa will be able to work 20 hours every day to supply the bread to the prison camp. You and me will be working extra hours."

"We will need Elsie more, too."

"Si, tell your little friend to plan more hours."

"Si, mama."

She watches her mother walk back into the kitchen carrying empty trays. And in no time she comes back with them full, ready to slide bread under the glass case.

"Your papa is very tired. I have decided to leave store at two in afternoon to talk to prison commandant. Maybe he will give us back our prisoners. You must drive me."

"Si, mama." Especially now that it is hurting papa. This is something even Elsie will be able to see.

"And try to get Jenoa Domenici back." Her mother studies her daughter.

"He already knows our way and he speaks English," she adds to belay her mother's suspicious glare.

Chapter Fifteen

The bakery is closed for the day when Elsie arrives. As she goes around to the back entrance she can feel the kitchen's radiating heat, although the windows and doors are closed. She knows that it is a sign that yeast-laden dough is rising. The temperature gauge next to the back door reads 98 degrees Fahrenheit. Once inside she can tell all four ovens are at full capacity baking 100 six-inch-long loaves of bread at 350.

"Keep the door closed," shouts out Giovani as he dusts his baking table with flour. He is preparing his next batch of dough, "Start on the dishes, little one."

Abra operates the two electric mixing vats while blending ingredients into one, then the other.

"This will be our last delivery," she says in a stern tone while tossing Elsie her apron.

Elsa is in another corner, quietly greasing stacks of baking sheets. Elsie starts washing stacks of dirty dishes in another corner, wondering what happened.

Giovani always watches the clock before he dares open his ovens to pull out each batch of loaves. Waves of heat hit his face before spreading throughout the kitchen. But the wonderful aroma compensates for the heat. With a towel wrapped around his forearm and hand, he grabs the foot-long brush positioned inside a can labeled Bertonelli's Extra Virgin Olive Oil. He generously sweeps it over each loaf, giving them a glow before quickly closing the oven door.

Unable to stand the silence, Elsie asks, "Well, what happened?" She is silent while keeping her back turned away from everyone there.

Abra answers: "Because of riot in camp, the Mayor Tingley ordered the camp closed."

Elsie persists, "Riot? What caused that?"

"Newspaper contraband is all commandant would say."

Elsie stares at her silent friend who continues to keep her back turned.

"I am sorry," she says. "I know how much business that brought the bakery. I'm really sorry." The silence is almost deafening.

"Can we at least turn on the radio?" She asks, as she wipes sweat from her face with her sleeve.

Elsa finally turns to her mother who glances at her father, who nods his approval. She turns on the radio and Big Band trombone music soon fills the kitchen. The two teenagers immediately recognize the song.

"I love Frankie," Elsie comments, smiling.

Elsa takes small dance steps in place. "I saw his picture in the movie magazine. His eyes are so blue."

Elsie tells her friend's parents, "The magazine says that he's Italian too, from New Jersey."

Giovani's hands and arms pause kneading pounds of dough on his flour-laden table. He tells his wife, "Italian? No wonder these girls like this kid."

Abra delivers another load of dough on the table. Giovani reaches for his wife, pulling her toward him while placing his arm around her. He enjoys that he still can use the same arm length around her as the day they were married nineteen years ago in the old country. Their mutual attention is focused on the sight of their baby dancing in front them. He softly kisses the palm of his wife's hand.

As the girls finish their tasks Giovani says, "Ah, bambina, load this batch of bread in the truck. We must deliver this last load to Camp Albuquerque."

"Last load, already," asks Elsa, thinking of Jenoa.

"Si. The prisoners are being moved out," answers her papa.

His daughter answers back, "The prisoners are leaving? The prisoners are leaving," she asks, then tells Elsie.

He is obviously depressed about it. "*Si. Si.* We lose the bread contract." He leans on his wife for support.

As if she heard wrong, his daughter asks again. "The prisoners are leaving so soon? I mean, are we losing the bread contract work so soon?"

Both girls show their concern.

Her father just nods. "I must deliver the bread now," he says.

"Papa, let me make the delivery," Elsa says. "You look very tired. Let me do it." A knot has grown in her stomach.

He yawns, which reminds him that he hasn't slept since yesterday. He yawns again. It is easier to continue to nod yes to his daughter.

***

The bakery truck passes through the front gates of the POW camp. "Do you see him?" Elsa asks anxiously.

Elsie rubber necks. "Not yet."

Elsa drives around the corner of a row of wooden barracks and into the open compound and says, "Oh, my God, look!"

Rows of troop trucks are parked with their rear gates wide open. Elsa slowly drives by. An MP signals them to continue on. Both girls are silent as they pull up to the camp mess. The usual prisoner swarms are not there. A lone MP stands guard. He signals for two prisoners to double time out to unload the truck. Both girls start to get out of the vehicle before the MP signals them to stay inside.

"Not closing the doors quick enough," the MP barks. "I said stay in the truck." He moves closer. "Close the doors," he orders. Only then does he signal to the prisoners to open the truck's rear doors to start unloading.

Trying not to let the unusual ominous atmosphere shake them, Elsa asks again, "Do you see him?"

Elsie shakes her head.

In quick order, the truck is unloaded and the doors shut. The MP signals the girls to leave at once.

"This place has become scary," observes Elsie. "I see only a handful of Italian prisoners here." Elsa swings the truck around the rows of troop trucks. Under her breath Elsie says, "My God, look..."

Hundreds of newly arriving prisoners jump from troop trucks parked in front of each barrack.

"Those must be the Nazi prisoners papa said are coming," Elsa tells her.

Across the compound, the girls glance to see the Italian prisoners filling up troop trucks one by one. A MP holds out his hand to stop the bakery truck as rows of Nazi prisoners cross in front.

"My God, it's actually happening," exclaims Elsa. Out of the thousand prisoners, both girls silently keep an eye out for one, Capitan Jenoa Domenici. "Do ya see him?"

"No, I don't."

The line in front ends and the MP signals the bakery truck forward. Elsa purposely drives slowly.

"Keep an eye out."

The truck convoy starts rolling. And again another MP holds his hand out to stop the girls at the front gate. The trucks carrying the prisoners start rolling by.

As a break in the procession occurs, the MP waves the bakery truck through the gate. Elsie looks back to see what she can under the Camp Albuquerque portal sign, but there's nothing.

"I want to cry," Elsa murmurs.

She steers the bakery truck close behind a prisoner truck, allowing the men behind its open flap to notice them. While madly pointing at the girls, they shout something.

"There sure is a commotion from those guys. It's like they've never seen us before."

Prisoners start changing seats. Elsa's eyes light up as she sees Jenoa Domenici moving up. He waves at her. Elsa becomes so excited, she stops the truck and gets out to wave back.

Jenoa blows kisses to Elsa. "*Arrivederci, bambina. Arrivederci.*"

Trucks behind the bakery truck start honking.

Elsie shouts, "Let's move before the MPs come."

As Jenoa's truck starts to move, Elsa wants to follow. But she stops in place as more troop carriers circumvent the little bakery truck to muscle in behind the truck carrying Jenoa Domenici.

Tears trickle from Elsa's eyes. So, Elsie hugs her friend. Both girls watch helplessly as the procession of vehicles command the road around them and head south out of town.

Chapter Sixteen

Early Summer

Clouds of steam spit from under a seemingly endless line of rail cars as they slow to a stop. The Grand Union Railroad Station public address system informs patrons: NOW ARRIVING, THE SANTA FE CHIEF FROM CHICAGO, ST. LOUIS, OKLAHOMA CITY, ALBUQUERQUE, FLAGSTAFF AND SAN BERNADINO.

Rear hatches open down the line. From a middle car, two lovely young ladies step down while holding onto their hats. Both laugh with excitement.

"We're in City of Angels!" they shout.

From beyond the steam they hear someone calling: "Elsie. Elsie! Over here!"

Elsie sees arms waving several rail cars down the line. She giggles when she glimpses her smiling sister. "Esther!" she cries out.

They run across the railroad platform into each other arms in a hug that conveys the years since they've seen each other. Elsa catches up, carrying their suitcases.

"Elsa! You're even more beautiful," Esther says, pulling her into a hug.

She directs attention to the tall fellow standing next to her. Taking his hand, she says, "Ladies, this handsome fellow is Ambrose, my husband."

Elsa raises an eyebrow while making a show of scanning Ambrose from his well-shined shoes to his razor thin mustache. "I see why you married him," she observes.

Holding out her hand, Elsie says, "Hello, Ambrose."

"Is that any way to greet your new brother?" He embraces Elsie, lifting her like a feather, giving her cheek a smacking kiss. Elsie laughs.

"The second bedroom in our little house is ready for you two," Esther tells the girls.

"Thank you," Elsie says, adding, "We will start looking for our own apartment as soon as we can."

As the group walks away, Esther asks, "Any news about Johnny?"

Elsie shakes her head, "His last letter said he was sailing somewhere into the Pacific Ocean."

Esther gives her husband a puzzled look.

"That's where most of the US Navy operates," he explains.

The sisters nod in a somber moment, which Elsa interrupts. "So, this is Los Angeles. How far is Hollywood?" she asks, struggling with the bags.

***

A sign over the entrance reads Hughes Aircraft. Deafening machinery sounds blend with protectively clothed female assembly line workers. All shout instructions amongst themselves. The combined sounds echo off the walls of the cavernous structure.

Workers step over and climb through, in and out of rows of partially assembled B-10 Army Air Corp bombers. Intense flurries of bright sparks fly in all directions as they solder aluminum beams together. At the half-way mark along the assembly line, huge shadows start to bounce off each shiny plane.

One of a long row of welders finishes a task. She turns off her torch and places it aside. Pushing up her mask, Elsa wipes sweat from her face with a dirty sleeve while inspecting her work by walking the length of the 250-foot aluminum wing from tip to tip.

Cranes slide overhead along rails delivering sheets of aluminum to the next lot of air frame skeletons. Gloved female workers, standing in designated spots, carefully guide each eight by five-foot sheet into place. As quickly as the crane moves in, it moves out, clearing way for the next shining sheet. As her coworkers do, Elsa's gloved hands expertly guide one side of the razor-sharp sheet into place. A team of rivet gunners step in to bolt the sheet to a designated portion of the frame.

A rivet gunner climbs out of the plane's cockpit frame. She puts the tool on a work table and pulls off her goggles to adjust the bandana around her head. Elsie's shirt sleeves are rolled up revealing newly developed muscles that ripple with each move. She takes a deep breath, then loads her gun with more rivets before joining the line again. Soon, the siren echoes throughout the hangar, signaling a shift change. One crew quits for the day while the next shift continues where they left off.

The sun sits on the horizon as the two friends walk out of the front gate together, where they jump on a waiting bus. It moves through the San Fernando Valley below the San Gabriel Mountains, where it is dark in West Covina when it drops them off. After walking and walking, they finally open the white picket gate to Esther and Ambrose's house. Their jackets are thrown over their shoulders as they see the Christmas tree glistening in the window.

"Back home we'd be wearing a coat," says Elsie, smiling.

Before they open the side door they can hear Glen Miller's "Moonlight Serenade" coming from the radio. The song finishes directly into another Miller song: "Juke Box Saturday Night."

"Remember when this song first came out?" Elsie asks. "It was a Saturday night and we were out with my brother and his buddy."

"Yeah. That buddy had his hands all over me," Elsa recalls. "Yeah, I remember."

"Where are my sis and her husband?"

The girls sit down to rest after hanging up their jackets. "It's not like them to leave the Christmas lights on."

They rest until the next song starts. "Little Brown Jug? Isn't that another Miller tune?"

"I want to hear something by Frankie," Elsa says with a sigh of exhaustion.

Elsie asks, "Isn't that the third Glen Miller song in a row?"

There's a moment of silence until the announcer speaks. "If you have not heard yet, the BBC in London reports that an airplane carrying famed American swing band leader Glen Miller is missing over the English Channel and is presumed lost."

Miller's somber "Fools Rush" fills the room.

The girls seem to go into shock. Tears fill their eyes as they hear some-one—Esther crying in one of the bedrooms.

Through the paper-thin walls, they hear Ambrose say, "That's okay, baby. Go ahead, it's okay."

"She's always been a big Glen Miller fan," Elsie tells Elsa.

The mournful sound of Miller's solo trombone smoothly fades away.

Chapter Seventeen

January 1945

The factory workers enjoy a momentary diversion when two fifty-foot banners are raised into place on the sides of the cavernous facility. One reads, "Loose Lips Sinks Ships!" while the other exclaims, "Slackers help the Axis!"

Workers on the line experience a slight boost in motivation, while those on their thirty-minute lunch break simply take it in stride. The majority sit at break tables finishing their sack lunches or cigarettes.

Elsa and Elsie sit silently next to each other unable to hide their mutual humdrum outlook. They split and share their one stick of rationed chewing gum. A gal sitting next to Elsa notices this and graciously offers her a cigarette.

Elsa smiles while shaking her head. "Ah, no, thank you, Betty."

"It'll help you relax," Betty insists.

"Aren't they rationed?"

"Listen, it's time to relax. Besides, these cigs are pushing their stale limit."

Out of curiosity, Elsa accepts. "I've never smoked before." She offers to share half with Elsie, who nods.

Elsa breaks the Lucky Strike cigarette in two and hands her a half. Both fumble with it, only to learn that the action spills valuable tobacco. As each carefully lights her half with their one rationed match, both cough as they try inhaling.

Betty asks, "Elsie, aren't you from New Mexico?"

"How many times have I told people around here how much I miss home?" Elsie asks between coughs.

Betty takes a worn envelope from her pocket. It is obviously military with all the markings all over it. "I have been writing a soldier from New Mexico, but I can't anymore."

Elsa's leans towards her. "I thought you were engaged to a local boy?"

Betty nods. "In good conscience, I can't do both anymore."

As Elsa reaches for the letter, Betty hands it to her.

"My thinking was to ask you, Elsie, if you'd be interested in writing to your fellow New Mexican? He's cute. I don't have his photo anymore, but he is cute."

Elsie snaps the letter from Elsa and looks it over. "Sure. Why not? I always wanted to. It's a small way to do my part."

When the assembly line whistle blows, Betty carefully stubs out the cigarette, putting the remainder in her pocket. Elsie and Elsa quietly drop theirs.

As they head back to work, Elsie slips the letter into her overall pocket.

***

"Happy Valentine's Day, ladies," Ambrose says as the girls arrive home from work.

He and Esther stand over a pot simmering on the stove. They watch Esther hug her husband who holds her shoulders while she brings a dripping spoon to his lips. He smiles with delight.

The girls exchange a look that silently says Esther and Ambrose should get a room—but this is their house. They drag themselves into the living room and plop down on the sofa, dead tired.

"It's Friday night," Ambrose calls to them. "Why don't you gals go dancing or something?" They exchange another look when they hear Esther practically swooning.

"The USO Club would welcome a couple of pretty ladies," Ambrose adds unnecessarily.

"Not a bad idea," says Elsa, nodding.

"It has been a while since we went dancing," observes Elsie.

Still too pooped to move, they feel the pressure to get out of the house.

Esther puts the spoon on the stove so she can run her fingers through her husband's hair. He kisses her, grabbing hold of her buttocks with both hands. Esther giggles loudly.

Annoyed at the pet sounds, Elsie says, "Let's go."

Elsa stands, walking towards the bathroom. "I want to clean up first."

Ambrose and Esther purr in each other's arms as he carries her to their bedroom, right past the girls.

Elsie turns off the flame below the simmering stew after serving herself a bowl knowing that her sister is an excellent cook, just like their mom.

Mom! Elsie realizes suddenly how much she misses her. I must write her my weekly letter, she vows.

Elsa walks out of the bathroom brushing her long jet-black hair. "It's yours," she announces.

Tomorrow, Elsie thinks as she scurries into the vacated room.

***

The mirror ball spins colorful reflections throughout the USO Dance Hall. The former East Covina warehouse beside the railroad tracks is decorated with red, white and blue bunting. Flags with emblems from the military services wave over the dance floor. An improvised stage is home to local musicians swinging away with their Big Band, Artie Shaw sound. The dance floor is soon filled with youthful uniforms and local ladies.

Elsie and a sailor do a swing step on one side of the dance floor. She enjoys her sailor's confidence as he leads by swinging her into the air, then through his legs. The watching crowd applauds.

On the opposite side of the dance floor, Elsa tries watching until she is asked to jitterbug by a Marine private. Naturally she accepts, then immediately regrets it when she tried to follow his clumsy lead. Silently—but obviously counting out steps, he accidentally places a boot on top of Elsa's open-toed sandals. She holds in a scream as pain shoots through her consciousness.

While helping her limp to the chairs, he says, "I am truly sorry, ma'am. Thank you for the dance," and quickly walks away, turning red. Elsa massages her toes.

The teenage kid playing the trumpet on stage wipes hair out of his eyes as he blows the last high notes of "Begin the Beguine." Elsie is pulled to a standing position by the sailor as they finish the dance. She laughs while catching her breath. Thirsty, she walks to his table and picks up a glass, downing half of its contents with her first gulp before looking around for Elsa.

Elsa continues to massage her foot until she sees Elsie approaching with a beer mug in her hand.

"It looks like you need this more than I do."

Elsa grabs it and chugs the warm beer. "Thanks. You're a lifesaver."

A crash from the other side of the room attracts everyone's attention. The very table that Elsie walked away from is broken in two. The sailor Elsie was dancing with has a Marine in a headlock. "You stole my beer," he shouts. Others move away as military security rushes in.

With urgency, Elsie says, "We'd better get out of here."

"I don't want to walk on this foot yet."

"You must learn to listen to me. You are drinking that sailor's beer."

"Oh!" Instantly understanding, they both walk to the exit.

Once outside, they erupt in laughter. In the cool of the night, they start walking home.

"How I missed dancing. I love it, love it," says Elsie.

Elsa winces with each step. "That clod hopper!"

Both giggle as they walk under the clear night sky with only the full moon to lead them home.

Chapter Eighteen

Ocean waves roll lazily onto the sand around the Santa Monica pier. Among many weekend beach combers' blankets on sand, four are positioned side by side. Countless people play in the waves, shouting their enjoyment.

Elsa sits on one of those blankets watching Elsie dunk herself under a wave while Ambrose tosses Esther off his shoulders into the water. She is uncomfortable sitting under the sun, but the thought of jumping into all that water is unnerving. A large brimmed hat offers some protection but she constantly rubs lotion onto her pale skin as she hears faint shouts from her friends in the water to join them.

Shaking her head, she applies more lotion. Finally, the three run back to their blankets, inadvertently kicking sand onto her.

"Hey, watch what you're doing," Elsa snaps. "Now I'm covered in sticky sand."

"Then get in the water," Ambrose says.

The husband and wife laugh.

Elsie comes to her defense. "She can't swim. It's not her fault." She then runs back toward the water.

The three watch Elsie test a wave with her foot. Elsa opens a magazine with a picture of Casablanca movie star Bogie on the cover.

"When do you report back?" she asks Ambrose.

Listening, Esther's smile fades and she looks as if she's about to cry.

Ambrose says, "Two days."

"I almost forgot," says Esther with deep sigh.

"I'm sorry for bringing it up. I'm really sorry," Elsa says.

Ambrose pulls his wife into his arms. "Don't worry, *mi corison*. Forget it for today."

Some time passes in silence. Elsa shades her eyes as she looks toward the ocean. Fighting off the glare from the water, she winces, then sits up.

"Where's Elsie?" she asks.

"Oh, that chica," says Esther, as she too starts to look for her sister. Then, so does Ambrose.

Elsa stands up as the Pacific waves roll in. But there is still no sight of Elsie.

"Seriously, I don't see her."

Esther and Ambrose's attention now become acute.

Stretching his view, "Me neither," says Ambrose.

Elsa jumps and points into the distance. "Look!" she screeches.

All three see Elsie frantically waving an arm, struggling as a wave washes over her, pulling her down.

"Oh, my God, she's not coming up." Elsa cries. "Oh, my god, oh, my God!" she shouts.

Ambrose kicks up sand as he runs toward the incoming waves, soon diving into the water toward Elsie.

"I can't see her," shouts Esther. "Hurry, Ambrose! Hurry!"

The girls run to the water's edge as Ambrose power strokes toward Elsie.

They try to shout directions to him, but he can't hear them. Elsie pops in and out of the waves, but it is obvious that she is tiring fast.

"The ocean is pulling her out farther and farther!" cries out Esther.

"Oh, my God," says Elsa. Moments later shouting, "Oh, my God!"

Ambrose's training kicks in. Without assistance, he propels himself above the water to locate Elsie, then swims toward her.

At last, he says, "It's okay, Elsie. I'm here." He spits water as he grabs her wrist. She's about to go under again but he pulls her closer, looping an arm under her shoulder, almost pulling her onto his back.

"Don't worry, sis, I've got ya."

Elsie says nothing. Ambrose breast strokes toward the beach but soon starts getting dangerously tired. "We're almost there, sis, almost there."

Esther shouts from the water's edge, "You're almost here, Elsie." She dives in and swims out to them. Unexpectedly, Elsa too runs into the water, dives in and starts clumsily slapping at the waves.

As Ambrose paddles, he says, "Can you hear them? Even Elsa's calling from the beach. Can you hear her? Can you, Elsie?" he asks.

"I'm stopping to rest." He feels terrific strain. "We're getting closer," he tells her.

Elsie is still silent as Esther reaches them. She stretches her arm under Elsie's other shoulder, so she and Ambrose can begin pulling her together.

Elsa standing up to her waist in the waves, follows Ambrose as he pulls Elsie onto the beach. A crowd grows around them.

Ambrose is so tired he falls to the sand, gasping for breath.

"Give her mouth-to-mouth," he gasps.

Not knowing what that is, both girls fumble, looking at each other.

Still breathing hard, Ambrose crawls over to his sister-in-law, pinches her nose closed and opens her mouth. He takes a deep breath, then blows air into her lungs. Repeatedly, he blows breath in her mouth—which at last produces results.

Elsie starts moving—coughing, gagging and spitting out water. Finally breathing!

The crowd around them applauds. Ambrose falls back, exhausted.

"You're okay, *amica*," Elsa tells her dear friend. "That's right: breathe, baby, breathe. You're okay now."

Esther tends to her husband. "You're my hero," she says, kissing him all over. He smiles and pulls his wife to him.

Elsa helps Elsie sit up, wiping her face with a towel as she coughs up more water.

Finally, Elsie looks around, startled. She asks, "What's happening? Why are all of those people standing around us?"

Then she notices Elsa. "Look at you," she points. "You're all wet!"

***

A week later, warm spring rolls over the steel braced, colossus air plane factory. The place bustles with technicians moving around their work stations. Conveyers move series of four prop propellers overhead.

Elsie flips open her welding mask to catch her breath as she finishes touching up a particular weld on the B-10's armored sheet metal skin. At another station, Elsa cleans tools from a table filled with them. By coincidence, both adjust their bandanas at the same time as a sudden, shrill alarm echoes off the walls. The assembly lines come to an immediate stop. All workers look around in amazement. This has never happened before without a shift change.

"What's wrong?" Elsa asks the worker next to her.

The alarm stops just as suddenly, followed immediately by an excited voice that bounces off the hangar walls from the rarely used public address system.

"Attention, ladies and gentlemen. News from the War Department has been confirmed. Nazi dictator Adolf Hitler has committed suicide in his bunker. War in Europe will soon be over!"

A ripple of cheers combined with waves of applause break over the work floor. Elsa jumps up and down in delight. Elsie screams for joy. The friends quickly find each other so they can jump into the other's arms. They begin dancing with excitement.

Fellow workers pat each other's backs while shaking hands. They hug each other in congratulations. Some men go as far as kissing the closest woman. "The war is over!" they tell each other with excitement. They shout, "The damned war is over!"

A lonely coworker stands silent among the celebrants, thinking about the war still raging in the Pacific. She shouts into the jubilant crowd, "What about the Japs?"

Chapter Nineteen

Sunday June 3, 1945

The Hilton Hotel coffee shop is still busy after the Sunday lunch. From behind the counter, Rose pours coffee into the diners' cups as she walks the line. She refills the pot and moves out onto the floor to refill the cups at her tables. Most customers are reading the morning paper.

An elderly woman with a younger man occupy one of her tables. Rose sees he's making notes on a map of the town. The lady seems to be examining a couple of railroad tickets.

"Do not lie to the conductor again about having asthma," she tells her son, who makes no reply. "Why must you act like a limp wrist?" she asks. "I raised you to be a man's man."

"We'll head back to Philadelphia at five tonight," he says, checking his watch.

Back behind the counter, Rose looks again at the younger man. His weasel-like facial features twitch and he is small in stature. Other than that, this short-sleeved, white shirt-wearing, pasty faced customer is just another hotel traveler passing through. Still, there is something unpleasant about him. Something she can't quite identify.

"Rosie, order up!" calls the cook from the grill.

Rose carries the two prepared plates to the lady and younger man, along with their lunch tab. The fellow scarfs down his meal, scrutinizing the charges. After glancing about, Rose watches him pull out his wallet and carefully squeeze out coins, which he places one at a time on the table, until the $1.22 sum is reached. Then, after retrieving a nickel, he looks over his shoulder while placing it back inside his wallet.

Taking his fedora from the table, he puts it on as he steps away.

"I should be back in an hour," he tells his mother.

Wincing from the clear Albuquerque brightness, he dons his sunglasses and walks east up Route 66, retracing his early morning trek. He passes under the Santa Fe railroad bridge and quickly past Albuquerque High School, studying street signs as he passes. Finally, he spots the HIGH St. sign. Wiping sweat from his brow before turning left, he walks north a block and a half and stops at a brown and beige brick house. Double checking the address on a slip of paper—209 N. High Street—he walks around to the back entrance. Thinking once, then twice, he glances about and quickly walks up the back steps, where he enters through a screen door.

He knocks on Number 4. As he does, he hears Benny Goodman Big Band radio music coming from the inside. He likes Benny Goodman's music because Benny is a good Jewish boy. The rented room's door opens slightly. On the other side stands Dave, the Army uniformed soldier from New York. His wife Ruth stands behind him.

"Good afternoon, Bumblebee. If you recall, this morning I told you Julius sent me," says the stranger.

Ruth grabs her husband's arm causing the stranger to take notice of the corporal T5 insignia on his sleeve.

"Julius sent me," he repeats.

Dave and Ruth both seem to recognize the name of their brother-in-law Julius Rosenberg in New York.

"Come in," says Dave.

As he enters, Dave quickly closes the door.

"When I was here this morning, you were dressed in pajamas." He glances around a one-room kitchenette. "I wasn't expecting a soldier."

"He returns to Los Alamos this afternoon," says Ruth. "But we're going to the USO Club first."

"Then let's take care of business."

From his wallet, the stranger retrieves a little jagged piece of cardboard. Recognizing it, Dave takes a book from under the bed and flips through the pages.

"It's in here. Ah, ha." He displays a similar piece of cardboard.

They slide the two pieces of raspberry Jell-O box together on the table, where they match.

"My name is Harry from Philadelphia," says the stranger.

"I'm David and this is my wife, Ruth. My brother-in-law sent you?"

"I do not know. Do you have the information?"

"Let's sit," Dave says. He pulls out a tablet and finds one to write on.

"I drew several drafts of THE GADGET I am now fabricating. They are calling it the Fat Man and it is designed to withstand an implosion of uranium elements."

Harry from Philadelphia studies the designs from different directions, although it is obvious he doesn't grasp the idea.

"It is due to be tested in early July, probably between the 15th and 18th. Locations are now being prepared down in the southern desert." He hands the courier another page.

"I have also made a list of individuals who could be sympathetic to Mother Russia."

Harry takes the list. "It is unwise to recruit. I do not advise that course of action."

Dave appears puzzled until Harry pulls out his wallet and counts out five one hundred dollar bills. Ruth instantly grabs them.

"This will come in handy." She counts the five hundred dollars again. "We can walk you back to your hotel, if you like. We're anxious to get to the USO club."

Harry nods.

Within moments, they walk down the back steps. Half way to the hotel, they split up. Harry is anxious to get out of town on the 5:15 PM Super Chief.

***

July 4th, 1945

A somber Esther, Elsie and Elsa sit at their kitchen table. All three take drags from their rationed cigarettes, then grind them into the ash tray in front of them. They silently pass around a simple one-page letter.

A cloud of cigarette smoke hangs above them.

Elsie reads the letter again, saying nothing as she tosses it onto the table. They are all on the verge of tears.

Elsie's older sister says, "You can tell mama's heart is breaking."

"Getting news that Johnny's missing in action on the same day we get fired—makes me want to cry." says Elsie.

"Today is shit!" exclaims Elsa. "I've never been fired before!"

"The boys are coming home, one way or another. And they're clearing us out to give them jobs," says Elsie, not for the first time.

"I wish Ambrose was coming home," says Esther. "If only I could hear from him."

Elsa pulls out a fresh pack of cigarettes. The others watch her strike a match and, with a single experienced move, she lights up.

Esther says, "Give me a fresh one."

Elsie watches her sister light up. "Me, too."

The smoke above them soon grows larger.

Esther looks across the table at her sister. "At least Mama is going to be happy to see us." She leaves the table to walk into the bathroom.

Elsie nods. As they finish their cigarettes, a long moment's silence is broken by Elsa.

"Sounds like it's time for us to go home." She slides two rivets from the assembly line across the table. "Pick one."

The others nod as Elsie puts the memento in her blouse pocket.

They hear Fourth of July fireworks exploding outside.

Chapter Twenty

5:15 AM: Thursday, July 16, 1945
The Morning the Sun Rose Twice

It is the peak of summer as Rose dons her best light-weight clothing. For this is a special day. She will walk to work, as usual, but about 1 PM, she will walk a couple of extra blocks to the train station—because her babies are coming home this afternoon!

Checking herself in the full-length mirror, she smiles in approval. Locking her empty house and screened porch, she pauses so her eyesight can adjust to the darkness. The air is clean and crisp from a light drizzle a couple of hours earlier.

After swinging open the gate of her white picket fence, she side-steps rain puddles and looks south down the dark street to the lonesome streetlight at the end of the block.

Rose knows this will be an unusually busy day. By 10 AM, as chef, she will have prepared a specially catered breakfast to a large group of government VIPs. Since the hotel's permanent chef is busy with the day's normal workload, he recommended her for the assignment. That was after several big-wig Army Officers interviewed her for the job. Rose was complimented when told she, herself, has a reputation as a top chef.

She can hear her fast-paced footsteps over the sidewalk rain puddles during this lonely, early morning walk. She thinks again about the coming day. Did she order enough eggs? She tries to remember. The sous chef did her the favor of baking extra loaves of bread for today. She remembers she must be at the hotel early to receive the delivery of fresh vegetables. Her watch reads 5:29 AM. She must be out by 1:00 PM to make it to the train station in time.

Suddenly, in the southern sky—directly in front of her—an extremely bright light begins to grow and rise slowly above Albuquerque's buildings, fully lighting the street she is walking along.

What the ...? The sun doesn't rise from the south, she thinks.

The brightness grows in intensity. Her eyes flutter at being forced to unexpectedly adapt. She grabs hold of her neighbor's fence till they adjust. "This is loco..."

Seconds pass like minutes before her eyesight adjusts when, just as suddenly, the street becomes dark again. After another heartbeat or two, the ground she is standing on begins to vibrate with growing intensity.

Instinctively, Rose sits down on the wet sidewalk while gripping the fence for dear life. She feels the vibrations strengthen—and realizes it seems to be coming from the same direction as the light. From the south!

Then, suddenly, it's gone. The ground grows still. A slow minute passes before Rose dares to release her hold on the fence.

What the hell was that? she wonders, getting to her feet.

As she considers trying to walk again, she realizes that dawn is lighting the sky over the Sandia Mountains to her east, just like it has her entire life.

"That's more like it," she murmurs, trying to breathe deeply and control her shaking legs.

Moments later, as the bright yellow ball of the sun peaks over the mountain's crest, she feels its warmth and is encouraged.

She remembers that she must get to work, but it is the thought of her babies coming home that brings back her smile. She continues walking.

***

Five Hours Later

The tall gentlemen with a pencil thin mustache is elegantly dressed. Yet, he paces nervously just inside the entrance of his Hilton Hotel off Route 66. He again checks his watch recalling how New Mexico's governor had called him from Santa Fe yesterday to ask for a favor. A favor that quickly became a command.

"Conrad, possibly anticipate an extraordinary and rare gathering for lunch. Understand, it may or may not happen."

"But, governor..."

"Don't ask questions! Just roll out the red-carpet."

"May I ask for..."

"Listen to me! I am grateful for your help in my recent election, so I am returning the favor. This luncheon—provided it happens—will be the highest-powered VIP function your young hotel has ever hosted. Got it?"

"Thank you, governor..."

"Let me know how it goes. I will soon bring my lovely wife down from Santa Fe for a weekend getaway. You can return the favor then."

That is all Conrad Hilton hears the New Mexico governor say before he hangs up.

Rose, now changed into a crisp, white chef's uniform and chef's hat, approaches her boss.

"The best of the best of our service is laid out, sir. The banquet room is ready."

Hilton's attention is on the government-green Packard limousine pulling up to the front entrance.

"Thank you, Rose. You make this gathering easier." Mr. Hilton steps out of his hotel entrance to welcome his guests. He stands between his two gray haired doormen.

The lengthy Packard's two guest doors fly open. Two Army officers exit and stand at attention. The tank Army limo dips a bit as a tall, extremely rotund, bear of an Army officer gets out. The two officers salute him.

Conrad Hilton recognizes his rank as he approaches. "Welcome to my hotel, general. We await you and your guests."

The general barely acknowledges Hilton as he bulls his way inside. Rose stands by, then leads Mr. Hilton, the general and his guests to the small banquet hall.

When she stops beside an open door to allow them to enter the room, she is reminded of baby goslings walking in line behind their momma goose. The general is followed by a tall, very lean fellow with an unlit pipe in his mouth. Behind him is a short, stout, bushy eye-browed man whose quick speech is peppered by an accent.

"We should be proud, Oppy. This morning's test exceeded our expectations."

Gripping the pipe between his teeth, Oppy nods and asks, "Mr. Teller, have we calculated the yields well enough to know who won the pool?"

From her friends, the Santonis, Rose recognizes the Italian accent coming from the third fellow.

"I am a hungry. Could not eat this morning," he says to the guy behind him.

The fourth fellow replies with a teasing smile. "Enrico, it is time to replenish your tremendous brain energies."

Fermi laughs. "Lawrence, it's obvious that you are from that California bunch."

Lawrence Livermore joins Fermi's laugher.

Rose realizes that the limo carried many men. Mr. Hilton closes the banquet doors behind them as the two Army officers stand at attention in the hall.

Meanwhile, a crowd is collecting outside the hotel entrance. Kids, teenagers, couples and singles, old and young, Hispanic, Anglo, Native Americans have never before seen the such a sight. The Army sergeant chauffeur stands in front of his Army green stretch limo. With pride, he allows the growing citizenry to visually examine its every nook and cranny.

Six Weeks Later

For being a dry, arid climate, the early September monsoon rain still pounds at the bakery's front glass window. Mr. Santoni turns the Closed sign to Open at the entrance. He smiles and winks at his daughter as she comes downstairs to start her first day back at work.

"Ah *bambina*, I am sure you remember everything here."

With a decided lack of enthusiasm Elsa says, "*Si*, papa."

She looks through the front window and knows why she's depressed. It's not because of the grey outside. It's because she thought she had escaped the bakery. When papa walks back through the swinging doors to the kitchen, she reluctantly ties her apron tight around her waist.

The front door bell tinkles as a wet customer hurriedly enters. Elsa recognizes him as the neighboring haberdasher. She waits until he places his wet newspaper on a table and removes his dripping jacket to reveal his professional trademark: arm bands. He is seated as she brings him a pot of coffee and a fresh cup.

"Good morning, Mr. Stromberg," she says with a smile.

"Well, if it isn't little Elsa Santoni. How are you, young lady?"

"Back home once again," she replies, while filling his cup.

"Your papa and mama were telling me almost every day that you were working in an airplane factory in Los Angeles."

"It already seems like a life time ago."

The older gentleman laughs. "You make it sound like it was years instead of just weeks." He smiles, "Oh, child…"

"It seems the only thing to be grateful for is that the war is over, Mr. Stromberg. Thank God."

"In case you do not remember, I will have my usual: a bagel with green chili cream cheese."

"Of course I remember, Mr. Stromberg." As she walks away, he spreads out the paper and pours cream into his cup-o-joe.

"Will your friend Mr. Baca be joining you?" Elsa asks from behind the counter.

"I am sorry to say that my close friend Elfego passed shortly after you went to Los Angeles."

"I am very sad to hear of your loss."

Elsa slices a bagel and toasts it while preparing a scoop of the green chili laced cream cheese. In a moment, she delivers it to her customer.

Mr. Stromberg pulls his nose out of the paper to comment. "You can tell the war is over because the paper runs happier photos once again."

Elsa looks at the black-and-white front page dated September 2, 1945 where a photograph shows American generals sitting across a table from Japanese diplomats dressed in top hats and tuxes. The headline reads General MacArthur Signs Jap Surrender on Battleship Missouri

"It's hard to remember when we didn't have war," she says, walking away.

Mr. Stromberg rolls the page down and starts reading the next front page article. Its headline reads, Atomic Weapon Secretly Tested in Southern New Mexico. The front door swings wide open. Elsie rushes in wearing a raincoat and a hat. She sees Elsa with coffee pot in hand.

"Sorry I'm late for work." Taking off her dripping coat and hat, she hangs them on the rack. Elsa hands her an apron.

Elsie recognizes the only customer in the room. "Hello, Mr. Stromberg. Good to see you again."

Breaking away from the engrossing New Mexican atomic news story, he says, "Well, well it's Elsie Lovato on this unusually humid day. I am happy to see you, too. I know that the war is really over now that I see you both back at Santoni's."

From the kitchen side Mr. Santoni peers through the portal window of the swinging doors. He waves his wife over to him.

"*Mio amore*, look." She walks across the kitchen while wiping her hands on her apron. She glances out the window.

"See what I see?" he asks.

She smiles, nodding. "Like old times. Like old times."

"Thank God, the war is over. Thank God," he says.

Chapter Twenty-One

Cooler temperatures accompany cloudless blue skies. The red, white and blue proudly waves in front of every business along Gold Street. At the 2nd Street intersection, town workers stretch a banner over the street proclaiming: NEW MEXICO WELCOMES BACK THE STATE FAIR.

More people are walking under those banners every day. Increasing numbers wear military uniforms returning home. Complete strangers approach them with handshakes and back pats. Veterans smile and again enjoy the New Mexican `Hello Neighbor' attitude.

The style of dress is changing. More western wear such as boots, cowboy hats and blue jeans recapture local State Fair fashion. Santoni's Bakery customers line up behind the counter to pay for their purchases. Elsie and Elsa giggle at the sight of Mr. and Mrs. Santoni happily modeling their matching his-and-her cowboy hats.

In the Hilton Hotel's kitchen, Rose Lovato shows off her still youthful figure by modeling new blue jeans to her fellow workers. Embarrassed, Esther pulls her mother away by asking her to inspect baking talents. The mother shows pride at the sight of her daughter's decoration of a three-layer cake. Trimmed in New Mexico's colors of yellow and red, it is topped by a cowboy waving his hat while astride a rearing horse. Rose hugs her eldest daughter for her well accomplished work of art.

***

Not long after, Mr. Santoni finishes carving a toothless pumpkin and places it in the bakery's front window display, which is bordered by American flags. Mrs. Santoni places a candle in it. Elsa embraces her parents. Elsie, dusted with a light coat of flour, contributes a tray of decorated orange pumpkin cookies. She enviously watches the Santonis as she slides it under the glass display.

That night, Rose and Esther don similar Hilton uniforms. To capture the Halloween mood, fellow hotel employees wear half masks. Mother and daughter carry pans of different foods to a display table. The ballroom is filled with Dracula, Frankenstein, Civil War and Marie Antoinette costumes on the party revelers dancing to a live ghoulish faced orchestra.

***

More automobiles travel on a late November Gold Street under the latest banner that reads HAPPY THANKSGIVING. Half of the stores and offices still display their flags. Wind-blown piles of fall leaves tuck into building and street crevices where they are soon carried away by an occasional burst of wind.

Santoni's front window displays a closed sign next to a large picture of a primly dressed pilgrim turkey. Folks walking past pull their jackets and coats tighter while scurrying along as crystal blue skies begin to darken. The sun sets earlier these days as Indian Summer prepares to meld into winter.

The lights above the bakery are out with exception of a lone candle burning brightly at the center of the kitchen table. Giovani and Abra Santoni with their daughter, Elsa, hold hands as he says grace for his family. All three bring the tips of their right fingers to their foreheads, then their hearts, and then right and left sides of their chest.

"*Grazi, grazi,* Lord, for ending the rationing restrictions on food."

He makes another sign of the cross with joy and laughter. The ladies watch as the man of the house carves the large turkey. Abra pours chianti into waiting glasses.

Six blocks away, three Lovato ladies sit at their kitchen table which is laid out with bowls of salad, mashed potatoes, brown gravy, candied yams, red and green chili, and a basket of bread, surrounding a medium-sized turkey. In the middle sits an unlit candle.

Two vacant chairs attend the table with full place settings.

Esther sits next to one place setting that has an U.S. Air Corp table tent on it. Rose sits next to the other, which is adorned with an U.S. Navy placard. Elsie sits between her mother and sister.

Silence reigns as the two sisters bow their heads while their mother performs a ritual she had done every Thanksgiving feast since they were kids. She strikes a match and slowly lights the lonesome candle in memory of a long-lost husband and father. Esther remembers her father walking her to school on her first day. Elsie's memory of her father seems to fade more every year. Rose recalls about two decades ago her salesman's last kiss before he left home on his last sales trip where he suffered a heart attack.

Rose makes the sign of the cross as her daughters follow suit. No sooner does she say "Amen," that all three dig into the feast before them.

***

Christmas tree-lined streets all over town are decorated with American flags along with the usual tinsel and trimmings. Public building roofs are lined with luminarias and their windows dressed with multi-colored lights. Lengthy garlands with candle-like decorations stretch across Gold Street.

Standing on a chair to decorate the Christmas tree, Elsie waves through Santoni's front window at passersby. She is distracted by a ringing sound from behind the cash register. Elsa dashes through the swinging doors in her white-floured apron and a hair net. She quickly picks up the receiver of their newly installed telephone.

"Thank you for calling Santoni's Bakery," she says. Suddenly acknowledging the caller with a large and joyous response, "You are at home?" She shows her giant smile along with outward and excited shock, "Yeah. She's been working here... You sound great!"

Elsa immediately adopts a tearful smile. She summons Elsie to the phone. Stepping off the chair, she approaches her friend with great apprehension.

"Me? I've never talked on a telephone before. Besides, who would telephone me here?"

"Hurry, darling. You don't want to keep him waiting," says Elsa says, holding back tears.

Elsie hurries to grab the receiver.

***

An hour later and two blocks away Esther, her mom, and fellow employees scurry across the Hilton kitchen as they perform their daily tasks. Esther blends sugar into her mixing bowl. It's the first time since the war has been over that she is freely adding previously rationed commodities. She can't wait till tonight to pull out her new bobby pins and let her long hair down. She wants to put on her new nylon stockings, too.

Rose walks through the hotel's filled pantry. Canned goods, butter, coffee and tomato catsup are well stocked. And now she's able to wrap and chill her meats with tin foil. She wears her first new shoes in many years and her work dress has zippers.

The hotel owner enters the kitchen through its swinging doors. The staff works nervously at their stations since the owner never comes into the kitchen. They watch as he summons the head chef who briefly confers with Mr. Hilton. The head chef nods and points toward Rose and Esther. A moment of dread covers everyone's faces. They think someone is going to be fired, probably Esther. She is still here on a trial basis. Mother and daughter both stand rigid as Mr. Hilton waves someone in from behind the swinging doors.

Elsie walks through with a beaming smile as Mr. Hilton points her toward her mother and sister. Through happy tears, Elsie signals an extremely gaunt young man enter the kitchen. Still in a sailor's uniform, he enters slowly with the aid of a cane.

"Mama," he says, "I'm home."

The kitchen utensils in Rose's hands clank onto the floor. Not believing what she is seeing, she covers her mouth as if to hold back a cry of joy, then walks to her son with trembling opening arms. Tears well in Esther eyes as she watches her mom grasp her brother.

"My baby, my boy," is all Rose can say.

Esther joins their embrace, and Elsie can't resist the hugging. The kitchen staff breaks into applause, some with tears in their eyes.

Conrad Hilton leaves the kitchen wiping his eyes with his suit jacket sleeve.

"Merry Christmas," he says under his breath.

Chapter Twenty-Two

The shimmer of falling snow flakes is enhanced by Gold Street's colorful Christmas lights and flickering luminarias as day becomes Christmas Eve. The delightful aroma of pinon wood smoke wafts from fireplaces.

Upstairs from Santoni's Bakery, a Christmas tree is fully lit and decorated. The joy of the season fills the room as the Santoni's host the Lovatos. Dressed in his only clothes, his naval sailor's whites, Johnny Lovato hypnotically stares into the fireplace. While stoking the wood with one hand, he takes a drink of eggnog from the cup in the other. Rose and Abra discuss a recipe in the kitchen. As they sit around the kitchen table, Elsie, Esther and Elsa laugh at Giovani's jokes, so he pours more eggnog into their cups. Esther sips from her cup then whimsically steps away and toward the beautifully decorated tree. She examines each decoration. Her imagination naturally places significance and purpose for each. At this moment, everyone in the room cannot help but hear the front door bell from downstairs. It rings once again before anyone reacts.

Elsie quickly glances at the 8:30 PM on her watch. She thinks to herself, 'Right on time.' She then glances quickly at Elsa who nods back in acknowledgement.

"We are closed," Mr. Santoni exclaims.

"Mio Amore," his wife says. "It is sure they cannot hear you from there."

"Please papa. Answer the door," Elsa urges.

As the downstairs bell rings again, Mr. Santoni resigns himself to having to go downstairs. The bell rings again as all the ladies watch him leave the room to step down the stairs. From the bottom step and through and past the darkened bakery, he studies the dark silhouette on the other side of the bakery front door.

"We are closed." He walks closer.

The knocking continues. But because the silhouette outline is dressed like a police officer, he reaches to unlock and open the door.

Upstairs, the women sit around Johnny on the sofa.

"I am so glad that you are home Johnny," says Rose. She kisses his forehead. "This is my best Christmas in years."

"Cheers." Esther offers the toast as all in the room clink their eggnog mugs together.

Focus is directed to the stairs as curiosity pounces on Mr. Santoni. But before a single female question is thrown at him, he side steps on the top and final step.

"Esther, do you know this man?" he says with a smile.

All study a tall, straight, fully uniformed Air Corp. Lieutenant as he steps up the last step into the room. While taking off his hat, snow falls from it.

"Hello Esther."

A heartbeat of silence captures the room. Then suddenly all wince at Esther's screech of happiness at the first sight of her husband in almost a year. She runs into her husband's arms.

"Ambrose!"

He braces himself from falling backwards down the steps as she smothers him with kisses.

Mrs. Santoni comments to Rose while sipping their eggnog cups.

"It looks like you have a handsome son-in-law."

"This is my best Christmas in years," Rose says again.

"But how did you know we were here?" the wife asks the husband.

"The only address I had was the bakery's so I came here earlier. Elsie was working and said you'd be here later tonight. Here I am."

Esther gives off a grateful stare at her sister and friend, then, as if it is her first duty, Esther leads her husband over to her mother with her arm locked within his.

"Mother, this is my husband Ambrose. Ambrose Jacob Ornales."

Rose takes a deep gaze into her new son-in-law's eyes.

"I am very happy that you have come home to us safe and sound, son." She takes his hand before whispering, "Take care of my baby and you will always be my son."

As she kisses him on his cheek, the room cheers.

Elsie joins her mom. "And he also saved me from drowning." She kisses her brother-in-law.

"He's only been in the room a minute and all of the Lovato women have already kissed him," states Johnny. "Maybe I should kiss him too." He stands while placing his weight on his cane, he proceeds to limp.

Instead, Ambrose quickly steps to him. "So, you're the Johnny I was always hearing about."

Instinctively, the sailor snaps to attention to salute the air corps officer before him.

"Sir, yes sir!"

Ambrose smiles "At ease sailor." He holds his hand out to shake, "Hello brother."

Johnny smiles and shakes his brother-in-law's hand.

Elsa walks up to him, "Remember me?" she asks.

"How can I forget you, doll." He kisses her cheek. "I've met your father. Now introduce me to your sister."

"Who?" Then she realizes who he means. "You mean my mama." Elsa slaps Ambrose's shoulder while Mr. Santoni rolls his eyes back. "She's my mama," Elsa repeats.

Everyone in the room laughs as Abra shakes Ambrose's hand.

"Let's eat," says Mr. Santoni. "We must allow time for midnight Mass."

Everyone nods except the two military personnel, who just go with the flow.

"Is that green chili stew I smell?" asks Ambrose, inhaling.

Esther says, "Set another chair at the table, next to me."

Mr. Santoni obliges, smiling.

Everyone gathers their chairs around the table topped with holiday food including the stew. Giovani and Abra Santoni carry a tray with a huge turkey to the table and proudly present it to their guests. All eyes widen.

"This is the best Christmas in years," Rose says again.

Giovani Santoni makes a special effort to pull out the chair next to his wife at the head of the table. Only after his wife sits, does he.

"Shall we all say grace?" he asks.

All nod.

Chapter Twenty-Three

New Year's Eve

Although scheduled to work at the hotel, Rose decided to spend her happiest New Year's Eve in years with family and friends. Asked to fill in for her mom, Esther also turned down the offer. She, too, wanted to be with family and friends, especially her husband. And since mom and sisters were partying, Johnny accepted the invitation from the Santonis.

Still up, the Christmas tree sports new decorations saying *Y Prospero Nuevo Ano*. Everyone has egg nog in hand. The only thing different from last week is that Ambrose is dressed in crisp new civvies, and Johnny knew to bring a bottle of rum for the nog. He smiles with eyes open wide as he examines the table holding several Italian dishes and breads.

Giovani raises his cup of rum. "To all my friends and family, I wish upon us for life to be at its best as we go into 1946 without war."

Ambrose agrees, adding, "Bravo, bravo!"

The downstairs doorbell seems to jingle on cue.

"*Lasciare lo squillo di campana*," Mrs. Santoni tells her husband.

The bell chimes again, seeming louder. "Let them ring," says his daughter.

Giovani Santoni pushes himself toward the exit. "They can see our lights. And besides *E' Natale*! It is New Year's Eve!"

"Well hurry back, Bene. *Affretti indietro*," says Abra.

Giovani Santoni carefully makes his way down the dark steps to the bakery below. He thinks it's zero degrees when he notices new snowfall behind the silhouette of a man at the front door.

"We are closed," he shouts. The chiming bell is replaced with loud knocking.

"We are closed." Giovani insists.

Hearing a familiar voice, the silhouette speaks. *"Il Signor Santoni, e' che lei?"*

Giovani vaguely recognizes him. *"Si. Si.* This is Giovani Santoni." He steps closer to the door, "This is my bakery." The front door lock pops open as he turns the handle.

Back upstairs, Elsa washes dishes. Esther embraces her husband and presses her face into his chest. Rose and Abra visit. Johnny stares into the fire and takes a swig of eggnog. Smacking his lips, he pours an extra shot into the glass from his side pocket. Elsie adjusts decorations on the tree. As they hear Mr. Santoni coming back up, they all move back toward the table.

Arriving at the top of the steps, they see the amazement on Giovani's face.

"Elsie, do you remember this fellow?" He nods toward a tall, well-dressed man.

"Well, I'll be..." says Elsie.

Elsa seems stunned. She drops a dish, breaking it.

But Abra Santoni welcomes their guest with arms open wide. "Ah, bambino..."

All he can say is, "Ah, mama."

Certain memories flash back to a year and a half when Giovani, Abra, their daughter Elsa and her *amica,* Elsie, last saw this fellow. He was wearing a grey tunic with a large letter P on the back—which is the only way they saw him dressed. Now, they see a manicured young man with slick, jet black hair. As he is welcomed, he takes off his ankle length tan felt coat and shakes off the snow. Under the coat, he wears a tailored black suit with a gold colored tie. His slacks have sharp creases. His patent leather shoes reflect the Christmas lights.

Mr. Santoni guides him into the room. "For those who were not here, Jenoa was a POW in the camp at the zoo. We worked him downstairs in the bakery when my back was not good. He has returned."

Jenoa is compelled to speak, obviously trying to minimize his accent. *"Grazie.* During war, the only experience I can smile to was the time I worked for Signori Santoni. Of all the places we were sent, I dreamed of coming back here."

He glances around the room. His smile grows as he spots Elsa in the kitchen. She smiles back. Giovani then leads him in further.

"Come, come, join the family and friends," he says.

Jenoa approaches Mrs. Santoni, "The memory of your gracious treatment during that time means very much to me."

He takes her hand and kisses it with a continental flare. She cannot hide her excitement.

"Jenoa Domenici is welcome in our home," she tells all.

Jenoa turns to greet Elsie, "*Law il bella' Elsie.*" Without a thought, he takes her hand in his and raises it to his lips. Elsie nearly loses her balance. "You are as lovely as I remembered you," he says.

After greeting everyone in the room, Jenoa turns and approaches Elsa from across the room. Elsa finds herself stepping toward him as well. Jenoa reaches her and holds out his arms to her, but changes his mind to simply hold out a hand. Without hesitation, she takes it. They both hold their touch as the room spins around them.

After glancing at the clock and the approaching midnight hour, Papa steps between the couple. "We can finally sit and eat now."

Elsie sees her friend's gaze locked on Jenoa's eyes. She side-tracks attention away.

"We need another chair," She says before kicking her friend's foot.

"Let's sit Jenoa between Elsa and me."

As if remembering something, Jenoa raises a single finger, "*Prego, un momento per favore.*"

He quickly steps down the stairs. While everyone waits at the table for his return, the sound of bottles clanking grows louder. Jenoa Domenici soon stands at the top of the steps carrying a large box. With youthful zest, he places it on the table next to Giovani. "As you say in English, Happy New Year!" He takes a bottle of wine from the straw-cushioned crate and hands it to Giovani.

"These bottles are samples from my family's cellar. My parents hid them. Now we clear space for our first harvest since before war." Jenoa pulls out another bottle. "From the Nebbiolo Grape, our best. *Domenici Barolo* 1936," and places it on the table.

"You brought these bottles from Italia?" Giovani asks while studying the next bottle label. "Domenici Chianti 1936!" Papa looks at another label, "Domenici Cabernet Sauvignon 1939, which I recommend for meals of beef and pasta." He pulls out the next bottle, "Domenici Asti Spumonti 1938," then the next, "Domenici Cepparello 1940."

"Because of war, it was last year of the grape till this year's harvest."

It has been a long time since Abra Santoni has seen her husband so impressed.

Also impressed is Ambrose. "I love wine, too," he says while reading a label. "How did these survive?" He offers his hand to Jenoa.

"And again, I have New Mexico to thank for this wine. Papa told me the story how negro soldiers from New Mexico, ah…ah…Buffalo Soldiers, battled Nazis to save my papa and mama and winery. I hear New Mexico and I know I must come back here." His eyes are glued on Elsa. "I am grateful to New Mexico in many ways." As he shakes Ambrose's hand, "Papa y mama buried them in cellar from Il Duce and the Nazis."

Without comment, Mr. Santoni removes the cork from the best bottle of Barolo and pours himself a glass. All intently watch papa Santoni, especially Jenoa, sniff the cork, then taste and savor the wine, anxiously waiting for his review.

"Ah bravo, bravo," he says, pouring wine into each glass around the table. Giovani raises his own glass.

"Happy New Year to my family and friends." He then drinks the wine down in one fell swoop, as all follow suit.

The clock ticks loudly into place at midnight.

As mama and papa embrace, so do Rose, Johnnie and Elsie. Esther and Ambrose wrap their arms around each other, Jenoa stands over Elsa's chair but says nothing. She instinctively stands to slide into his receptive arms, allowing him to kiss her, her arms around his neck.

Ambrose whispers to Esther, "This *Iti* works quick.

Chapter Twenty-Four

Seven Months Later

Sunshine at high noon glimmers on the crystal blue water and reflects off Elsie's fashionable, new sunglasses. The Zoo is a couple of city blocks away, and the now-crumbling POW camp is just beyond. She sits beside the newly reopened town recreational pond by the Rio Grande River known as Tingly Beach. While adjusting her beach umbrella and her wide brimmed sun-hat, sweat trickles down inside her swimsuit. Situated among other folks along the sandy, mile long beach in the middle of Albuquerque, they watch a motor boat sputter by. Geese flutter away from its wave.

She can hear the echo of fireworks going off from the other side of the beach. They are leftovers from the 4th of July. Lowering her sunglasses, she watches a man dive into the water from the ten-foot-tall diving buoy in the pond. This is the first time she's come close to this much water since her brush with death in the Pacific a little more than a year ago.

She returns a cigarette to her red-lipstick covered lips as she chooses between two letters yet to read. One is from her military pen pal. The other she received this morning from Tuscany, Italy. It is an easy choice.

Bona Cera, my dearest *Amica*;

Can you believe I am a happily married woman? Every morning I am reminded that I am a woman, if you know what I mean. Jenoa goes out to the fields at 5 AM seven days a week and comes home about 3 PM. We then get lost till dinner. We now prepare for our next harvest. Papa and mama came back here to live last week. Money from the sale of the bakery allowed them to buy a house here. They seem to have fallen in love again.

I look forward to you writing me because I miss you and life in Albuquerque. It is so beautiful here, though.

Elsie, I miss speaking English. Only Jenoa, my mama and papa can speak it. But papa is getting weird on speaking English. It is as if all he wants to hear is the local dialect. Recently, I tried talking normal English to him and he insisted we speak Italian.

You'll be able to write me now that you have my address.

Elsa Domenici.

Elsie wipes a tear for her best friend from under her sunglasses. Most of all she misses the Santoni Bakery job and those delicious *canollis*. She glances at her watch and realizes she'll have to leave for her new job soon. But first, she wants to read the letter from her military pen pal. She's been writing him since her return to Albuquerque a year ago. At first, she wrote several letters that went unanswered. She dreaded thinking the worst so she kept on writing. Then, this past January, it paid off with his first letter. Since then, it's been a monthly exchange. She carefully slices open the military envelope.

Como esta, mi senorita;

Great news! I am finally coming home. As a matter of fact, I write this tremendous news to *you* before my family. I have not been in New Mexico since we shipped out in September of 1941. I am coming home!

I would like to meet you when I pass through Albuquerque before I go back to the family ranch down in southeastern New Mexico.

Please receive me when I come knocking at the door of the address on this letter. Your address is burned into this retiring soldier's mind. I arrive within the week.

xoxoxo, Julian Arias

Elsie figures it's her duty to meet the soldier she's been writing this long. Besides, her curiosity is high. She glances again at her watch she realizes that it's time to leave. The bus should be arriving soon, and will drop her off at Penny's Department store makeup counter.

After placing the two delicate paper letters between pages in her Clark Gable movie magazine, she slips on slacks and a blouse over her swimsuit. She rolls up her blanket and pulls the beach umbrella out of the sand. As she heads toward Tingley Beach's entrance, another boy dives deep into the middle of the shimmering body of water.

At the entrance shack window, she returns the umbrella. While waiting for her deposit refund, her attention is swayed to the bulletin board. Quickly bypassing the swimming lessons notice, she sees a posting on the center of the bulletin board:

USO DANCE
WELCOME HOME OUR NEW MEXICO WAR HEROS
Saturday night, 8 PM, El Rey Theatre

That's tonight, and she immediately decides she will be there!

***

Upon finishing her day behind the makeup counter, Elsie walks home and jumps into the bath tub. She must pick the right dress before she can leave to walk to the USO Dance. Luckily, it's only a couple of blocks west on Route 66 from the store.

Arriving at the El Rey, she reads the marquee over the entrance.

WELCOME HOME

Elsie remembers that it's been almost a year since Victory in Japan, meaning that this celebration of VJ DAY is while our boys are still trickling home. Insignias from all military branches are still plastered on the theatre's walls surrounded by welcoming banners of the red, white and blue bunting.

She's a solo female made up to kill, and knowing it. In a red dress, red heels and red lipstick, she is welcomed in without a cover charge. She hasn't danced since Los Angeles.

The orchestra's swing music seduces her. She smiles while passing the bar, unable to find a vacant spot to sit. Besides, as they always do, some uniform will come along and buy her a drink. Despite being early, the place is filled with young men, all in uniform. But… it is also filled with other ladies.

"Soldiers, sailors and marines, oh my," she laughs.

Yet, she can't help but take notice of all the other ladies who are filling the room and are also dressed to kill. She recognizes some and waves, even though she hasn't seen them since high school. Without realizing it, the warm July night and energy of the band has her feet dancing in the aisle. From behind, a soldier tugs at her hand without asking, pulling her onto the dance floor. Because turning down a soldier in this room may not be the thing to do, she doesn't resist. Tossing the long strap of her purse around her neck, she goes with the flow. Realizing how much she has missed dancing, she laughs as some strange soldier swings her over and about in the middle of a crowded floor. As the song finishes, the soldier leads her back to an empty table and chair.

"Thank you for the dance, miss. I will send a waitress to take your drink, on me," he says with a smile.

Elsie watches him move on to ask another girl. There was a time when she'd still be ready for the next dance. But instead, she's thinking about having been on her feet all day.

As the waitress arrives, she orders. "Rum and coke please, heavy with rum."

Till now she's only heard the orchestra, not watched them. Now she sees that all the band members are in military uniforms. During a silent moment before the next song, the trumpet player puts down his instrument and walks to the microphone at center stage.

"Ladies and gentlemen welcome to the El Rey's USO dance. After our many years of playing together, tonight will be our band's final night in uniform. Tomorrow we're civilians. It is a pleasure to play for you on our last night. So, let's slow it down for our next one by giving tribute to one of our fallen Americans. Let's remember Glenn Miller with "Along the Santa Fe Trail.""

The room goes silent, seemingly in respect. Piano riffs lead into distant muffled trumpets. Strumming rhythm guitar underscores the smooth, mellow trombone that simulates Glen Miller's style. The dancers applaud, then break into couples. Most of the uniformed men have just met their partners, but a common feeling among the ladies is that it's their duty to slowly dance with their military partner.

As each couple dances by, Elsie notices a rail-thin soldier. In the next brief moment some gal asks him to dance. He nods, and she sees that he has one gorgeous smile. She watches him take command by expertly twirling his dance partner onto the floor. The girl smiles in approval. Then out of the blue, a marine takes Elsie's hand and without saying a word, and leads her to the floor. He's the war hero so she decides to go with the flow.

The soldier behind the microphone begins to sing… "Angels stop to paint the desert nightly. When the moon is beaming brightly, along the Santa Fe Trail…"

She finds it easy to glide across the floor with this partner.

"Stardust scattered all along the highway on a Rainbow-colored skyway. Along the Santa Fe Trail."

After several more dances Elsie rests her throbbing feet with her third rum and coke, watching the activity around her. How fast time flies, Elsie thinks while tunes by Artie Shaw, Benny Goodman, Harry James command the floor. A quick glance at her wristwatch tells her that in the last three hours she must have danced with almost every guy in the room.

Her looks across the dance floor and sees that one soldier she still hasn't danced with. She notices that he's eyeing her, too. As their gaze meets, he smiles, then winks at her. All she can do is blush and look away. The band leader again takes the microphone.

"Ladies and gentlemen, most of us in uniform tonight will become civilians tomorrow. But now, the time has come when we must say goodnight. It is time for our last dance of the evening..."

Elsie, now standing, sees the soldier across the dance floor also come to his feet. Both keep their eyes locked as creamy clarinet riffs from Glenn Miller's "Moonlight Serenade" waft through the dance hall.

The spinning mirror ball above throws out sparkling stars. Elsie and the soldier cross the dance floor ignoring other dance requests along the way.

They move into each other's arms. Without a word, it is as if they've been dancing together for years. They stare into each other's eyes while floating across the floor. The clarinet sings, welcoming our soldiers home one last time. All couples fill the floor. Elsie smiles. He smiles.

"My name is Julian Arias," he says.

Elsie's memory realizes the name rings a bell.

"My name is Elsie."

Both silently question their dance partner with their eyes. Then, too soon, the song begins to wind down. But seemingly at that last moment, the soldier witnesses the mirror light flashing a star across her face.

"By some strange chance of the Lord, Is your name Elsie...Lovato?'"

"Why, yes," she says with surprise.

"Elsie Lovato? From 309 Third Street, Albuquerque, New Mexico, USA?"

As she nods, he sees her amazement. And as the clarinet fades away with the melody, he kisses her. Elsie returns his kiss.

Chapter Twenty-Five

One Year Later

Activity in the department store's coffee shop is winding down from a busy lunch. On her break from the makeup counter, Elsie sits at a corner table. With pen in hand she writes her thoughts on thin, wispy paper. She thinks how international postage has become more and more expensive in the last year. Especially, since she's becoming addicted to monthly exchanges with Elsa.

...Esther and her husband are concerned because they are not able to have a baby. I console my sis after long bouts of tears. I can't tease her anymore about the fun of at least trying to have a baby.

Mama went out with a man last weekend. He seemed nice enough. But I do not know if they will go out again. Mama said she didn't like his response to being introduced to my brother. Johnny does not make a good impression.

Johnny, oh, my God. He worries all of us. He hasn't been able to keep a job. Mom cleans his room but says nothing about all the clanking of bottles I hear her throwing out. The war still affects him badly. He has been going to the Veteran's hospital every week, but it doesn't seem to help. It seems whiskey is his only friend.

One good thing is that Julian and I are talking more serious. He says he'd like to get married but he still has several issues to work out for himself. Physically, he's strong. He's gained twenty pounds of muscle since being a prisoner of war and a slave laborer in Japan.

He says that It helps him to work at his family's ranch. He tells me the fresh air and the wide open spaces are great medicine for him. Oh, Elsa, would it be a funny thing in life if Julian and I did get married? You married an Italian POW. And I, an American POW? Wouldn't that be funny? The thought is, anyway...

Elsie glances at the wall clock. It's time to get back to the makeup counter. She has inventory to count.

***

Across town, Johnny sits under a tree in a vacant lot on a Girard Street corner. Before the war, this was his favorite spot to bring his dates on picnics. The view to the west seemed infinite.

To his left is the Rio Grande valley with endless miles that stretch to the western horizon. He scans the dormant volcanoes along the western horizon that precede Mount Taylor, some sixty miles away. But he can easily tell that these views will be blocked soon by the houses going up in front of him. This Ridgecrest neighborhood is obviously becoming desirable. It is growing and sprawling fast. New housing starts are being laid out all around him and the whole town is growing fast on both sides of the Rio Grande.

He takes another swig from his bottle as memories from only a few years ago overtake him. He can't forget no matter how hard he tries. Only his friend, Jack Daniels, eases his flashbacks of drowning in a burning, oil-slicked South Pacific, at a place called Leyte Gulf.

In an alcoholic stupor, he has little choice but to lay back. War memories force themselves into flashbacks in those days west of the Philippines. Kamikaze planes shot down left and right all around him—while he was in the water!

Some got through, smashing into the U.S. Navy battle group around him. He didn't think he'd see home again.

Mentally, he flashes back to the present, so he takes another swig. In front of him, across the street, home builders are in varied stages of laying out a development. Tractors are pushing down old adobe structures. Residential lots have survey stakes planted along the planned streets. Cement is being poured into some house foundations.

Unsteadily, he remembers that he's here today for a reason. To his right, across the street, is a single home at 900 Girard. A white picket fence surrounds its freshly painted white paneled walls and green shingled roof. A wide green ribbon stretches across the front entrance. A number of cars and city trucks are parked on the street around it. A KOB radio truck sits in the driveway. City workers plant a 5 x 5 foot sign in front.

From the people surrounding the new sign, he recognizes only one, Mayor Clyde Tingly. He can't hear what they are saying but can watch the mayor cut the ribbon. Johnny takes another swig as he reads the sign.

HOME OF PULITZER PRIZE JOURNALIST
ERNIE PYLE
Opening Soon
ERNIE PYLE
MEMORIAL LIBRARY

His alcoholic stupor encourages a torrent of memories that stretch back…

Chapter Twenty-Six

"Oh, God! The pain!"

Covered by black machine oil so thick it doesn't wash away as ocean waves slam down on him. "Ahhhhhh!" he screams as pain overcomes him.

Johnny can't feel his legs or move his left arm. When he wipes his eyes with his good hand the blood from the gash on his forehead mixes like oil with tar. But now he realizes he's at the bottom of a swirling water-dervish surrounded by ten foot waves.

"Ah, shit!" he screams as the ocean again forces him beneath its churning waters. When he finally surfaces, gasping for air, there is a show of carnage before him.

Just as quickly, another wave overcomes him, and again as he's pushed up, able to look through a tunnel of ocean water. Salt water stings his eyes and cuts. Another giant wave crashes down on him. As the last gasp of breath is squeezed from his lungs, the mighty Pacific carries him up to the crest of a wave. His seared torso makes him want to scream, but instead, he gasps for air.

In the distance, he sees his battleship—the USS Samuel B. Roberts—with its decks burning, somehow firing its five inch guns to shoot down a diving Kamikaze. To his right, loud whizzing reports from salvos of rockets launching off the USS Tennessee draw his attention. Both Fletcher class ships rip apart another swarm of enemy planes.

Countless black puffs of explosives detonate in the sky above. Hot shrapnel rains down around him, sizzling into the ocean that again pulls waves over him. He now realizes that the only thing keeping him afloat is his yellow Mae West life jacket.

As his body numbs from the pain, another wave carries him down, then up again. Hordes of shooting planes continue to fill the sky above. Johnny sees a Kamikaze Zero flying low over him. He is hypnotized by the Rising Sun emblazoned under its wing.

The Kamikaze aims at the middle of the Tennessee. Johnny watches it strike at water level below the port side of the ship. It's deck explodes into red and black smoke.

While watching his fellow sailors jump off or be thrown into the ocean, he hears their screams.

At last, he realizes what is happening. He was on the front deck when his ship took a direct Kamikaze hit on the port side, throwing him overboard. With black smoke belching from its side, but still under its own power, the USS Samuel B. Roberts sailed away, leaving him behind.

He remembers. They were charging directly into the biggest Jap ship he'd ever seen. They called it the Shokai. The Samuel B. normally sailed so close to the water that the Japs couldn't aim their guns low enough to pop them. Jap eight inch shells flew over his ship's bow while our five inch shells bounced off the Shokai's thick armor plating. He remembers they continued charging, getting close enough to shoot off three 24-foot Mark Fifteen torpedoes directly broadside. We sent that sonofabitch a message!

The waves crash over on top of him without warning. Struggling to breathe, he remembers he's from the high plains desert. He's not supposed to die in the middle of a nowhere ocean. His scream is greeted with a throat full of salty brine.

***

The remaining battle groups steam away in all directions to lick their wounds. Johnny grasps onto a bowl shaped piece of wreckage and struggles painfully to pull himself into it. The afternoon begins to pass slowly under the broiling sun.

"Remain calm, sailor," he tells himself, "so the pain won't get worse." Still, he winces at a type of pain he has never felt before. "Our guys will come back for us," he tells himself as he blocks the sun from his eyes with his good arm. "...the sun is so damn hot! I need pleasant thoughts, pleasant thoughts..."

Momentarily, pleasant memories come easily. Was it only three days ago that he sat in the middle of a thousand waiting sailors on the flight deck of the USS Saratoga Aircraft carrier?

The seas are calm and the sun warms the breeze. He remembers his anticipation of the most exciting experience he'd ever had. His excitement built as his fellow sailors stood up in waves to shout recognition of the big band music they'd heard for the last five years. And now, they would witness it live. Live, amid this nowhere South Pacific.

At last, famous clarinet riffs, big band sounds were amplified through the ship's speaker system. Along with the other thousand sailors, Johnny stood whistling and applauding at the sight of the twenty big band musicians rising from the lower deck.

The afternoon spotlight was directed on the back of the leader. In full sight of everyone aboard, he turned around to face his audience holding his famous clarinet. Instantly, his band began his national number one hit: "Begin the Beguine." The sailors increased their excited roars at the sight of international recording artist and now Naval Lieutenant: Artie Shaw.

***

A cold night dressed only in wet rags finally leads into an ironically beautiful orange and yellow glow rising over the horizon.

The night had been filled with never-ending cries of pain from other guys in the water. The sailors shouted out who they were every hour or so, keeping tabs on each other.

Soon enough the sun begins to bake him. The metal under him grows hotter. He splashes sea water in and out to cool it.

***

The temperature drop feels like fifty degrees as a darkness beyond belief encompasses him, bringing no moon or stars.

Someone shouts, "Anyone out there?"

"Jack Yuson," comes a response. "Dominick," another calls out. "Bob Higgens," comes out of the darkness. Then come the names, "Bob Golbaum, Jones, Padilla, Connors, Jose, Gunner." All calls are recognized as the sailors from the Taffy 3 Battle Group.

Johnny anxiously listens as hundreds shout. As the volume increases, he prepares to shout out with pride, "Johnny Lovato!"

But before he can, screams echo through the blind darkness.

Someone shouts, "Sharks!"

More horrific screams pierce the night. Johnny sheds helpless tears at their sudden and abrupt end.

***

The ball of fire rises in the sky again. He feels himself baking as he floats over calm waters. Red blisters start to grow on his legs, chest, and face.

He struggles to sit up, but he's unable to open his sun burned and swollen eyes. All he can hear are groups of sailors grasping onto anything for dear life. The brightness of the day hinders his ability to fully open his eyes, even though he suddenly hears more screams nearby.

He knows: Sharks!

***

The night's waves are dead calm. No one can keep count, but it is obvious that the roll call is getting shorter. A few hours of sleep are interrupted by a shriek only ten feet away. A struggle churns the water next to him.

Another sun rises over the horizon and into his face. As he feels its warmth, he's unable to open his eyes.

"Hey Green, are you all right! Green!"

He doesn't hear a reply. Suddenly, his bow shaped steel life preserver begins to rock violently. Being helplessly thrown side to side, he can feel the hard hit of a shark ramming his thin steel island. As Johnny feels the jolt he senses the shark's tall fin flop over the side.

Suddenly, he hears rifle shots. Countless numbers of shots ring out. As the violence from the shark encounter dissipates. He shouts his only thoughts: The damn Japs are back and they're picking us off one at a time. That's all he remembers as he blacks out.

***

He comfortably stares up through sterile gauze wrapped eyes to see the whiteness of a hospital ceiling. Even though grateful, he has no damn idea how he got here. A fog clouds his mind as he feels no pain. How long has he been in bed? He doesn't know. Must have been a long time.

He tries to think back, and recalls working in the ship's mess when the Battle Stations order came over the speakers. After quickly manning his station top-side, explosions rocked his ship. Slammed against a bulkhead, he bounced into the water.

Now through the gauze come faint visions of blinking Christmas tree lights before he fades out.

***

Thoughts race through his mind as he opens his eyes. Johnny breathes easier through slits in the gauze around his mouth and nose, despite the corset about his chest. Through fresh gauze he watches the nurse adjust red paper hearts on the wall. As the days pass, he feels dull pain in both of his legs raised in traction, as is one of his arms. The world fades out again.

***

Whether it's the sun shining through the windows or mild stirrings at the front of his ward, he awakens. He sees nurses and doctors with excited smiles hovering around a small man with grey hair as he walked into the ward through swinging doors. They all extend clipboards to him with their pens or pencils.

"May we have your autograph, Mr. Pyle?" someone asks.

With a matter-of-fact expression, the man gives them quick signatures. Johnny watches the old fellow's expression change to serious purpose as he makes his way through the ward in Johnny's direction. Ernie smiles warmly, waving greetings to each bed he passes. As he walks by, occupants excitedly sit up with a smile and wave back.

"Hey, Ernie, how's it going?" a guy shouts.

Johnny develops a quick apprehension as the most famous war correspondent in the English-speaking world approaches him. Doctors and nurses hover around this guy with grey hair as Pyle asks them something. They all are nodding toward his bed. He then steps toward Johnny, his entourage following. He motions to them to step back.

"Please." He moves to Johnny's bed side, "Hello, sailor." Reaching for Johnny's free hand, he clasps it without moving the arm. The entourage dissipates. "May I sit down next to you, sailor?"

Johnny's curiosity gets the best of him despite the drug induced fogginess. His partially gauze-wrapped head nods, and the man pulls a chair up to his bed.

"I understand your name is John Lovato," he says. "Mine is Ernie Pyle."

Johnny mumbles, "Sit."

"Well, John, I write for the newspaper, and I want to do a story about you."

"Why?"

"I understand you and I are from Albuquerque, New Mexico, USA."

"Wonder if I'll ever see home again," Johnny mutters as grogginess starts.

"My wife, Jerry, moved there three years ago, and we live in our new house on Girard Street," says the man, gently taking the sailor's arm to convey his empathy. "We like it because our front yard stretches as far as you can see. Mt. Taylor, 65 miles away, is like a picture framed by our front window."

"I know that place back home." The drugs coursing through his veins make him to fade in and out.

"Johnny, can I ask you a couple of questions?"

"Yeah."

"I understand you were at Leyte Gulf?"

"Oh?"

"And that you were in the water for days before they pulled you out."

"Seemed longer."

"Were sharks ever a threat to you?"

"Sharks! Sharks!" Johnny screams. "Get them off me!"

He kicks with his painfully broken body. Nurses rush to his bedside with more injections. Moments later, Johnny calms down.

"Hello, Johnny, Johnny, sailor..." is all he hears as he moves into a painless existence.

***

Still sitting across the street from Ernie Pyle's Girard house, Johnny watches the proceedings finalize. Only recently did he remember the brief encounter. Soon thereafter, America learned that the grey-haired old man had caught a round when he stuck his head out of a Le Shima, Okinawa fox hole. Johnny never learned if Ernie Pyle wrote that article.

A familiar grogginess approaches him. The crowd across the street dissipates, and he knows it's time to go home. Taking another swig from the almost empty bottle, he stands with difficulty.

After several woozy steps, he stumbles to the ground and passes out, face in the dirt. Above him is a sign that reads: Soon to Become the Duke City's Newest Subdivision of Homes.

Over all is a fiery red-orange ball slowly dipping behind the flat western horizon. What's left in Johnny's bottle dribbles out onto the ground.

Chapter Twenty-Seven

Corona, southeastern New Mexico
The Next Day: July 8, 1947

The same blazing July sun beats directly on the parched southeastern New Mexico desert. Endless flat and arid chamisa terrain surrounds Julian. He jabs at the earth with his pole digger. Planting barbed wire fence poles around his family's forty acre ranch is the task he's given himself. Being raised on the ranch has always meant hard work seven days a week. Hard work wasn't strange for him through his four years in a Japanese slave labor camp. It was starvation and disease, and the constant cruelty, that was hard to bear.

He knows hard work is necessary to regain his health. Having removed his shirt, he can see his sweaty arm muscles ripple as he pulls a full shovel of clay from a post hole. In addition to activity, he has New Mexico's endless blue skies and mom's steak, red chili, tortillas and beans. He packs on muscle while coming back from the walking skeleton he was two years ago.

He takes off his white cowboy hat and pulls a cloth from his back pocket to wipe the sweat from his brow, then from his broad chest. He carries the pole digger over his shoulder and walks back through scrub brush to the jeep. He must get used to the boots he wears after years of practically going barefoot.

He grabs the water canteen from the back seat and drinks a third of its cool, watery contents while putting back on his shirt. The sun is catching up with him as memories flood over him.

Five Years Earlier

A rifle shot cracks up ahead through the tropical April morning on the Bataan Peninsula island of Luzon in the Philippines. The order comes from the top: the surrender of 60,000 to 80,000 troops. Four months earlier, the

Japs wiped out the American Navy at Pearl Harbor. So, they all knew one thing: there was zero hope for resupply for this American base in the Philippines. They also knew: no Papa, no Mamma, no Uncle Sam.

Philippine and American soldiers, now POWs, half-heartedly form columns at the airfield in some hamlet called Mira Vales including several thousand men from the 200th and 515th New Mexico National Guard Coast Artillery. Many march behind Julian while the rest precede him.

He adjusts his pith helmet while studying the platoon of Japs that surround his men while aiming bayoneted rifles toward them. They are being bunched tightly together. Two, four, six, eight, ten Jap troop trucks pull alongside.

"All right! They're going to load us on them," someone says down the line from Julian.

A Japanese officer shouts an order causing the simultaneous action of the canvas covered truck beds being flapped open. Machine gun crews are revealed preparing to fire. As they cock their guns, the surrounding Jap bayonets retreat behind the trucks. As the commanding Jap officer raises his sword, countless flocks of birds come out of nowhere to fly off.

"Oh, my God!" Julian realizes this is his last moment.

Suddenly the ground begins to shake beneath his feet. Jap, Pilipino and American men are slammed to the ground. Foot wide fissures crack open beside the road. Screams come from all nationalities as they fall into newly cracked crevices. Trees and ramshackle buildings collapse. The heavy Jap troop trucks are tossed onto their sides, throwing out their machine gunners, crushing some. Battle hardened men scream as they're tossed about by the earthquake.

The shaking intensifies. Julian lays face down on the side of the road gripping its dirt in both hands. He prays. "Dear lord, *Dios Mio*, please, please, no, no." Tremors intensify.

Seconds seem like hours before the ground gradually settles down. POWs stay prone until that same damn Jap officer shouts orders to his men. Julian looks up at nervous Jap soldiers trying to regain their composure.

Obviously responding to their orders, their bayoneted rifles force the POWs to stand at attention and form into two marching columns. After an hour or so, endless lines of American and Pilipino soldiers begin marching out of *Mira Vales*.

Later that afternoon, Julian sees Japs driving by in a captured American car, then a truck. Inside are photographers straining to take photos of the dragging, marching troops.

Second Day

After sleeping on the side of the road for a few hours, the marching continues. More rifle shots come from ahead. Four columns of ragged men persevere without missing a beat. Julian reaches another body on the side of the road. The American's chest is half gone from a point-blank execution.

Forced to ignore the sight, his column keeps marching forward. He avoids eye contact with the Jap soldier standing on the back of a truck. "March! March!" he shouts.

Suddenly, Julian hears his fellow troop's prayers getting louder. He can't help but think he is down and out because he is so thirsty. But strong motivation forces him to continue marching. The decapitated corpse of an American sailor lies beside the road with a tin cup still gripped in its hand. The head with its cap still on, lies next to its shoulders. The prayers get louder.

Soldiers stand at each side of the marching columns with fixed-bayonet rifles. Along the way, each soldier pushes forward an American with the butt of their rifle. Julian suddenly feels that butt on his spine. Any breath he had left is knocked out as he stumbles forward. He catches his balance before falling, and somehow continues marching which amazingly puts air back into his lungs. He's grateful his lace-less boots and pith helmet didn't fall off. After all, some of the men are marching with bloody, bare feet.

***

A rustle in the New Mexican shrubbery draws Julian's attention back to the ranch. Hidden between some dried chamisa, a short snake wrestles with its prey. He can't tell what's in the snake's mouth because only a tail sticks out. He grabs his rifle from the back seat and aims at the squiggling snake. An unexpected nervous twitch disrupts his aim. Still holding the weapon, he shakes as he wipes sweat from his eyes. Changing his mind, Julian puts the rifle back into its rack. That the snake has a right to live, just like him, he thinks. No more killing.

It's time to get back to the ranch. He's hungry, and has big plans for tonight. He jumps into his jeep. He is careful to hug tightly to the crevices and gullies along the miles of fencing he's already put up.

"Landscape of New Mexico," he says to himself as he parks on top of a hill. Sunshine hits him from directly overhead, telling him that it's high noon. "It must be a hundred degrees," he tells his jeep. "I better get back to Albuquerque tonight to see Elsie. I'm starting to talk to the jeep already." He shakes his head.

As he drives toward southwest, he can see vultures flying directly above. He decides to investigate what they're circling over. Leaving the jeep, he suspects it's the missing cattle his brothers told him about. He stomps over broken terrain, past dried chamisa, and around prickly pear cactus.

He knows his suspicions are right when he detects a familiar, gut wrenching odor. There was a time when he would upchuck at this point, but now, with all he's experienced over recent years, he's just curious and moves closer, unfazed. He knows the smell is dead cattle. Dead humans smell sweeter. At last he stops to survey what is laid out in front of him.

"Well, hell!" He counts one, two, three, four, eventually ten dead head, all laid out in a perfect circle. "Ah, hell!"

Each carcass's eyeballs, internal and sex organs have been surgically removed. He steps into the circle in amazement. There is not a drop of blood to be seen. It is as if the carcasses were brought here and laid out perfectly. His eyes widen as he cannot detect a single tire track coming or going. Not a broken bush or plant to be seen. He shades his eyes as he glances up to the sunfilled sky.

Only then can he see a growing dust cloud in the distance. Getting his binoculars from the jeep, his view sharpens. Through the dust, he watches an endless convoy of military troops and flat-beds trucks rolling south. The flatbeds appear to be carrying tarp covered cargo.

"That's Mac Brazel's place," he says.

Driven by curiosity, he makes his way down the hill toward the road. As he gets closer, he is stopped by his own fence between his land and the neighbor's road. Through frustration he stops to watch the convoy continue past. Finally, the last of the flatbed trucks approaches, then pass, spitting out fine New Mexican dust. Its tarp blows open revealing shining, silvery smooth metal.

A troop truck following stops as the convoy continues. A sergeant and several privates, fully armed, jump off and approach, shouting at him. Julian continues to watch as the sergeant barks.

"What the hell's matter with you? Are you deaf?"

Julian shrugs.

"Get the hell out of here!"

"This is my property!" Julian shouts back.

Their advance stops at the barbed wire fence.

"There is nothing here for you to see. Get the hell out of here," the sergeant repeats.

Out of principle, Julian refuses to move. So, the sergeant motions to his troops to go through the barbed wire fence.

The thought of seeing Elsie tonight is more pleasurable than confronting this threatening squad. Julian smiles and jumps back into his jeep. His work with the fence is paying off. As the soldiers cuss and shout at being hung up in the fence, Julian chuckles. He drives away without looking back.

He wonders where the hell those guys came from.

Then he sees two planes flying patrol over the convoy. The rugged terrain makes Julian pull away from the fence line. Now headed in the opposite direction from the convoy, he thinks, that they probably came from the Army Air Field down in Roswell. So now for some strange reason, as he rumbles up and down the desert road, he thinks of ROSWELL. ROSWELL keeps coming to mind. Besides, he thinks, I've got plans tonight with a pretty lady waiting for me. Why am I here?

He smiles as the rough road bounces him around.

***

The ten-piece orchestra plays the big band swing tune to its end. The mirror ball stops spraying its light through out the Sunset Night Club Dance Hall along Route 66. Couples make their way back to tables. Overlooking them is a wall mural of a desert-scape. It features a skinny Navajo man riding a white horse. Walking behind the horse is an obese Navajo woman, with five Navajo children trailing behind.

Esther, Ambrose, Elsie, and Julian slip back into their booth behind a table filled with half full glasses. The ladies are in their finest dresses. The men loosen their ties. A man in a fine suit with a diamond and turquoise bolo tie approaches their table.

Smiling, he says, "Welcome to Route 66's own Sunset Nightclub. I hope everything is to your liking, folks?"

"Como esta, Joe?" says Ambrose. "How's the owner of the hottest night spot in town?" He puts his arm around his wife's shoulders, "You know my wife, Esther."

Joe nods. "Como esta, senora?"

"May I present this young couple? They are my new soon to be brother and sister-in-law, Julian Arias and Elsie Lovato."

The nightclub owner offers his hand to Julian. "I am Joseph Martinez. It is a pleasure to meet you." After shaking Julian's hand, he makes it a point to shake Elsie's.

"I understand you have the best T-bone steaks in town," says Julian. "We're here to celebrate." Smiling, he glances at Elsie.

"My sister just got engaged to this guy," says Esther, pointing to Julian with a smile.

With pride, Elsie shows her hand with the sparkler. Joe Martinez smiles. "Congratulations, ma'am. Your steak dinner is on me tonight." He looks around for his employee, a blonde lady who has a flash camera strapped around her neck. "If there is anything you folks want while you're at the Sunset Nightclub, just ask for me."

Within seconds, the photographer steps up to the couples' table. "Gentlemen, care for a photo? It's on the Sunset Nightclub."

"Sure. Flash away," Ambrose replies.

He poses while placing a kiss on Esther's cheek. Julian places his arm around Elsie's and grins. The ladies dab their eyes from the flash. The orchestra kicks in with a Benny Goodman swing tune. Without a word, Ambrose and Julian stand up and the ladies follow them onto the dance floor.

Ambrose wastes no time swinging Esther around the floor. Julian pulls Elsie into his arms. Before he can twirl her, she gives him a quick kiss.

"After what I went through today to get here, Elsie, you make me so happy." With exuberance, and the largest smile he can manage, he twirls her around the floor.

Chapter Twenty-Eight

Elsa beams with fulfillment as she looks out her third level bedroom window. Sunshine glimmers over drifts of blinding white snow that cover the fields as far as the horizon. Countless mounds of snow cover the grapevines below.

Joy fills her as she watches Jenoa playing with their 18-month-old son in the courtyard below. She smiles as he shows the baby how to make a snow ball.

Loosening the belt around her expanding waist, Elsa sits at a table next to the window. She picks up a pen while resting her other hand over her growing baby bump. She soon loses herself in a letter.

Dear Elsie,

Merry Christmas! We went to Midnight Mass last night. As I sat in the family pew, a beautiful voice grew out of the choir. As she sang AVE MARIA, my mind flashed back to Albuquerque. I recall our high school years, life in Los Angeles and especially working and living above that old Gold St. bakery.

But those years were a long time ago and another world away. Jenoa and I watch little Palo stand, then fall. How quickly he grows. All the while we prepare for our new one coming soon.

Papa's health seems to be a challenge. He's coughing more these days. Mama thinks it is the cigarettes he has smoked all these years.

The winery is growing. The Domenici family bought the neighboring winery which increases our land holdings to 500 acres. They have matured growths so we can improve our production without having to wait years for new vines to mature.

You would be surprised how much of a grape farmer I have become. And this week, I designed new labels for our bottles. Three different blends require a fresh design.

I am grateful for your friendship. You are my only link to thinking and writing in English. I miss you terribly and wish you could be nearer.

Love, Elsa

***

Elsie is drawn to the kitchen's wood stove by its enticing aroma. She feeds it more wood and, with a wooden spoon, soon stirs the bubbling pot of stew. After carefully bringing a spoonful to her lips, she decides it is a bit too thick. After adding a half ladle of boiling water from the side compartment, she adds a dash of salt and flips the flour tortilla on the grill while turning over the toasting green chili pod.

With care, she pulls her culinary creation from the stove and spreads butter on the tortilla before slicing open the chili pod. Then she lays it out onto the tortilla for her dinner sandwich. With a glass of milk, a bowl of stew and her sandwich, Elsie sits at the kitchen table. Paper and pencil await.

Dear Elsa,

HAPPY NEW YEAR 1950!

Weeks into our new decade, I received your latest letter yesterday. It is good to hear life in Italy is so satisfying for you. I can imagine how your baby and the one on the way can keep you busy. I can see Jenoa bouncing them on his knee.

Julian says that he wants sons. But I can tell you, if we had a daughter, Julian would be so over protective. He's been working the family ranch while he waits for his job application to come through for Sandia Base. He says once he gets that job, we'll be set. So, we wait. Having the job before we get married is our plan. But we did meet with Father O'Brien at St. Mary's and we're set up there. Till then it's still behind the makeup counter for me.

Esther is trying to get pregnant. My heart bleeds for her as she'd be a great mom. Ambrose has ordered her to quit working at the hotel, hoping that will help relieve the stress.

It's times like this that I am reminded of a former co-worker of mine from the store. She didn't last long on the job because of family concerns. The other day I learned what those concerns were from a story in the newspaper about her having her 9th baby. Plus, get ready for this: believe it or not, she has given birth to 35 kids! THIRTY-FIVE! But only 9 have lived. The problem with that story was that it was Esther who showed it to me. She was feeling both tearful and angry because of her difficulty in getting pregnant. I feel for her.

About getting a job, Johnny can't keep a job. I am angry at him. Mama still has to clean up all his empty whiskey bottles. It must be easy for you to imagine how it gives me great joy when Julian helps me escape to go look at houses.

You would not recognize Albuquerque. There is an explosion of new house construction because of the returning soldiers. Can you imagine houses are starting to stretch between here and the university on Route 66. Ever since the city council merged old town with new town, there has been talk about renaming Route 66 to Central Avenue because it runs through the center of Albuquerque from the mountains on the east and the desert on the west. The salesman said that building will soon stretch all the way from the bottom to the side of the mountains. Can you believe it?

Mama has been promoted to assistant chef at the Hilton. All I know is she's been home much less.

Please write back soon.

Elsie

The Following Spring

Elsa wants to find the perfect present for Elsie's special day. Even though she can't be there, Elsa thinks often about what that special gift could be. What can she send Elsie to represent herself? Not knowing Elsa's husband, her present won't be for them, but just her.

Then she realizes where the perfect present can be found!

She has looked forward to the day she can go on an enthralling adventure, and that day has finally arrived. It will be the first day on her own since the baby was born. She will travel while Palo and Victorio are with their grandmother, Abra, who was more than happy to look after them, more than happy. Jenoa will be busy in the vineyards today, freeing her for her first solo excursion into the city since they've been married.

First, she will make the two-hour train trip from the vineyard's spur. Jenoa kissed Elsa and smiled as he saw her off, calling this their own private train. She can simply sit back and gaze through the window as the family's winery and its buildings roll by. A grander view is provided by their tall green trees that shade the buildings' new Tuscan tiled roofs. Further out, lush green grasses are capped with beautiful crimson red and plumed flowers growing in the unused field behind the family house. The train slowly builds momentum uphill, over-looking the manicured rows of grape vines. Soon, Domenici Winery is off in the distance.

The colorful sight of the neighbor's fields is mesmerizing. Fields of leafy golden sunflowers spread farther and farther. Elsa knows the neighbors extract their oils and seeds for world markets.

Vibrations from the pre-war rails are felt up through to her seat. She already knows where she will go and how to get there because Jenoa showed her 'The City of the Lilies' during their honeymoon. Now, she adjusts herself by trying to stay in her bouncing seat.

Tumbling vibrations from the steam engine through the train tracks begin to slow. Steam belches past her view of the station rolling by. Slowing to a stop, she sees the station's sign: Firenze.

Now actually there, Else wonders how to reach her destination from the train station? Jenoa took her hand in hand there. She fell in love with the place. Little did she realize that the memory would come in handy.

Florence, Italy is famous for its grand churches that date back to the 13th Century. Jenoa showed Elsa the other side of town where tremendous architectural churches have gained fame through the ages. When they saw the abbey at *Santa Croce* where Michelangelo and Galileo are entombed, she was amazed by the all-encompassing grandeur of Renaissance beauty. Her memory of all this is still vivid.

But now, she purposely pictures the narrow cobble stone streets that were just a walk from the station. For her destination is the abbey of Santa Maria Novella. They say that 600 years ago Dominican monks opened this abbey with a little side shop, unaware of course that *La Farmaceutica* would become the world's oldest pharmacy.

While most monasteries developed their wine grapes, Santa Maria Novella offered herbal remedies, oils, and elixirs to help ease the human condition. But soon they added skin care products and exotic fragrances and perfumes. Since the 13th Century, the Santa Maria Novella has become the world-renowned Mecca of fragrance.

She remembers going with Jenoa around a dark corner of the abbey's entrance to a massive wooden door. She retraces those steps past the door and goes inside. The memory of aromatic riches lures her closer.

As she pulls the thick ageless wooden door closed, she surrenders to the scent of rose petals, Persian oils, soaps, and sachets. A path pulls her through large rooms with walls covered by elegant Renaissance frescos. Only now does her sojourn blend into the path that finally leads to her destination.

The *Farmacceutica's* shelves, filled with merchandise, seem to bloom around her. Gleefully losing herself while walking among them, she wonders how many people have walked these floors over not just years or decades—but centuries.

At the other side of the broad room, her eyes widen at a curiosity that draws her to it. Nestled in the center cabinet between shelves filled with countless apothecary tins and glass jars, sits an obviously old mechanism. A master invention of its time, it now seems simple. A foot wide, coffee-like dripper continues to drip distilled flower water with its heavy aromas. A sign states the flower of the day: Orchida.

It seems like minutes before she loses herself among the fragrances. But as Elsa glances at the clock over the back counter, more than two hours have passed.

Carefully examining every item one by one in the store, she makes her decisions. Selecting one sample at a time, she carries a potion, then an essential oil, a lotion, and a scented bar of soap to the front counter, behind which stands the pharmacist/clerk. To his side is a special display. Upon closer examination, glass encased diaries of fading documents trace back centuries. Metal placards on each describe that these are recipe ledgers dating back to the Renaissance. Their fading scriptures contain the Monks' ancient ingredients and formulas.

She places more items on the counter in front of the clerk, separating which to keep and which to send to Elsie.

"Can we arrange to send these items overseas?" she asks him.

The clerk smiles. "*Si, si senora. No problemo.*"

He sorts the items and seems surprised when he asks, "*No fragrancia, senora?*"

"*Fragrancia! Si, si grazi. Fragrancias!*" she remembers.

She quickly returns to the rows of fragrances. While dabbing several scents inside her wrists, she decides to keep the one labeled *Persion Lilach*.

The next bottle is labeled *Arid Sunshine*. A whiff encourages her to smile wider. She has a flash of a memory, a moment from years ago. She recalls another sunny day back in Albuquerque. Elsa picks up two bottles, one for herself and the other for Elsie. She knows that she's found the perfect fragrance for Elsie so she requests that her bottles be wrapped with a golden chain.

***

A Month Later

Sunshine fills the blue skies this Saturday morning. St. Mary's bells ring proud and loud. The church's double front doors are open wide. Joyous people dressed in their finest pour out and gather. Within seconds, Julian, in a black tuxedo, and Elsie, in her white flower-pinned dress and a white veil, walk through. They are greeted with cheers.

Relieved to finally witness one of her baby's wedding, Rose cries at the sight. Esther lifts the long train of Elsie's wedding dress with one hand. With the other, she tosses rice. From the groom's brothers and sisters more rice rains upon the newlyweds. As they move down the church steps the onlookers cheer louder as Julian kisses Elsie.

Julian's car awaits in front of St. Mary's with Just Married written on the back window. A string of tin cans is tied to the back bumper. His brother Gene opens the passenger door, giving his brother the keys. The brothers shake hands. Before the newlyweds climb into the car, Elsie turns to the crowd and pauses before tossing away her bouquet. The crowd cheers and applauds even louder as one of Julian's bachelor brothers catches it. Rose sobs happily as the newlyweds drive away.

***

Later, at the American Legion Hall, Julian holds Elsie's hand as they cut a section from their three-layer cake. Elsie whispers in her new husband's ear, "We'll save the top for our first anniversary, darling."

Cheers and applause fill the hall as the band plays a familiar New Mexican Ranchera tune. The newlyweds wipe cake frosting from each other's lips. Julian leads his bride to the center of the dance floor. Everyone watches the couple. The bride's gown becomes covered with dollar bills pinned to it as Julian leads her about.

"I look forward to dancing with you for the rest of my life," he whispers.

"We'll dance till we're old and grey."

The rest of room follows behind them. Even pre-teen boys bow and ask pre-teen girls to dance. Smiles from seated older folks grow as they watch the little ones dance.

***

Julian has pulled the tin cans from his bumper, washed the Just Married off the window, and loaded the trunk with their luggage. He leans against the front passenger door studying the road map. He can't help but watch his wife close and lock the door over the threshold he carried her over last night. Her open car door awaits.

She laughs. "Like that new song says, let's get our kicks along Route 66!"

Sitting behind the steering wheel, Julian is nearly overcome by her alluring fragrance. His lips find their way to nibble her ear then her throat. She giggles.

"You smell so good."

She smiles in amazement at how well her friend's Italian present works.

Soon the Chevy is rolling down the brand-new neighborhood street. So new that half of the planned houses are still being hammered.

Chapter Twenty-Nine

Two Years Later

Darkness fills the bedroom. Elsie lays next her husband squirming in maternal anguish. Their son cries loudly from the other bedroom.

Julian puts his arm across her torso. "You can't keep getting up every 15 minutes." His pillow muffles him. "Let 'im cry, he'll get tired out."

Lying on her back, Elsie stares into the darkness with building anxiety. Her baby is crying. And crying. And crying! Her husband forbids her instinct. Frustrated tears stream from her eyes.

When her baby stops crying everything seems to go deathly silent. A few seconds pass. The silence becomes intense. She decides to ignore her husband by pushing his arm aside and rush to her infant.

Sweet relief comes over her at sight of her baby Russell sleeping comfortably.

She steps carefully back into her bedroom. With great care, slips back into bed. Elsie can hear her husband whisper before he slips into slumber: "I told you."

She thinks about how he works hard every day at the laboratory and needs his sleep. She finds herself not wanting to wake the men in her house, her husband and son. She is married to a hard man and has learned why: He had to be to survive. Her eyes are open as she lays silent. In his sleep, Julian murmurs, tossing and turning. His reoccurring nightmare is back.

***

Eight Years Earlier

On December 7th, 1941, we heard that eight hours ago Pearl Harbor was bombed. As coast artillery gunners, we are already at our posts shooting down endless swarms of Jap planes at Clark Field in the Philippines. At least, unlike Pearl, we had notice they were coming.

Every day since my fellow troops have been pushed back by an endless onslaught of air raids and the landing of Jap troops. My artillery battery is ordered to fall back to Corregidor.

With our Navy wiped out at Pearl, there is no hope of supplies. Ammunition and rations diminish quickly. Remnants of my New Mexico 515th Coast Artillery merge with the New Mexico 200th Coast Artillery as we all fall back.

Radio reports from home say the newspapers are calling us the `Battling Bastards of Bataan.' Four months later, after being forced into underground bomb shelters throughout the Bataan Peninsula, all supplies are gone. After going hungry for days, the order comes down from the top: "Surrender."

As it is now, April's tropical heat suffocates the largest Army surrender in America's history here in Bataan. They say seventy thousand American and Pilipino soldiers have been ordered to quit.

For the next six days and seven nights thousands of my fellow broken and bleeding soldiers are forced to march… and march… and march. Dead and dying palm trees line the road. Rotting animal and bloating human remains putrefy the air. Stench causes marching men to want to heave their innards, but not having eaten anything, nothing comes out. Soon enough, the stench becomes second nature.

Columns of thousands of praying men are ahead of me, thousands march behind. Some are barefoot and bloody. But those with only one boot cause me to be glad I have both of mine, despite having no laces.

The crack of firing of a Jap rifle ahead vibrates down through his marching line. Another bloody soldier is thrown out of the formation ahead. Yet the columns of ragged men continue their march without missing a beat.

I reach the body, this one is of a Pilipino laying on the side of the road. His chest is half gone from another point-blank execution. Swarms of blow-flies are in a feeding frenzy over the corpse. Forced to ignore the sight, the men keep on marching forward. I avoid eye contact with the Jap standing on the back of a truck.

"March! March!" the soldier shouts.

I'm being pushed to my limit. I'm thirsty, but I don't dare to ask for water as I march by several corpses of decapitated American troopers beside the road. What was their skin is now infested with blowflies. I lower my head and keep my mouth shut so they don't fly in.

Soldiers with fixed bayonets stand at each side of the road. They realize their American enemy overwhelms their own numbers. To them we did the unthinkable, we surrendered. Therefore, we are now nothing more than pigs. To control us, we are to be kept weak.

Along the way, a Japanese soldier pushes forward an Albuquerque boy, Abel Garcia, in front of me, with the butt of his rifle. I suddenly feel the thud of a rifle butt in the back of my spine. With my breath almost knocked out, I stumble forward. Capable of catching my balance, I should continue to march hoping my lace-less boots don't fall off.

After what seems like hundreds of miles, a week of days turns into a week of humid nights, and the columns arrive at a train spur. We are forced onto the train transports.

***

Kept starved and thirsty while being crammed in like cattle for another day or so, we are finally unloaded. For those of us who survived, we are again forced to march. Finally, we reach our destination. At the entrance, we are pushed to march over one, two, three flat and pulverized human remains. Our common feeling is gratitude that their faces are down after every Japanese troop truck and tank has rolled over them. The only recognizable aspect of the remains is the 515th insignia on their uniforms.

Finally, the remaining American and Pilipino troops pass through an entrance with endless fences. Overhead, a dangling sign reads in American: Fort McDonnell. Other buildings have entrance signs in Spanish. I deduce this was once a Pilipino base. Well inside, the columns finally stop. An order passes through the ranks, a welcome order to sit down.

I look down the right of my ranks. At the head of column is Sergeant John Love. And next to him is the only Army Air Corp 19th Bomb Group guy I know, Pete Gonzales. As he scratches his mustache, he's one of the first to sit down. Then I nod to Agapito "Gap" Silva as he sits next to me. We start to count our fellow scruffy southern New Mexico troops. Clifford `Smokey' Martinez sits next to him.

"How are our Albuquerque Boys," I whisper.

"I'm going to escape this fucking hole," he whispers back.

I count while glancing down my left ranks to the Northern New Mexico troops.

"How are our Santa Fe Boys?" I ask the farmer Manuel Armijo who sits next to me.

He just scratches his unshaven face, and shrugs.

I start counting the store keeper Felix Aragon, the truck driver Jim Smith, Cocomo Joe Burrola, Floyd Bescher, the college boy Warren Graves who lied about his age so he could be here. Here? Filadelphio Cordova, Rich Swaim, Gustavo Lucero, Ernie Suttles, Jake Padilla who gave up a state job to volunteer for this shit, wine makers Wyman Parks and Santana Romero, and Faustino (the Devil) Olguin. Last but not least is the medic, Orlando Stevens, as far as I can recognize.

The late afternoon sun shines directly into my weakened eyes. I put my hand over them while I take count of who is sitting behind me. Adolfo Garduno, who always said he was happier being stationed in the South Pacific instead of Europe to fight that other Adolf.

Now look at him, bloody and bruised. Sitting on each side him is Eliseo Gonzales and Dag Rameriz. In front of him are more Albuquerque Boys, Billy Overmeir, the guy that sold houses, Ben Chavez, Jose Montano, Johnny Mosely, Joe Martinez, and the cowboy from Fort Sumner, Kildee Herring. As I see Las Cruces's Dave Johns, the sun continues to burn my view. But I smile when I notice Roswell's Chuck James sitting next to Tom Barka. I still owe him five cigs from our last poker game.

We all hear the sudden crackle of the camp public address system. A voice addresses the thousands sitting throughout the compound in broken English. Everyone easily understands the domineering martial tones.

"You are slime, wild animals now owned by his Majesty, Emperor of the Rising Sun... From this time forward, when you are in the presence of your God, any proud citizen of Japan, you are to fall to your knees and bow to your lord..."

Negative grumblings roll down the ranks at hearing the Jap voice. In front of me, from Albuquerque, 515th's Evans Garcia grumbles while shaking his head. Sitting somewhere behind me, Lorenzo Herrera is mumbling.

"That sonofabitch."

To Herrera's right squats Jack Aldrich from Roswell. With his 200th Coast Artillery patch still prominent on his sleeve, he calms down his buddy as the voice continues.

"Now you are to hear the voice of your God, your commander for the rest of your existence in this farm filled with you pigs, animals..."

Whispering under his breath from two rows in front of me is Dion Trujillo.

"They're talking about themselves." A couple of guys in front of him chuckle under their breath.

"Everyone bow your heads for your commander Lieutenant General Masaharu Homma..."

All Japanese troops snap to attention at the mention of his name. The speakers whine, then crackle.

In broken English, "...Swine! My command. You bow to your Land of the Rising Sun superiors! Now bow. This is what will happen to you. Escape or disobey me? This will happen to you..."

From the end of the front column a ragged blonde soldier is pulled out of place by three hefty Jap guards. The soldier's nearby weakened buddies stand in his defense but are quickly beaten down by Jap rifle butts.

"Isn't that Harris from Silver City?" someone from the Albuquerque Boys asks.

Harris' weakened condition offers meager resistance and proves futile as he's dragged onto an elevated platform. His ragged shirt is torn off as he's tied by the wrists to a post in the center.

"Stop! Stop!" A ragged man stands among the thousands. "You can't do this," he shouts.

The far off individual makes his presence known.

As we sit around, I hear someone ask, "Isn't that Eddy?"

Another voice says, "It's the kid from Iowa."

The speaker shouts, "Pigs, this is what will happen to you..."

The crack of the bamboo whip across the soldier's chest brings shattering screams. All sitting soldiers wince.

"Stop this madness!" Eddy shouts out as he steps between the ranks to approach the whipping post. The guards prepare to knock him down with their rifles causing him to raise his bible and rosary.

Someone behind me whispers with amazement, "That's Chaplain Eddy Sullivan."

Finally, the chaplain reaches the front where he is quickly beaten down. And like a mass movement, the sight brings the thousands of American soldiers to a slow stand. But their weakened state prevents them from moving further. Nevertheless, the guards notice the respect for this single individual. They take notice of the chaplain's religious articles. An officer orders his guards to drag the chaplain to the base of the whipping post.

The bamboo whip has become frayed as Harris receives two, three, four more slashes. All Chaplain Eddy Sullivan can do is pray from his bible and count his Catholic rosary beads while everyone listens to intense screams. Sullivan wipes a combination of sweat and helpless tears from his eyes. Harris' fellow troopers look away as he suddenly goes limp and dangles in mid scream.

"...and what do we do with dead pigs?" says the General's speaker voice.

One of the Jap soldiers on the platform jabs his bayonet into Harris' chest to rip it open. His entrails spill out under the hot, humid sun.

I cannot help but wish I did not know my men so well.

***

Julian flails his arms while sitting up in the bed, screaming. He is covered with sweat. Elsie receives a forearm across her chest. She cries out, causing the baby to scream from the other room. Elsie bends over in pain and rolls out of bed to run to her sobbing baby.

Moments later, trying to calm and sooth Russell in her arms, she watches her hardened husband tremble and shake vigorously.

"I'm sorry. I'm sorry. I'm so sorry," he cries into the palms of his hands.

Chapter Thirty

The Fifties (July 1951)

Freshly picked, scent filled, prickly pink and red roses from the bushes out front lay in wait. They are wrapped in old newspaper on the coffee table in the living room. Baby Russell naps as Elsie picks up his toys and puts them into the toy box before closing his bedroom door. She picks up the roses and carries them into the kitchen to find a vase.

Her smile grows from the rich yet delicate aroma from the water filled vase as she places it back on the coffee table. Elsie reads again the headlines of the old newspaper as she has done many times. She is amazed at the ongoing story. With pen in hand, she anxiously begins to write a letter.

Dear Elsa,

My friend, the news from here is international. I wonder if you heard it in Italy. It is in the local newspaper every day! It's about those spies, Julius and Ethel Rosenberg. They were testified against by their own brother and sister-in-law. All of them were investigated by the FBI here in Albuquerque!

Their photos are on the front page of the newspaper. I remember and recognized them!

During the war when we were waitresses in your folks bakery, do you remember that young New York couple we served every week? I do because they are still the only people from New York that I have ever met. Their pictures are in the paper every day. The guy, David Greenglass, admits he passed atomic bomb secrets to his brother and the Russians, while he was here in Albuquerque. Albuquerque? Of all places!

They testified that he worked up north in Los Alamos and he'd bus down to here every weekend to be with his wife. They lived at 209 North High Street.

That's just a few streets east of our high school. Can you believe it?

You must remember because we served them every weekend till we took off to Los Angeles. Can you believe that? It's amazing. Let me know...

Other than that, Julian works 8 am to 5pm, 6 days a week. The baby eats and eats and is gaining weight very well. Julian has been talking about having another baby. Of course, I do not argue. It would be nice to have a girl.

Elsie

August 1951

Elsa sits at her bedroom table under the only nightlight on in the room. Jenoa, asleep under the sheets, snores as he turns over. The only other sound is Elsa's pen scratching over paper.

Dear Elsie,

What a surprise development! It reads like a true espionage novel because it is real. Yes, the Albuquerque news reaches us here in Italy. Poppa, mamma and me and even Jenoa have been following the story. It is on the daily international radio news reports. Plus, yes, I remember them from their photos in all the newspaper stories. Of course, I remind Jenoa about them because I have him recall that they were in the coffee shop when he was there, too.

I even remember that I once bumped into her on the street. She said she worked around the corner from the bakery. I mentioned this to my parents. They just laughed because they have no memory. But Jenoa is serious about me forgetting it. Anything to do with the war he wants to put behind us.

The war negatively affected Jenoa's entire family. An area in the vineyard behind a distant isolated barn is still avoided to this day. Apparently, the Nazis caught seven partisans, lined them up for their firing squad. They are still buried on that spot. I did not learn of this until the day I was roaming the property. I came across the weather worn orange and brown stains on barn wall. Around it were bullet holes.

Elsie, it is obvious you and I had an easy time during the war compared to everyone else.

But as of today, after much hard work and sacrifice, our winery is doing good. Our families are healthy and satisfied. I wait for your monthly letter.

Elsa

***

Summer of 52

Today, Rose is walking home from work in a different direction than she has for decades. Route 66's route is longer and a couple of blocks out of the way. But she wants to see what's in the windows of the dress and shoe stores. She especially likes the flowers through the florist shop windows. Only then does she see her reflection. Despite the graying streaks in her hair, she spins around to see with pride that she has kept her youthful figure. She thinks it is because of all the walking she does. Suddenly, the beautiful summer afternoon seems brighter with not a cloud in the sky.

137

"Hello, Rose Lovato."

The male voice jolts her into reality as she recognizes the shop owner standing outside his entrance. His distinguished graying temples match his mustache.

"I didn't see you there, Mr. Dagmar."

"Ben, please." He smiles.

"Oh, ok." After years of serving him across the hotel's coffee shop counter, she now puts two and two together. "So, this is your shop, is it? I was just admiring your beautiful flowers. They all are lovely."

"I only see one beautiful flower."

Rose suddenly feels blood running through her cheeks.

"Have a beautiful afternoon, Mr. Ben Dagmar."

As she starts walking, the florist reaches into his shop to grasp a single long stem rose.

"Young lady," he calls. "After trying to get you to come by my shop for years, you don't think I am going to let you walk by, do you?"

Rose turns around as the florist approaches and hands her the flower. "A rose for a Rose," he says.

"It's beautiful, thank you," she says, smelling it. "I guess I will see you at the coffee shop sometime? I'll make sure your coffee and pie come quicker and are hotter than usual."

"Um... listen," he says. "I can close the shop so we can get that coffee now—served to us by somebody else." He doesn't hide the hope in his voice.

"Well... Ben," she glances around the busy street. "That would be very nice."

Ben Dagmar wastes no time locking up his shop and grabbing his Fedora. He offers Rose his arm as escort. She accepts as they stroll down bustling Route 66, smiling.

***

Summer 1953

The tranquil Tuscan afternoon sun casts lazy shadows. Cottonwood fluff floats on the air from the trees bordering the creek. Grey haired now, Giovani and Abra are content as they lounge in their flowery courtyard, holding hands.

They watch their grandchildren Palo and Victorio toss a red ball. Little Victorio falls as he tries to catch it. And for that moment he looks as if he will cry. Abra sits up but Giovani firms his grip on her hand. She looks at him, but he shakes his head. Both watch as the older brother Palo helps his baby brother. They toss the ball back and forth once again.

"They must learn to be brothers in America," says Giovani in broken English. He lights a cigarette and smoke wafts above him as he coughs. Abra turns towards him while bracing her astonishment. "You are surprised, wife?"

Also in English, she says, "Yes, I am, husband. I have not heard you speak in this tongue in years." He shrugs. "To say our babies in the same breath with America, surprises me."

"They would get best education there," he muffles a cough. "Am I wrong?"

Abra shakes her head. "But it's Jenoa who is to decide."

Giovani throws away the butt. He takes his wife's hand in both of his. "I remember many times in our life together you, you, Abra Santoni, worked miracles with a kiss and a whisper."

They pause to watch the cat dash about the yard as it is chased by their dog. As the couple sit back, Abra thinks of the talk she must have with her daughter. As the summer sun sets, they smile and Palo embraces his puppy and Victorio his kitten.

***

February 19, 1955

A huge ball of flame explodes across the rugged 10,000-foot face of the Sandia Mountains east of Albuquerque. If the resulting vibrations had failed to catch the attention of early morning residents, 7 AM echoes of the horror pouring west over the city from the Santa Domingo Trail did just that. Even without those signs, anyone in the Duke City knew something terrible was happening when every siren in town blared at the same instant—across the southern farmlands, the dormant volcanoes, downtown, to the height's suburban stations—all morning long.

The Kirtland Air Force Base Fire Unit Brigade did air reconnaissance and established a base camp below the snow-packed terrain. All suspicions have been confirmed. Cause: Airplane crash with fatalities. Not knowing what to expect, the firefighters prepared to do battle against wind-blown flames by climbing over rugged terrain to the isolated location, 5,000 feet above camp.

The report was concise. Missing: TWA Flight 260, a Martin 4-0-4, Eastern Airlines livery, Registration N40416. 13 Passengers, 3 Crew, Survivors unknown. Flight Origin: Albuquerque International. Destination: Santa Fe, New Mexico.

By mid-day all affected local, state and federal agencies are on alert including CAP, the Civilian Air Patrol. Crew chief Ambrose Ornales is bundled up for the rigorous undertaking of the day. In their makeshift tent, as CAP crew chief, he maintains radio communication by reporting their status.

"Concentration of manpower assets are being sent up through the Domingo Baca Trail," Ambrose tells his command via the camp's PA system. "Combined search and rescue assets are expected to be around one thousand." He pauses briefly to accommodate steady traffic through the CAP tent. "Severe snow conditions have hindered the spread of fire. Next report in thirty minutes."

Ambrose scratches his bristly whiskers. This morning's sonic boom caused him to open his eyes and gaze directly into Esther's lovely face. The call came soon after, causing him to rush from the house before having a shower or breakfast.

He picks up the microphone again at 1300 hours. "There are no survivors. Body extractions expected to start tomorrow. We are proceeding with overnight preparations."

Little did he know that, by the time he would again see his beloved Esther, participating in retrieval for the rugged campaign would take a couple of months. By April, he had helped bring down sixteen body bags and partials.

***

Autumn 1955

"Father Jacob almost put me to sleep with that sermon," Julian says.

"Everyone in the pew could see you nodding off," says Elsie with a smile.

He walks up behind his wife and whispers in her ear as he purposely lays his hand on her behind. "You did keep me busy last night, you know."

A moment passes before Elsie goes to the boys' bedroom to attend the baby. With a light kiss, she undresses him. The newly installed telephone rings, then rings again. As she pulls the blanket over the baby, she hears her husband answer.

"Who has a phone that would call this early on a Sunday?" He picks up the receiver grumbling.

"Arias residence." He listens. "Yes, this is Julian Arias. Yes, sir, I did register." He watches as his wife goes past him into the kitchen. "What? Are you kidding? Who is this?"

Elsie notices her husband's annoyance. "Is this that, what do you call it, the party line?" His voice becomes excited. "Wow! I can't believe it. Are you really serious?"

Elsie walks back in to the living room to see that her husband is very excited, with a giant smile on his face. "Sure. Of course, I could be right down. Of course, I'll be right down." Elsie's curiosity is peaked. "Thank you. I will see you soon."

Elsie watches Julian replace the receiver. "Elsie. Elsie. Remember I registered for a drawing at the grocery store last week?"

"Yeah. You didn't want to but, with your luck, I said you'd win the whole store."

He looks stunned. "Well, we did win."

"You are always lucky!" she kisses him. "We can use those extra groceries."

"We didn't win the groceries."

"Well, the gift certificates will be nice."

"We didn't win any gift certificates either."

"The only other thing they were giving away was a car."

He nods. "A 1955 shiny tan Chevy Bel Air car."

"Are you saying what I think you are saying?"

Still stunned and subdued, "Baby, I guess we won a new car."

Elsie screams in excitement. Julian winces at her screech but still laughs. The baby starts crying. Little Russell runs in to the living room to see his mother jumping into his dad's arms.

"I'm going to be driving a brand-new car!" she says.

"Shouldn't you get a driver's license first?"

***

July 1956

Seven-year-old Russell dribbles his cereal as he sits at the kitchen table. He watches his baby brother Freddy sitting in his high chair playing with his food while his mother sits. She pushes aside the stack of grocery coupons she clipped from this morning's newspaper. Now she anxiously prepares to continue on another letter to her far away friend.

> Mama babysat for us last night. Julian and I went to the opening night of Rainbow Gardens Armory. Tickets were one dollar and fifty cents. And the food was great! We want to start some memories there because we haven't been dancing in a while. So now our first memory of the Rainbow will be celebrating our third child. I am two months along. We want a girl.

Julian drank many beers but I only had one orange juice. I didn't think we'd dance as much, but the band—from Tennessee of all places—was good. They played the latest craze called Rock and Roll. The lead singer was darling. And he did a strange performance by wildly shaking his hips. I thought he was very sexy. The other women thought so, too. The men did not like him much. Especially when all the girls threw themselves at him. And he was kissing them back! Once the band started playing a song about a hound dog, Julian was anxious to leave.

Write back soon.

E.

Russell continues to watch his mother fold the letter and slip it into an envelope. He sees her bend over and grasp her side.

Elsie had shooting pain earlier that morning, too. She sees Russell's worried expression.

"I just overdid the dancing last night, that's all," she says.

The pain passes. She methodically places four stamps on the envelope and remembers when she only needed three. She clips the envelope to the mailbox outside the front door.

Russell watches her go back into the kitchen to start washing dishes. He can see her lift plates. He doesn't see his mommy crying in pain, but he knows something is wrong.

Elsie checks the wall clock. It reads nine thirty. It seems longer than two hours ago that her husband left for work.

Little Russell hears her suddenly cry out and lean over the kitchen counter gripping at her tummy. He wants to cry like his mommy, but instead he quickly goes to her. He lets her lean on him.

"Mommy, do you hurt?"

"Help me to the couch."

Elsie tries not to frighten her son, but the pain is excruciating and she is unable to hold back sobs. She lies down on the couch where her crying intensifies. Freddy calls from his high chair.

"Oh, my baby!" she cries.

Russell notices red stains on her clothes between her legs. With his mother and little brother both crying, he is pulled to the front door to escape. Without a thought, he decides to run to the neighbor.

He frantically knocks on the front door. "Mommy's hurting. Please help her!" he tells the nice lady who opens it.

For Russell, the next hour is a blur of activity. He and Freddy sit on the living room sofa and watch, where he finds his little brother's pacifier.

As the ambulance carrying his mother pulls away, the little boy can't hold back tears any longer. Holding him close, the neighbor says, "Your mommy will be all right. Daddy is meeting her at the hospital. You are a brave little man."

***

Several Months Later

Filled with depression, Elsie is in her bath robe. She sticks her face outside the front door to grab in the mail. As she thumbs through the bills, she breaks a smile. After several letters to Elsa, she finally has a reply with Italian postage. She rips it open on the spot.

10/15/1956

My dear, dear friend;

You have not heard from me, I could not answer your letters. Poppi died, heart attack. And because of your loss, please understand why I have not, could not, give you more bad news.

My dear friend, I have been crying every day since I buried him in his and mama's native town of Palermo, Sicily. I was born there and had not been back since we escaped *Il Duce*.

Amica, our hearts break. Now my mama is staying in bed. She is very weak and has not eaten since poppi was buried. I wish you were here so we could be there for each other. I will finish this tomorrow.

11/14/1956

I write to you now, I couldn't before. Elsie, Elsie, my mama died. So soon after poppi. She couldn't live without him. She never got out of bed, nothing. All she would do is talk about him. Her wish was to be buried with her husband.

This is the most I have been back there in 16 years. She didn't want to live without poppi. Write me soon, I need you.

Your friend forever

December 15, 1956

Elsie sits at her kitchen table watching her babies play in front of the Christmas tree. She smiles at their curiosity. It gets the best of them as they juggle the presents. After all, if not for those kids, she would not have put up a tree this year. She didn't want to ruin Christmas for them just because she had a terrible year.

Elsa, Elsa, Elsa,

My closest friend, we need each other during this dark part of our lives. Esther and mama's hearts broke when I told them about Giovani and Abra.

145

Mom suggests you study the dear faces of your babies to see your parents. We are both living through major changes, and will be different than we were just six months ago.

I feel like life will never be the same. Then, my heart heals more when I see the little faces of my Russell and Freddy. I know I must live my life for them. But then I get nudged by the other man in my life and realize that Julian wants me to live for him, too.

When I see his handsome smile and feel his embrace, I am reminded of the lives ahead of us. My thoughts to you are grab hold of your babies and kiss Jenoa. Start looking forward to your life ahead.

I am happy to say, my dearest *amiga*, you have me as your friend on the other side of the world here in little ol' Albuquerque.

Why? Because I know I have you as my friend.

E.

***

May 22, 1957

The United States Air Force Convair B-36 silver leviathan super bomber soars 10,000 feet above the clouds on its way to Albuquerque. Its six giant propellers in front of the wings and four turbojets behind them roar. The crew prepares to land at Kirtland Air Force Base. This delivery flight is from the 95th Bomb Wing, Biggs AFB, El Paso, Texas.

This crew of twenty men of the 334th Bomb Squadron includes some sandbaggers. These non-essential crewmen are anxious to log in extra flight time with a weapons training mission that includes simple takeoff, navigation leg and landing experience.

It was hoisted in place by a special sling that looked like giant bicycle chains. But now it is wrapped around a twenty-foot-long, five foot wide Mark 17 nuclear payload. It is one of two hundred in America's arsenal. It fills the rear two of four bomb bays. It is due to undergo modifications at Kirtland.

The entire crew, in their pressurized compartments, feel the cruising altitude play with the plane's long fuselage air frame as it normally interweaves and moans in reply to turbulence.

The pilot flips on the radio on his head gear as he receives incoming instructions.

"Kirtland here. You are cleared for landing on Runway 27," he hears.

"Roger. Clearance Runway 27."

Each B-36 member begins descent procedures by completing their landing checklists. They feel the plane's descent.

The pilot relays to ground control. "Now entering the downwind leg to seventeen hundred feet, "he informs.

The payload specialist leaves his pressurized access hatch to enter the bomb bay. His eyes adjust to the cold temperature and darkness. In securing his payload, he stretches over the top of the MK 17, AKA the Big Green Monster. The fuselage moans and creaks from the normal flexible structure of the airframe. He grabs hold of the locking pin from the holding chains and adjusts it as per the manual release cable requirements. With no unusual pressure or stress, the locking pin falls into his hand. He tries to place it back in the holding chains. But that moment in time coincides with the adjustment of the plane descent to seventeen hundred feet. His wrist watch reads 11:50 AM.

Seconds later, sunshine floods the compartment as air pressure swoops in. Strapped into his seat, the payload specialist can only watch in horror. He thinks he has committed suicide while taking his flight crew with him along with hundreds of thousands of citizens below. His stunned existence is cold and numb as he watches the bomb accidentally release itself from the airframe, taking the bomb doors with it. He continues frozen within his view of the Mark 17 dropping nose first. With a jerk, suddenly a large parachute slows the descent of the bomb aimed toward the cattle pasture below.

Within seconds, the plane climbs two hundred feet. The pilot fights to control the sudden increase in elevation. Both he and the copilot wonder why it happened, which is answered when they hear the navigator: "BOMB AWAY!"

The pilot announces over the address system: "Men, we are officially now a BROKEN ARROW status."

***

In less than half an hour Kirtland crews are surrounding the crevice of the crater. Men from the Armed Forces Special Weapons Project are inspecting the remnants of the impact and explosion. Inspectors are measuring the depth and circumference of the crater. They all carry Geiger Counters. Even though most of the men are military, a few of them are civilians. One of the civilians exits a government truck with lettering on the door that says AFSWP.

Ambrose asks for an update from the first Air Force officer he sees. "How are the radiation levels?"

"Practically zip radioactivity beyond the rim of the crater."

"I'm informed that your 2700 Explosive Ordnance Squadron from Hill AFB, Utah is enroute."

"Roger." The brass nods acknowledgement.

With an attitude more serious than any since the war, Ambrose grabs the truck radio microphone. "Hello, sir? We have kissed and been saved by the almighty. It was close. We are looking at only .5 milliroentgens per hour. This is only ten times a hazard level considering what this cargo was. Cleanup crews are enroute from Utah."

He is asked, "How is your crew holding up?"

"We'll vacate once Utah arrives. We expect the disposal equipment and bulldozers to arrive any time."

"Ambrose, the order just came down that we are to keep today confidential. The Air Force is taking over."

"Roger that. I guess I'll be taking the wife out to dinner tonight. Then letting her know how much I love her."

"Actually, plan on dying with this story," Ambrose hears as a large diesel truck in the distance carries two bulldozers on its flatbed. A moment later, the radio squawks again. "AFSWP, AFSWP, come in please."

Ambrose grabs microphone. "This is AWSWP, over."

"This is Kirtland tower. The crew reports the ordinance had a fifteen second trigger. It hit ground at eight seconds. The 2700 Explosive ordnance will be enroute momentarily.

"We will clear out upon their arrival. All requested equipment has arrived."

"Roger."

In each following moment as he waits, Ambrose wonders how damn close his world almost came to a stupid end, by a lousy seven seconds. And now no one will ever know about it!

***

February 1959

Julian sits calmly in the Lovelace Hospital waiting room. He's been in this room twice before. When Elsie gave birth to Russell ten years ago, he paced waiting room floor, sucking down a pack of cigarettes. He wore out the soles of his shoes. He was grateful to his brothers and sisters who came and went that day.

Three years later, Elsie gave him little Freddy. Again he paced the waiting room floor, but without the cigs. When Freddy came into their lives, he was battling nightmares. Also, his growing smoker's cough was troubling him.

One day he walked into the company's medical clinic.

The doctor said, "Give them up and start walking every day."

With the responsibility of his young family, he took the doc's advice. Now his cough is gone. His lungs are strong. Even the nightmares have dimmed, although the memories will always remain.

He impatiently looks at his wrist watch. It is early on a work day as he sits alone. A third child Elsie was to give him two and half years ago miscarried. Roxanne would have been her name. Elsie was in great physical pain then and later suffered emotionally. She needed time to heal.

Julian wipes the tears of memory from his eyes with his palms, tears at the thought of their lost child. He pulls a wallet from his back pocket and flips through photos there. He can finally smile as he gazes at photos of his two sons.

His wrist watch reads 11 AM. He arranged for this day off from work months ago. Paternity emergency is now a fringe benefit won from the hard fought, six month Teamster's strike at the Labs last year. He never thought he would carry a picket sign, especially for 6 months. But he's glad he did.

Elsie's water broke this morning about 6 am. In no time, he was pulling into the emergency entrance where a nurse quickly wheeled Elsie away. An hour ago the ward nurse told him it would still be a couple more hours. He wishes he could be with his wife.

Julian decided he can't stand it anymore! The confines of this waiting room is driving him nuts. Then it dawns on him that he doesn't have to stay put.

Without a second thought, he finds himself in the alcohol sanitized corridors, wondering where to turn. It feels natural to step into the gift shop.

"Hi! How are ya?" he greets the grey-haired lady behind the counter.

He sees shelves of candy, flowers, and gifts, which all seem premature. As for the magazines and newspapers, he doesn't have the patience to read. Leaving the shop, he takes the first corridor that comes his way. After walking past offices, he steps into an elevator that opens in front of him. Randomly, he pushes the 3 button.

Soon, doors open. He gets off and begins to follow his only path. Within a few steps he sees geriatric patients walking on canes and crawlers.

"Hello, sir," Julian says with a smile to an elderly gentleman in a wheelchair.

"Hi to you, too."

Julian goes back to the elevator. He wants the opposite direction and pushes button B. The arrow points down and past the ground floor. When the doors open, he's lured into a beautifully warm hallway. He sits on the only bench he finds.

A few minutes later he counts as, one, two, three, four, five, six fellows tumble through the swinging doors. All slide down the shining hospital floors in their paper shoes and open gowns. Toned bare back sides are wide open to the breeze. All of them have crew cuts. There's not a six-footer among them. They tease and push each other as they make their way to the elevator.

"All you pod-knockers, wave them proud and wide," says the last one.

They wait for the elevator doors to open. A seventh crew-cutter walks through the swinging doors. Instead of joining, he sits down next to Julian.

A little uncomfortable next to a half-naked guy, Julian asks "How's it going?"

"How are you, sir?" the fellow says as he sits ram rod straight.

"Doing fine, doing fine. Name's Julian."

The fellow looks forward. "Name is John."

A moment passes. Julian asks, "You guys military?"

"I'm Marine-Air," the fellow says with pride.

"Former 515th Artillery Army Air Corp. here."

"Europe?" the marine asks.

"Philippines, Bataan."

The marine looks at him. "Bataan? Were you a P.O.W.?"

Julian nods.

The marine knows what that signifies. His expression is of sudden respect. "Are you here for medical exams?"

"I'm waiting for my wife to give birth, third time," Julian says with pride.

"Congratulations, sir."

The guys down the hall shout, "Finally!" as the elevator opens and they pile in.

A guy shouts, "Hey, Glenn, what the hell are you waiting for?"

"Gotta go, sir," the marine says. He shakes Julian's hand and starts walking away when he turns around. "Congratulations again."

"Thanks," says Julian.

Julian watches as the marine, with his gown open wide, jumps into the elevator.

With this, Julian decides it's time to go back to the maternity ward. As he stands, two bald men in white lab coats step through the swinging doors. He detects a heavy German accent.

"*Zeez astronaughts?*" They smile while nodding. They leave in the opposite direction.

Julian reads the emblem on the back of their lab coats. He discerns the letters N.A.S.A. As he heads for the elevator, he wonders what it stands for.

***

Six Months Later

Sunday night. Julian, Russell, and Freddy inhale with anticipation their usual weekly dinner: fried chicken, mashed potatoes, vegetables, and biscuits with brown gravy.

Julian is reading the Sunday paper while the boys are in front of the TV watching The Wonderful World of Disney.

Baby Peter starts crying in the bedroom. Elsie crosses the living room to attend him but stops in her tracks at the same time Julian moves the paper aside. Both stare at the screen.

"We present an American legend from the old west, a story so popular last year we decided to show it again. From the autobiography, "The Nine Lives of Elfego Baca," it starts soon after the American Civil War.

"Julian, take care of Peter," Elsie says as she perches on the sofa. "I have to watch this."

Julian watches his wife's unusual interest in an old west cowboy shoot-out with letters across the screen that read Old New Mexico Territory. Soon, he's in the bedroom subduing the baby. When he returns into the living room, he sees that Elsie is still glued to the TV screen.

"Is supper ready?" he asks.

A moment passes. Then she says, "Take care of it, Julian. I knew Elfego Baca—he was my school superintendent."

"You knew him?" asks Russell.

When she fails to respond, her sons' attention is doubled and her husband, carrying the baby, accepts the situation and heads for the kitchen.

They see handsome Elfego in his gun-slinging youth as he matures into a sheriff's deputy, followed by his bona fide history of winning a gun fight with an armed gang of 30. This boosts his image as Disney shows the story makes eastern U.S. newspaper headlines. Soon he becomes the marshal.

"I didn't know that," Elsie says.

Rugged Elfego, a decade older, studies and eventually becomes a lawyer. (Elsie doesn't remember him being so handsome.) Time passes into the early 20th Century. Elfego Baca defends a captured Mexican general from the famed Pancho Villa army. But his sympathies are questioned as the general mysteriously escapes from his Albuquerque jail cell, never to be heard from again.

"My God. I never knew that!" Elsie exclaims.

They watch Elfego in front of an elementary classroom writing the alphabet on a chalkboard. The story fast forwards to a classroom of teenagers discussing American History, orchestrated by none other. Soon enough, the camera pans past a sign that reads Principal of Albuquerque High School with Elfego Baca sitting behind a desk.

Elsie stands. "Hey, that's my high school!"

Signs morph smoothly from Principal to Superintendent. Finally, they see Elfego as much older man with a head of thick grey hair. Elsie remembers him as a balding, hunched over old man. At least that's how he was when she last served him in the bakery.

As the show's credits roll, the kids assemble around the kitchen table.

For a moment, Elsie stays on the couch. Elfego Baca's respect grows in her mind for the old man she remembers and for the accomplishments she just learned about him. Her boys hungrily shout when she fondly joins them at the table which Julian has filled with dinner.

She laughs and shakes her head at how Hollywood improved his appearance.

Chapter Thirty-One

January 15, 1960

Elsa stands in the winery office that overlooks the bottling floor through a glass wall. She watches as assembly line workers guide and inspect every bottle when the family's Merlot fills it. She bites at her fingernails as the bottles are corked.

In actuality, wine is the last thing on her mind. She paces, sits, then stands again as Jenoa enters the office. As he nods, Elsa screams with glee. Through the glass walls, family and workers can see Elsa jump into Jenoa's arms and plant kisses all over his face. When he leaves, she sits down at her desk to write on the winery stationary.

Hello, my oldest friend,

Greatest News! I am coming home! The family winery is doing very well. Our wines are now selling throughout Europe. For years I have been whispering in Jenoa's ear about expanding the family's holdings to America.

He has always talked about remembering his short time in Albuquerque. Before he started working the bakery, he was sent to work the fields of the farms north of town. He remembers the soils there as rich and perfect for grapes. He wants to return to those fields, buy land, and expand the family winery. And the family has just given him the go ahead!

We are making the arrangements. I am coming home! Before poppy and mommy died, they advised us to take the babies to America for an education. It was their last wish. Jenoa wants to honor their wishes. It has taken years for him to convince his family and he was finally able to by showing them it would make financial sense for them, too.

I am now 33. It is time. After 15 years, I look forward to seeing you again. And I am happy to show my boys where their mother grew up. Even though they do not know English well, they learn from me and from Disney cinema. It will be a great experience.

It is months until we leave, and so I look forward to your next letter. I want to meet Julian and help with your new baby.

Your friend.

Elsie unloads wash from her prized, new washing machine. After loading another batch and sprinkling in detergent powder, she carries the basket out to the backyard clothes line. Item by item, she smells the clean dried laundry already hanging and folds each piece before pinning up wet replacements. As wet clothes snap in the cold breeze, she shivers.

The baby cries inside so she knows it's time to feed him. Looking down, she realizes she's stepped into an ant hill. She brushes off the few ants from her shoes and knows she'll have to insist that Julian plant a lawn this spring.

Full basket in hand, the screen door slams behind her. She warms a pre-filled bottle on the stove and tests it by placing a drop on her wrist. Perfect. She also hears the postman deliver mail outside the front door.

She's happy when the baby finishes the bottle, and wonders if he'll grow up to eat a whole cow like his brothers. Before she goes to the bus stop to meet her two oldest coming home from school she grabs the mail, smiling when she finds a letter from her dear Italian friend.

Once the boys are enjoying a snack back home, thrills overwhelm her as she rips open the envelope. She is compelled to reply immediately.

February 15, 1960

Dear *amiga*,

Oh, happy day! My friend is coming home! My dearest friend is coming home!

When I tell Julian about my best friend, he always says he'll be very happy to finally meet this mysterious friend that I have been writing to since he's known me. He says that because your husband is also a former prisoner of war, they will have something to talk about.

Let me know how I can help you from this side. Because you and *la familia* will need a home right away. Julian and I can help you find a house to rent till you find something of your own. With the kids, you will need a big house. Just let me know. I can also send you names of realtors that Jenoa and you can contact, if you like.

For me? I have been driving the car! I finally got my driver's license. It took years for me to get Julian to let me, but having doctor's appointments, grocery store errands and school for the kids, he is relieved now that he doesn't need take off work. Especially, because that he doesn't have to give me any more driving lessons.

I look forward to your next letter.

Elsie

Six Months Later

Three cars pull up along acre after acre in Albuquerque's north valley alfalfa fields. Distant borders of mature hundred-foot oak trees surround the fields. To the north, tractors move mountains of bales waiting to be hauled away. Alfalfa remnants waft in the humid air as cicadas sing their late afternoon song.

Three groups exit the vehicles and separate into groups. Russell and Freddy run into the fields with Palo and Victorio. Jenoa leads Julian and Ambrose into the plowed and harvested fields. He points to the north, south, east and western boundaries. Elsa, Elsie and Esther remain close to the cars. Elsie carries baby Peter. Elsa watches him play with the fine gold necklace around her friend's neck. Elsie removes the gold rivet on it from her baby's mouth noting her friend wears the same necklace and rivet. When the sisters' noses start twitching they share a laugh.

"You can tell we're city gals," Esther says. "We're both sniffing from the aroma of manure and freshly cut crops."

"This is a dream—to be back home," Elsa says.

Elsie pats the back of her baby. "Fifteen years seems like forever."

"Before the war I remember kissing my first boy somewhere out here," Esther says. "Of course, the alfalfa was tall and uncut then."

The ladies laugh as their men take off their sunglasses to better view the expanse of the property. Julian and Ambrose follow Jenoa's lead and scoop up a handful of soil.

"I always remembered this soil rich in nutrients for the grape," says Jenoa in his think Italian accent.

"I know ranching, not farming. But I know enough to say this land is prime real estate," says Julian.

"Where do you plan to build your house?" asks Ambrose.

Jenoa waves toward the far north center side. "Where those tractors are now. In several years we will place it there." He waves to the far northeast corner. "And there we must build the winery and cellar." He spreads his hands out wide. "But first we must clear this land, fertilize and plant the vineyard. We will soon plant midway the first five acres with the white grape."

"Impressive," says Julian.

Ambrose says, "You have your work cut out for you."

"Domenici's are used to hard work. There is no other."

Putting on their sunglasses, they walk back to their ladies.

Julian waves to his boys. "Common kids, let's go."

"Aw, dad," says Russell.

The cicadas in the trees seem louder.

***

July 4, 1961

The backyard barbeque flames sizzle as the meaty juices drop through the grill. Julian flips the burgers as Elsie brings out more hot dogs. The radio plays top 40 pop tunes.

"Who wants a toasted burger or hot dog buns?" he asks his guests.

Rose raises her cola bottle to make a toast. Esther, Elsa, Ambrose, Jenoa and Johnny raise their beers and colas as they sit comfortably in a circle of folding chairs placed over the cool, backyard lawn.

"Tomorrow I start my new job at the newest and upscale hotel in town, Western Skies. And there is no better way to celebrate than being with my family shooting up fireworks."

In the middle, baby Peter takes a few steps, then falls, giggles as he stands again. On the dirt portion of the backyard Russell, Freddy, Palo and Victorio carefully set up bottle rockets.

"Mom makes the best mustard potato salad," says Johnny.

He drops an empty beer bottle to his side before taking a swig from the one in his other hand.

"My mayonnaise potato salad ain't too bad either," says Esther.

"Hey, Dad, the fireworks are ready. Can we light them?" shouts Freddy.

"Wait for the sun to go down," Julian says.

The radio is playing Nat King Cole. "It's the lazy, hazy, crazy days of summer…"

As Julian watches Elsie sashay by he grabs her hand and swings her around to dance over the grass, being careful not to spill his beer. She laughs as she melts into her husband's arms. Everyone smiles as they watch.

As the song ends and they catch their breath, Ambrose reaches for the beer at his side. "I want to make a toast." The ladies raise their cans of soda while the men raise their bottles of beer. "To our Italian friends, may this be the first of many 4th of July family and friend gatherings we celebrate together."

As all raise their beverages, the phone rings. Elsie walks inside.

Johnny says, "I can taste those hot dogs and burgers now." He takes another swig.

Julian says, "Come and get it."

He starts to hand out the paper plates as Elsie comes back with a giant but nervous smile on her face.

"It's for you, Esther. You better go with her, Ambrose."

Both rush inside to the phone.

With her large smile on their return, Elsie tells her guests, "It's the adoption counselor. A baby has come."

Rose gasps and places a hand over her mouth, "Oh, my baby."

She too quickly rushes inside as Johnny takes another swig beer.

"We can come and pickup our daughter now," she says to her husband as she jumps into his arms.

"Now?" asks Rose. "It's a holiday."

"Yes, mama. The adoption system must be swift. Besides, holidays don't stop babies. You are a grandma again." Tears of joy fall from Esther's eyes. "We have to go now, Ambrose, our baby is waiting."

"Let's go!" he smiles.

"I must go with you, baby. I must," says Rose.

"I'll want to take the ladies. We'll follow," says Julian.

Elsie hugs her joyous sister.

"We'll stay and watch the kids," says Jenoa.

Esther, Ambrose, Rose, Elsie and Julian are out the front door. Johnny staggers in the back door.

"Hey, where is everybody?" he asks.

As two cars roll down the street, fireworks shoot high overhead, spreading wide into the dark summer sky.

***

ELSIE AND ELSA

Wednesday, December 12, 1962

Until word came at 3 PM this afternoon, Rose has never seen so many men in suits and dark glasses in her kitchen.

She was putting on her white chef cap and tunic when the general manager told her that these strangers were mandated to step throughout her Western Skies Hotel kitchen. So now, as her staff works, they carefully avoid eye contact with these new men.

This is, until Rose catches one of them removing a lid from the big pot of green chili simmering on the stove. She cannot believe her eyes as he raises the spoon to his lips.

"Who are you to taste my chili?" She demands, taking the spoon from him.

"Secret Service."

"Hmmph. Didn't your mother teach you any manners?"

The agent looks subservient. "Yes, ma'am."

Rose stirs the pot.

"She sure did and I am sorry, ma'am. But your chili smells so good. And it's been a long time."

"You just have to ask." Rose says as she hands him a bowl full of chili. "Be careful, it's hot in both ways."

His eyes widen. "Thank you, ma'am."

He takes a quick taste and whistles. Rose tries not to smile as she hands him several packets of saltine crackers.

"Thank you," he says again, smiling.

The Presidential Suite is occupied by an appropriate designee, which was a last-minute surprise. Rose has the honor—and the pressure—of preparing a private dinner to be served in the suite for him and two guests. She tries to ignore the pressure. Pressure, yeah, sure.

She decides to wait until the head chef returns from vacation to find out what he missed. As the assistant head chef of the Western Skies Hotel, the honor goes to her. This morning's paper said John F. Kennedy was flying in, then out of Albuquerque. Obviously, his plans have changed. He requested the epitome of the New Mexico meal.

Rose feels a private pride. With no high school diploma and being one the last Harvey Girls who soon became a widowed single mother with three kids, she's done all right. She credits her culinary talent for satisfying taste buds.

She watches the agents in her kitchen smacking their lips as one of them enjoys her chili. As the agent requests another serving, she orders portions for all of them.

After a few quick phone calls, her family is excited. She's the head chef for one night to the most powerful man in the world, the president of the United States of America.

***

As the elevator doors pull open, Rose's two assistants push the dinner carts into the hall from the elevator. She glances at her watch. It's now 8pm, right on time. Two big men in dark suits step out of nowhere to lead them down the familiar hallway. She's done this before, but for only senators, governors and movie stars.

***

Rose remembers a year earlier when her team pushed food carts down this same hall. Hollywood royalty had come to her hotel. Little did she realize it would be a wild experience. She had more time then to prepare dinner for a famous Hollywood wrap party for the movie "Lonely Are the Brave."

When they entered the presidential suite, she didn't see the movie star she had watched for decades, although she recognizes other actors. She remembers them talking about Academy Award nominations for their boss for a gladiator movie called "Sparticus," which he had just completed. That was when the room broke into applause. For a moment, Rose thought they were clapping about the arrival of her food. She learned better when Kirk Douglas walked in.

***

But that was then, and this is now, the ultimate assignment. Two guards stand in front of the Presidential Suite door. Rose checks the plate covers and glasses one last time to make sure her food is on the best china the hotel has to offer.

A guard knocks on the door before opening it. Rose's excitement has become unbearable. Both of her staff members take deep breaths. The other guard signals them inside. Rose leads the carts to the center of the world, and looks up to recognize the most handsome man she has ever seen: John F. Kennedy standing in front of the roaring fireplace. He holds his hand out.

"Hello. I'm John Kennedy."

Rose bravely conveys confidence and professionalism. "Good evening, Mr. President. I am your chef, Rose Lovato."

"Are you from New Mexico?"

"Yes sir, as is my staff," she says with pride.

"I am sure you brought a healthy sample of New Mexican cuisine."

"Yes, sir." She lifts covers to reveal her presentation. "We have for you thick enchiladas with sides of red or green chili." She hands him a fork.

Despite the lack of propriety, he succumbs. The aroma seduces him to taste both red and green.

She removes covers from the other dishes. "Mr. President, I hope you and your guests enjoy rice and beans. All these ingredients were harvested from New Mexican farms." She watches him take a taste, his eyes opening wide with pleasure.

She folds the cloth off the bread basket. As steam escapes, she says, "Sopapillas are the uniquely New Mexican bread, especially with honey." She hands him another spoon.

"They look like little pillows," he says.

"Finally, Mr. President..." she presents a colorful array of diced tomatoes, bell peppers and onions, along with strips of beef arranged on a marble cutting board. "I am anxious to prepare our New Mexican fajitas." She snaps on the grill while signaling for the second cart. "And to enjoy alongside..." she removes the cloth from that cart, revealing several bottles of wine on ice.

"Well, now I've become hungry. Start up those fajitas, please," he says.

"Yes, sir."

Before she pours a touch of oil in the pan, she shows him the bottle of virgin olive oil.

"This is the only non-New Mexican ingredient. I apologize."

"I won't tell your senators, if you won't," he says with his engaging smile.

The vegetables and beef strips start to sauté. Minutes later the sizzling intensifies.

"This is marvelous. Rose Lovato, I am impressed."

She controls the emotions welling up inside her.

"Thank you, Mr. President. That means much to me and the Western Skies kitchen staff."

A man enters from an adjoining room, his head covered with a towel. "Hey, Jack, what smells so good?"

Pulling the towel away, he eyes the dinner carts. As he approaches Rose and her staff, their jaws drop. Rose is amazed how blue his eyes are.

He examines the feast. "This looks great," he says.

"Dig in, Frank. It's all New Mexican cuisine, isn't it Rose?" JFK winks.

"Hello," the man greets Rose. "Are those enchiladas?"

"Yes, Mr. Sinatra."

"May I?" he asks. "And are those fajitas?"

Rose nods and prepares him a plate.

"I favor green chili," he says.

As she hands Ol' Blue Eyes his plate, Rose is amazed at how Mr. Sinatra knows New Mexican food. While the fajitas continue to sizzle, he examines the wine.

"It's good to be president, isn't it, Jack?"

An elegant lady enters from the adjacent room. She wears a form fitting beige outfit with matching shoes, with a gold scarf around her neck. Her red lipstick complements her flowing jet black hair. Rose hears a whispered mumbling from one of her male assistants: "She's so beautiful."

"Dig in, Ava. A banquet awaits," Frank directs her to the feast. "The lady dines first."

Miss Gardner offers her hand to Rose. "The aroma is appetizing. Since the guys like your creations, I'm sure I will, too." She flashes that Hollywood smile.

"Thank you, Miss Gardner."

Rose hands her and Sinatra plates of fajitas.

"Hey, guys, look," says JFK as he opens a large box. "I'm taking this to Caroline." He displays an Indian head dress adorned with countless feathers. "Isn't it glorious?"

Pouring himself and his lady glasses of wine, Sinatra says. "Yeah, glorious, Jack. Glorious."

Ava Gardner runs her fingers lightly over the feathers.

"They're eagle feathers," he tells her. "From the Isleta Pueblo."

"Isn't this more for you than your daughter, Jack?" she teases.

Ava Gardner takes a bite of food from her plate, and says "This is excellent." As she finishes, she adds, "Frank, I like New Mexico." She selects the largest sopapilla. "I am glad you have a concert here tomorrow night."

Carefully putting the feathered head dress back into the box, the president says, "You must learn to appreciate the finer things, Frank."

Sinatra moves to Miss Gardner and slides his arm around her before kissing her cheek, "I am."

She succumbs to Sinatra's nibbling her ear with a giggle.

The president becomes formal. "Rose, please thank your staff for their efforts."

"Thank you, Mr. President." She allows her assistants to leave the room before her.

As the door closes behind them, Rose hears the president say, "Ah, Frank, not in public, please."

Rose and her assistants pass the hallway gauntlet of Secret Service agents. When they are finally alone behind the elevator doors, they shake hands and pat each other's backs.

"I can't wait to tell the girls!" says Rose. "I can't wait!"

***

The Next Afternoon

The tall elm and pine trees cast long, late afternoon shadows over the entrance of Our Lady of Fatima Elementary Catholic School. Elsa makes the sign of the cross as she enters under the huge cross over the entrance.

As soon as the call came about an hour ago from the principal's office, she hurried across town. Victorio is in trouble. Anger at her boy simmers all the way there. But she tells herself to calm down until she finds out what he has done.

The school halls are empty as she finds her way to the office. Victorio is sitting outside the office door. She glares at him like she never has before. He sits there with guilt written all over his face. Before she can say anything, the principal's door is opened by a fresh faced nun who smiles.

"Mrs. Domenici? I am Sister Marie."

"Yes, sister."

"Come right in and have a seat. You too, Victorio." She points to chairs in front of a desk. Both see the sign there that reads Principal.

Sister Marie smiles as she pats Victorio on the shoulder. "Our principal will be back in a minute," she says. The young nun leaves them alone in the room.

Elsa's gut churns at the feeling of supreme authority that surrounds her. For some reason her mind flashes back to when she was a girl. The thought of *Il Duce* weighs on her mind.

"Mom," Victorio says, "I didn't think it was such a big deal."

"Don't say anything to me. I am mad enough. I want to hear what your principal has to say."

The silence continues causing her to examine every article in the austere office. She's amazed at the absence of religious symbols. Minutes later, the door opens.

"Good afternoon Mrs. Domenici, Victorio."

Elsa and Victorio stand, practically at attention.

"Afternoon sister," they say at the same time.

The older nun makes her way to the seat behind her desk. The black and white habit drapes her small frame. Deep riddled lines on her face are emphasized by her frameless round glasses.

"Mrs. Domenici, I am Sister Zoe, principal here at Our Lady of Fatima. Are you aware what Victorio did that has caused us to summon you?"

Elsa glares at her son. Summoned? She hates being summoned. "No sister, not yet."

"With something like this, we like to have both of our student's parents here."

"Is it that serious?"

"Mrs. Domenici, Victorio is being expelled for a week. This should be serious enough for both parents to be here, don't you think?"

"Expelled?" Elsa looks over at her son. "What did you do?"

Victorio seems to melt into his chair.

"Mrs. Domenici, I personally witnessed the incident. We abhor and will not allow desecration under any circumstances."

"My God! What did you do?"

Victorio squeezes back into half of his chair.

"Mrs. Domenici, I am sorry to say that I saw Victorio—excuse me—it is so hard to say.

Elsa's tension increases.

"Mrs. Domenici, I am afraid we caught Victorio playing Rock and Roll on the church organ."

Elsa's gaze on the old nun goes dull. "And...?"

"Mrs. Domenici, you don't seem to understand. Victorio was playing Satan's music in the house of the Lord."

"Excuse me, sister. Do I understand that you are expelling my son for simply playing music?"

"Yes, for one week. A sacrilege was committed. The penalty is mild, considering."

"Let me get this straight. You are kicking out my son for playing the organ?"

"He was playing Satan's music, Mrs. Domenici. Satan's music."

Elsa feels her temper rising. "Sister, in my opinion, and I am sure my husband will agree, that is ridiculous."

"Mrs. Domenici, Victorio sinned. He committed a major sin. He must be punished for being a sinner."

Her son is being accused of being a sinner for playing music? Elsa's face is red with anger. She fights to hold her temper. Her son is not a sinner! As she perceives the penguin costumed old lady in front of her, she says, "The only sin I see here is the ridiculous tuition we struggle to pay to get both of our sons in this school."

"I am sorry you feel that way, but your son must learn a lesson."

"The only lesson here is that you won't have to expel my son. I am pulling him from this school right now. And as far as that is goes, I am pulling both of my sons right now, along with both tuitions."

An alert expression suddenly covers the nun's face. "Mrs. Domenici, I am sure we can work something out."

"Not necessary, sister. Victorio is not a sinner!" She smiles at her boy. "He is a gifted musician. This gift should be encouraged, not stifled."

Victorio relaxes.

"As a matter of fact," she adds, "My husband and I are very proud of our boys. She becomes resolute. "Sister Zoe, the Domenici boys will not be returning to this school tomorrow or any day. Good afternoon."

Elsa grabs Victorio's hand and drags him from the office. As the door closes behind them, they both almost bump into the young Sister Marie.

"Excuse us, sister," says Victorio.

"Victor, you play well. Keep practicing."

"Thank you, sister."

Elsa drags her son down the hall and out of the school as fast as she can. "I am happy to hear you at least played the church organ well."

"Mom, I was only playing 'Louie Louie.'"

***

November 22, 1963

The mid-morning sun is unusually warm. Elsie makes sure the kitchen table is properly dressed to host the girls. Because it is Friday, she knows that finger tuna sandwiches will do just fine. This is despite her craving for roast beef. 'Such is the life of us Catholic girls,' she tells herself. We'll fill up with the colorful salad with juicy red tomatoes.

She glances out the back window, smiling at Peter gleefully playing on the swing set. His brothers say they are too old for that. As her four-year old swings higher, the doorbell rings. She lets herself in and lifts the baby carriage over the threshold. She has carefully made sure she is protected from any chill.

"She'll soon be too big for this," Esther tells her sister.

"I have the table ready for our luncheon."

"And I already have ideas for next month's meeting at my house."

Moments after she closes the door, the bell rings again and Elsa walks in carrying a brown paper bag.

"*Ciao, bambinas.*" She raises the bag, "Guess what I have?"

"Break it open." Elsie says as she glances out to check on Peter. "Shall we try a little guilty pleasure?"

"Darn good idea. Do it," says Esther.

Elsa pulls the vodka from the bag. "Let's continue the tradition we started back in L.A."

"Glasses, half filled with orange juice for the screwdrivers are ready to go," says Elsie.

"But, ah, *bambina*, I'd prefer a cosmopolitan," says Elsa.

Before Elsa can finish her statement, Elsie is handing her a bottle of cranberry juice from the refrigerator. Then again, without thinking about it, she glances at Peter again. Esther pulls her sleeping baby from the carriage.

"Diane is getting big," says Elsa.

"She eats like Elsie's boys."

"I have the water simmering to keep her bottles warm," says Elsie.

Perry Como is soon crooning on the radio and the ladies are laughing. The finger sandwiches are gone and the salad bowl is empty. The ash trays are filled and overflowing. And little Peter plays in his bedroom.

Esther laughs as she packs away some dirty diapers. "Next month we meet at my place." "And I'll bring the Vodka," says Elsie.

"I'm changing diapers, I could use the vodka now," says Esther with a grin.

As the ladies laugh, the radio begins to play the haunting melody, `Smoke Gets in Your Eyes.' The phone rings. With Elsie's hands full, Elsa automatically answers it for her friend.

"Arias residence," she says. "Oh, hello Julian, this is Elsa." She watches Elsie pour the last of the Vodka into her glass. "Of course, she's right here." She hands the receiver to her friend.

Elsie takes the receiver in one hand while holding the glass in the other.

"Hello, husband." Her friends watch her happy expression change as she drops the glass. "No! Oh, no! "Elsa and Esther suddenly stand. "You are lying!"

Elsie points to the TV. "Quick. Turn it on… They do… You're coming home early?"

The friends are still watching Elsie as the black and white television warms up. She hangs up the phone with difficulty.

"My God, what's wrong?" asks Elsa.

Elsie can't speak and just points to the TV. Soon they are all watching CBS newsman Walter Cronkite sitting at a desk.

"Shot," is all she can say.

"For God's sake, who was shot?" Esther asks.

Walter Cronkite can barely speak as he looks at the wall clock behind him.

"Moments ago, John Fitzgerald Kennedy was pronounced dead." He adjusts his dark rimmed glasses as he wipes his eyes.

"Oh, my God!!" exclaims Esther.

With her face in her hands, "Ah, *dios mío!*" cries Elsa.

Elsie, Esther and Elsa are stunned as they watch Cronkite report. They don't notice little Peter walk into the room. He wants to watch Captain Kangaroo, but instead he sees broken glass on the kitchen floor and his mommy and his aunties crying. He's never seen them cry like this before so he joins them.

***

The Western Skies Hotel dining room is filled with the usual lunch crowd. Each table feels free to spread the dreadful news.

"Oh, my God!" a female patron shrieks.

The dining room empties. All tables abandoned. The waiter steps back into the kitchen.

"Did you hear?" he asks the crew.

He sees the usual hustle and bustle come to a complete halt. Everyone stands at their stations in disbelief. One by one, as if their legs are knocked out from under them, several female workers sit down on the cold kitchen floor. Tremendous grief grips their faces.

Soon enough, the General Manager rushes into his kitchen. He wants to say something to his grief-stricken professional staff, but he too feels helpless as he shares the most horrible grief he's felt since World War II.

He moves around the kitchen, looking for his chef… then in the kitchen and outside the delivery door. He finally finds her in the cubby hole of a kitchen office.

Rose sits at the desk crying, gripping an autographed photo of JFK that reads: To Rose and her staff, thank you. I look forward to tasting your excellent enchiladas and red chili again, JFK

The manager quietly closes the office door as he too walks away in tears.

***

Sunday, February 16, 1964

Pushing himself from the dinner table, Julian says, "That was a very good Sunday dinner, Elsie."

"Yeah, mom, the fried chick was groovy," adds Russell. Trained to do so, he carries his plate to the kitchen sink. The fourteen-year-old kisses his mother's cheek as he anxiously leaves the kitchen.

"I like the mashed potatoes with brown gravy," says eleven-year-old Fredrick. He too carries his dish to the sink, returning to kiss his mother's cheek before following his brother.

"Me too, mama," says little Peter as he jumps off his kitchen table seat. He starts sucking his thumb as he follows his brothers.

"Don't forget your dishes to the sink," Elsie reminds Peter.

"Turn on Sullivan," says Russell.

"It's already six o'clock," says Fredrick.

"The show is already on. One of my friends has a drum set like them," adds Russell.

Peter follows his older brothers' lead.

Julian shrugs. "Have you ever seen them that anxious to see Ed Sullivan?" he asks his wife.

Elsie shakes her head with a smile. "No."

The boys pile in front of the black-and-white screen, glued to it. The parents glance at each other as they sit back, amazed at the screaming girls in the audience that drown out Mr. Sullivan.

With his signature position—stiff body and folded arms—Sullivan says, "They will be on now and later in the shoe."

The audience screams. Elsie says, "I like how he says show."

"We also received a telegram," Sullivan continues. "Colonel Parker says Elvis welcomes these boys from Liverpool, England to America." The screaming audience makes it hard to hear him. He throws out his arm and spins him around. "Ladies and gentlemen, the Beatles!"

Julian and Elsie are amazed how their sons' attention is only a few feet from the picture screen. The TV camera cuts to the audience of screaming teenage girls, crying and pulling at their own hair.

"She loves you, yeah, yeah, yeah..."

"Someone should give those kids a haircut," Julian says.

"Ssshh!" say all three boys at once.

Fredrick turns up the volume as mom and dad stare at each other in wide-eyed bafflement.

***

Summer 1964
Western Skies Dining Room

White coat-wearing bussers clean tables. Servers wearing tuxes carry trays out through the kitchen's swinging doors. All the dinner tables are full. Waiting patrons gather around the maître d'. Sounds of tinkling piano music softly serenades them all.

Jenoa, Elsa, and Palo proudly sit up close to watch their tux wearing Victorio playing the grand piano. With nimble fingers, he expertly plays a tune he just heard on the radio that morning. His eyes close while he loses himself in the melody.

Elsa tells her husband, "He looks so handsome."

Rose Lovato walks into her busy dining room wearing her chef hat, a clean white tunic and a smile. She approaches the Domenici table.

"Enjoying yourselves, folks?" she asks them.

Elsa stands up to hug her. "Rose, thank you very much for getting Victorio this job."

"For you, anything, darling. You are like my daughter, you know."

Jenoa hugs the chef as well. Through his heavy Italian accent he says, "Grazi, mama Rosa, grazi. We are grateful to you for giving our son his first job."

Rose gazes around her dining room. "It appears folks are enjoying the piano as much as I am."

"The food is great!" says Palo in his near-perfect English.

Victorio finishes a tune and bows to the applause. "Ladies and Gentlemen, my name is Victorio Domenici from the Domenici Winery." He glances over to his parent's table. A proud papa gives his son the thumbs up. "Even though I am almost seventeen years old, I would like to try to play your requests." He sits back down.

"Enjoy the evening, Domenici family," says Rose.

Elsa kisses her cheek, "Thank you again, Rose."

Rose moves to another table where a grey-haired couple sit. "It is our hope you are enjoying your dinner, folks," she says.

Palo watches his brother. Then he scatters his view over the entire dining audience. His scan reveals a pimply, skinny kid with a military crew cut. He is dressed in baggy blue jeans and a white shirt. He stands from a table across the room. At that table sits a uniformed naval officer and a lady who appears to be his wife, a teenage girl, and another teenage boy—all around a birthday cake.

The skinny kid is drawn to the piano. Victorio smiles as the kid approaches Victorio and watches intently.

Victorio finishes the tune without missing a beat.

"That's great man. You're good. Is that a tune from that new group from Liverpool?" asks the patron.

"Thanks. You know your music," says Victorio as his fingers continue to experiment with different piano keys.

"I stay up with the latest. It's my thing. As a matter of fact, I've always wanted to learn to play piano, but never had the time," he says.

"I've been playing since I was a kid. Mom brought over a piano when we moved here from Italy. Been on it ever since."

"I'm a Navy brat." Says the younger fellow. He points to his father at the table. "There's never been time for me to learn with all the moving we've done." Victorio continues tinkling the keys. "Isn't that a song from that group from England?"

Victorio nods. "It's called Michelle."

"I like it." He listens while looking around the room. "I always wanted to play piano but my dad said it wasn't the pay grade for a son of a Navy man."

"Mom's pushed me into music all my life. It's ok."

"Well, it's too late for me since I'm now transferring out of college in Florida."

Victorio gently fades away on the piano.

"I'm finishing junior high school myself."

"Oh, yeah? I went to Monroe Junior High here. That was before we got transferred to Florida. But we got stationed back here at Kirtland. So, I graduated from Sandia High a couple of years ago. I'm now planning on going to film school at UCLA."

"I still have a couple more years before I have to decide," says Victorio.

The young patron offers his hand. "My name is Morrison, Jim Morrison."

While his hands tinkle away on the keys, Victorio says, "It's good to meet you."

"We're celebrating Dad's birthday. Can you play Happy Birthday for us?"

"I'd be happy to." He transitions to the appropriate piano chords. "See ya around, Morrison."

The fellow goes back to his table. As Victorio plays Happy Birthday, he can see the dining room patrons focus on the birthday table. The officer's wife kisses her husband. He's then hugged by his daughter. Victorio smiles when the young fellow salutes his father and shakes his hand. Victorio then notices his boss, Chef Rose, exit the room through The Doors.

***

Across Town

Russell carries two bags of groceries past his mom as she holds open the front door of her mother's house for him.

"Your grandma gets home in a few hours from work. It would be nice to have dinner waiting for her," she says. She straightens up a few items in Rose's living room.

"I'll put things away in the kitchen," says her son.

Russell puts the bags on the table. As he starts putting things away, he notices Johnny's adjoining bedroom door is open.

"Uncle Johnny, are you home?"

Hearing no response, he steps into the dingy, unkempt room where he sees his uncle spread out on his bed, eyes closed. A bottle of Jack Daniels dangles from his fingertips, barely touching the floor. Russell goes back to the table.

As Elsie walks in, her son says, "Uncle is passed out in there."

Elsie sighs and moves to close the bedroom door.

"Your grandmother doesn't need to be greeted by that when she gets home from work."

She takes a quick peek at her brother. He seems too still. She steps inside and sees that he doesn't seem to be breathing.

"Johnny," she says. He doesn't move. "Johnny, wake up," she says louder.

Russell joins her. Elsie shakes her brother, but he doesn't respond. "Dammit, Johnny, wake up!" she cries. "Johnny!"

"Russell, call an ambulance!"

***

The procession of limos and private vehicles arrives from Albuquerque, soon weaving their way past acres of deep green lawns covered with gravestones at the Santa Fe National Veterans Cemetery. Soon thereafter, Julian, Ambrose, Jenoa, and Russell roll Johnny Lovato's coffin out of the hearse and escort it to his final resting place.

Four U.S. Navy honor guards await. They shoot three volleys of blanks into the sky. The rifle cartridges fly onto the grass below. They shoulder their rifles in unison and step to the red, white and blue covered coffin. With reverence, two of them lift the stars and stripes, folding it tightly into a triangle, which is handed to the third who carries it to the fourth sailor standing in front of black-dressed family members sitting graveside. The sailor bends at the hip with the flag over his forearms to present it to Rose. Elsie and Esther put their arms around her. Behind them, Rose's three grandsons place their hands on their mother's shoulders. Seeing this, Esther's four-year-old daughter, Diane, in her father's arms, begins weeping.

Ambrose whispers to Julian, "He's better off. He could never recover."

Julian nods. "The war still got him."

The former Air Corp. officer and New Mexico National Guard sergeant salute their fallen Naval comrade.

Early Spring 1965

A tractor maneuvers around acres of grapevine poles, cleaning the fields between the growing sprouts. Wide brimmed sun hats and hand gloves are worn by all as Elsa, Jenoa, Victorio, and Palo carefully prune the side-by-side rows of young vines. Day laborers add to the work force that spreads between the rows. In the distance, more laborers are laying curved Tuscan orange-brown tiles on the roof of the main house.

"Winds will slow us down if we do not finish this today," Elsa tells her sons.

"We'll get it done, mama," says Palo as he wipes away his sweat.

"Yeah, no problem mom," adds Victorio.

Jenoa steps away from his family as another truck pulls beside them carrying a large spindle of irrigation hose.

"Where do you want this laid out, sir?"

Through his accent, Jenoa says, "We have the trenches dug along the east acre side." He can see a question on their faces. "Let me show you." He jumps into the back of the pickup as it drives away.

Elsa takes off her hat and wipes away her forehead as she watches her husband ride away. She glances at her almost completed home in the distance. As she watches her hard-working sons, she smiles.

***

At the same time in the heart of downtown on Route 66 in front of the KiMo Theatre hundreds of costumed citizens gather. Motion picture klieg lights shine over the intersection of streets. A motion picture camera on an elevated platform aims down the street. A man sitting high on an elevated crane perch next to the camera calls directions. A cast of hundreds is in front of him, all local extras that are directed to gather around a decorated Native American parade float.

"Okay, folks," the director says through a PA system," when I say ACTION, the street extras all gather around the float smiling with excitement. Reach in high as if you want to touch Flap. Shout out your lines until you hear CUT! You look great. Let's do this, people."

Elsie, Russell and Freddy stand in the crowd dressed in Native American clothes. All wear head bands with a feather in it.

"What did you say the name of this movie is?" Freddy asks his brother.

"They said it's called, 'No One Loves a Drunken Indian."

"I think they will change the name to FLAP," says Elsie.

A roar from the crowd grows louder. Film crew techs create a path through the extras so the principal actor can make his way before he climbs onto the float. Crew members climb up behind him, attended to his costume and makeup before climbing back down. Both Russell and Freddy study their mom's hypnotic amazement.

"Who's this old guy?" asks the younger Freddy.

"Apparently, he's been in a lot of movies since before we were born," says Russell. Neither has ever seen their mom so attentive on any guy like this. Russell says, "Hey, mom! What's this guy's name again?"

"Anthony Quinn, baby. Anthony Quinn."

The boys shrug it off as the director shouts. "Okay, quiet on the set. And... Action!"

Hundreds of extras surround the float while reaching and shouting for Anthony Quinn, AKA Flap.

Late July 1965

Elsie and Elsa stand while sipping goblets of red *vino*. Both stare through the glass wall of the living room at row after row of grapevines. Their voices echo lightly in the empty, tiled room.

"Too bad Esther couldn't be here now," says Elsie.

Elsa, after studying her growing fields through the wall-sized picture window says, "She and Ambrose must be enjoying little Diane at that Disney place in California." She takes another sip of her Rose wine. "Remember twenty years ago, when we sat around that little Los Angeles kitchenette table puffing cigarettes?" asks Elsa. "In that small L.A. house, I never imagined this."

Elsie takes another sip from her glass. "Life has been good to us, Elsa. This merlot is excellent."

"It's good for the heart."

Elsie watches their boys working the fields in front of them. "We're both outnumbered by the men in our life." She loses herself to the beautiful view in front of her. "What you've created here is wondrous," she says.

"We have four varietals out there. Our plan is to have many, many more." Elsa grows silent. "I wish mama and papa could be here to see what their daughter has done."

"How long has it been?"

Elsa's eyes tear up at the thought. "Almost eight years. Mama didn't want to go on so she gave up on life only a month after Poppi."

Finishing her merlot, Elsie can now see her sons pruning and weeding the fields. "Thank you for the summer jobs for the boys. They come home with stories about all kinds of wine. I learn about the process by listening to them."

"We are grateful to have them here. The last couple of years have been difficult since the family in Italy's underwriting expired. We desperately need your manpower just to keep up."

"Sounds like Italy kicked you out of the nest," Elsie says, looking around the empty home. Tuscan Moorish arches divide the bare hallway walls of this two-level house. "But still, thank you so very much."

"Outside of these promotional samples, Jenoa says it takes about ten years to produce the first saleable bottle of wine." Elsa refills Elsie's glass.

"Come on! Look around, gal," Elsa enjoys another sip.

"You guys are doing great!" says Elsie.

The double front doors swing open. Jenoa and Julian make their grand entrance by stumbling inside, each carrying an open bottle of wine. Behind her hand, Elsie says, "Our POWs have arrived."

Elsa smiles.

"Hey, baby," announces Julian. "Today I saw how wine is made."

"I was showing Julian the wine cellar. One thing led to another and..." Jenoa trails off.

Elsie smiles, "Darling, it sounds and looks like you learned by drinking it."

"Of course," Julian grins and takes a swig from his bottle.

Jenoa starts coughing. Julian puts his arm around his shoulders. "Clear your throat. Take another swig of your excellent Pinot Noir."

As Jenoa does, both laugh with glee.

Elsie says, "I hate to break up the drinking buddies, but I'd better get you home, Julian."

"Yeah doll, let's go." He tosses her the keys. "You drive while I finish this Cabernet."

Elsie rolls her eyes and slides her arm around his waist as they exit. Elsa takes Jenoa's hand they follow their guests outside to the circular driveway.

As they wave to their departing guests, Jenoa coughs again. Then says, "I love you, *mi corazon.*" Elsa kisses his forehead and leads him inside.

***

ELSIE AND ELSA

August 1965

Elsa sits up in bed into darkness and places her feet on the floor. She crosses the room and opens the drapes, flooding the bedroom with sunlight. It reveals rows of green vines that seem taller than the day before.

She hears Jenoa turn over under the covers and knows he needs a day away from the fields. The idea of going to the new Winrock Shopping Center in the heights to buy furniture for the front room is exciting. Because they now can afford it, Elsa decides to pay themselves back by splurging.

She steps in the bathroom and turns on the shower before arranging her long jet-black hair inside a shower cap.

Hearing the shower, Jenoa pushes away the covers and sits up as he coughs. He brushes his mouth with his pajama sleeve. Blood covers it. Guilt grabs him again because he hasn't told his wife about the doctor appointment he has this afternoon. He doesn't want to worry Elsa or the boys.

He steps onto the balcony to enjoy the elevated view of his vineyards where farm hands are already at work.

***

A Week Later

With a smile, Jenoa watches Elsa bustle about their living room. The prospect of decorating has energized her. She clears the way by moving borrowed side tables and lamps, and readjusting paintings to various spots in the room. Changing her mind, she moves them again.

The doorbell rings.

"That must be the furniture!" she says.

She throws open the doors and sees uniformed movers moving down a ramp from the back doors of a delivery van.

When the phone rings Jenoa says, "I'll get it," as Elsa disappears outside.

Jenoa searches around boxes in the dining room—their temporary office—pushing them aside, to finally find phone on the third ring.

"Hello." He pushes more clutter aside with his leg. "*Si, si,* this is Jenoa Domenici. Ah, *si doctori, bona cera...*" What he is told causes him to drop suddenly into a chair.

***

The front screen door swings open. Freddy steps inside and tosses aside his baseball glove. His dad, mom, and two brothers are seated around the supper table.

"He's here," says Peter, the youngest brother.

"You are late for supper again," barks his father.

"Baseball practice was longer today," Freddy says.

"Go wash your hands," says his mother.

Moments later Freddy returns to the table carrying a small tan box with an antenna sticking from it.

"We've already said grace," Julian says. "Before you put fork to mouth, say yours."

"Yes, sir." Freddy sets the box on the table, makes the sign of the cross, folds his hands and bows his head.

Big brother Russell picks up the box. "What's this?"

"Pass the mashed potatoes, please—and the chili," says Julian.

"It's a transistor radio," says Freddy. "It plays all the local radio stations."

"Cool," Russell says, turning the dial. Rock and roll blares from the speaker. "This is groovy."

"Turn that off!" says Julian as he dips a tortilla into the chili on his plate. Russell passes the radio to Peter who fumbles turning louder rather than off.

"I said turn that thing off!" Julian yells.

Peter hands the radio to his mother.

"Where did you get this?" asks Elsie.

"I traded my baseball bat to Jimmy for it."

"That bat cost me money, boy," says his father.

With obvious reluctance, Elsie hands the radio to her husband. "I'd rather you played baseball than this thing," she says.

Julian inspects the new contraption.

"But it plays great rock-n-roll, pop."

Glaring, Julian spits a mouthful of food onto his plate, a red flush covering his face as he pushes away from the table.

"This damn thing says SONY on it. It was made in Japan!" he shouts. "I don't want this in my house!" He slams it onto the table. "Don't bring it into my home again!"

Julian slams the kitchen screen door behind him. Through the back window, the family watches him pitch the radio to the ground and grind it with the heel of his boot.

Having never seen their father act this way, the boys are startled. Tears well up in Freddy's eyes. "That's my radio."

"Someday, you'll understand your father," says Elsie.

"But it's my radio," insists Freddy.

The phone diverts them. Through the open door, Julian sees his family staring at him with astonishment. He paces back and forth to calm himself.

Elsie answers the phone. "Oh, hi darling," she says. "Listen, things are not so good right now...What? What?"

The boys are still watching their father angrily pace back and forth over the lawn. Elsie goes to the door.

"Julian!" she calls to him.

He ignores her.

Elsie opens the screen door and moves closer to him. "Julian, Jenoa is in the hospital!"

Chapter Thirty-Two

Late Summer 1965

"Such a beautiful sight, *mi amori*," Jenoa tells his loving wife. She hides her despair at her husband's weight loss. His emaciation is punctuated by endless coughing. She eases his head into the palm of her hand, swiping his once jet black, now gray, hair out of his eyes.

"*Grazi, bambina.*" With effort, he pushes himself into a sitting position. "Has the tests come in from the *doctori* yet?"

Elsa shakes her head as she sits by his side. The previous doctor's report wasn't good. So, she refused to listen when he began suggesting that afterlife arrangements be considered. She calmly tells Jenoa, "Still, they find nothing to the cause except they continue to insist it is chemical induced."

"The boys?"

"They are working and managing the harvest. You trained them well. But don't think about it..." She lovingly palms her hand over her husband's face, following with multiple kisses as the sun shines into their bedroom, then over their bed.

"The sun embraces my love for you, *mi amori*," she whispers in his ear.

Both enjoy the view that they built.

***

Victorio and Palo halfheartedly oversee the realignment and roll-over of the full storage barrels and smaller kegs of wine. Sunshine squeezes through every crevice in the otherwise dark and dry wine cellar. Empty wine containers are rolled off the shelves to eventually be refilled before returning to the shelves. One by one, Vic rolls in a new shipment of empty five by six foot barrels on a hand dolly.

"Sugar levels are high on this year's harvest, but the yields are strong."

"We barely harvested in time," says Palo.

Without thinking, Vic says, "If papa wasn't so sick, we would have harvested sooner. I wish he could be here."

"If he was here to advise us, we'd do the work," says Palo. Being taller, he rolls wedged three by four foot, empty kegs off the overhead shelves. "He's getting weaker every day."

"I know and mama has been with him ever since the hospital."

As fine dust falls on his face, Palo says, "It's up to us to keep this place going." He grunts while pulling and pushing a stuck keg from a dark corner, wiping off cobwebs before lowering it to the ground.

Vic notices an open sack of something wedged under it. "What's that?"

Palo uses both hands to pull it out, almost falling backward as it gives. Granules of something spill from it. He studies the chemical name on the bag. "Fertilizer," he says.

"I remember that stuff," Vic says. "Pop used it some. He said he gave up on it because it was so acidic." He thinks for a moment. "As a matter of fact, that was about the time I saw him covered with the stuff. He said the open bag fell off the overhead shelf." Both look up at the shelves above them. "And he was spitting like he had some of it in his mouth."

"When was that?"

"Oh, about five months ago, I think."

"Isn't that about the time he started getting sick?"

Their eyes widen before they rush to the elevator, bag in hand. Carefully placing the fertilizer in the back of the trunk, they jump into Palo's '62 silver Thunderbird.

"Do you know where the doctor's office is?"

"Hell, yes," Palo says, flooring the pedal.

Gravel spits out from under the back tires.

***

Three Years Later
June 1968

The American Legion Post 13 banquet hall is packed. From the stage, Vic Domenici's college rock 'n roll band plays the Beatle song, `She Loves You.' Behind them hangs a banner that reads, `CONGRATS RUSSELL 68 GRAD!'

Teenagers dance to what is their favorite local band. The girls stand at the edge of the stage to watch Vic's fingers' dance over the piano keys, occasionally swiping his long hair out of his eyes. Parents, aunts, uncles, and friends of the family sit at tables lined up from the dance floor to the banquet table in the back of the room. Still others, mostly friends of friends, pick and choose food and drink from the banquet table. Men, some wearing American Legion caps, walk to and from the room with paper cups of beer in hand. Comfortably sitting at the front tables, Elsie, Elsa, Esther, and Rose watch their kids dance. As the band's lead vocalist, Vic belts it out.

"Ladies and gentlemen, here is my favorite from Jay and the Americans: "Cara Mia Mine." He belts out the lyrics in falsetto. The girls swoon and cheer.

Elsa watches her son perform with pride, knowing their investment in his music is paying off. Then she watches her other college underclassman, Palo, dance with his girlfriend.

Grandma Rose says, "Elsie, this room hasn't changed much since your wedding reception." She smiles at being surrounded by her family. "I wish I could have thrown you girls a graduation party during the war."

Esther watches her little Diane dance with her much taller cousin, Peter. The seven-year-old stands on her cousin's shoes as he walks her through the dance steps.

"The war steered all of us in other directions," Esther says.

Elsa looks around. "Where are the men?"

"They're in the bar, probably watching politics on TV," says Rose.

Elsie smiles. "Julian is so deep into politics that even though he's a Republican, he's watching the California Democrat Primary."

Vic is now singing, "Baby light my fire, light my fire, light my fire..."

Elsa says, "Jenoa is at fault there. He is anxious to learn American politics."

Elsie can see her high school graduate dancing with a pretty blonde with generous endowments. "Russell is dancing very close to his little friend," she says.

Elsa replies with a teasing smile. "Elsie, there is nothing little about her."

Elsie continues to watch them without smiling.

As the song ends, Russell kisses the cheek of his partner.

The band goes directly into the next song. Vic sings, "I wish they all could be California girls..."

Another girl from Russell's class asks him to dance.

"So popular with the girls," Elsie says with pride.

Julian arrives and hands his wife a vodka tonic. He whispers to her.

"The guys are ready in the back room."

Immediately she stands to face her husband.

"Oh Julian, must you now? We're having such a good time. Why spoil it?"

"Elsie, we've talked about this for years. He's not a boy anymore. And the time has come."

As her husband walks away to wait for their son to step off the dance floor, she sits down with a sudden depressed expression on her face.

"What's wrong Elsie?" asks Esther.

Not wanting to hear the question, Elsie watches her son take notice of his father's signal to come over to him. She nervously stands to watch. Rose immediately whispers to the others, informing them of the plan. Glum expressions overcome their faces as well. Elsie wants to join Russell and Julian. But as she stands to join them, Rose grabs her arm.

"Elsie. Elsie," she says firmly. "You may not like it, but Russell's a man now. Let it happen."

The daughter surrenders to her mother's advice. She watches her husband place his arm around their son's shoulders. Their son is lead unsuspectingly into the backroom. She slowly sits back down as the door closes behind them.

Esther shoots in, "Look at all the girls dancing with your Freddy and Peter."

***

As the backroom door closes behind them, Russell evaluates his surroundings. He's surprised to see that he and Pop are not alone. The small room's walls are covered by flags, American, New Mexican and from the various military branches. Most of the light in the room seems focused on a lone empty chair in the middle of the room. Five of his dad's cronies sit in a circle that surrounds it. All five have their American Legion caps halfcocked.

"Sit there, son," orders his father.

Russell complies, but apprehension kicks in when his father leaves the room.

One of the shadow-faced American Legion caps asks, "Your father has never told you what he did in the war, has he?"

"No, no sir," stutters Russell. The muffled rock 'n roll music in the background evaporates.

Another says, "That's why we are here. We all served with your dad, kid."

A sudden respect sweeps over Russell. He sits up straighter.

"My brothers and I have asked him about it. But he just gets mad or changes the subject. So, we stopped asking years ago."

Another of the men says, "We all find it difficult to tell our kids. And that's why we're here today. We all shipped out together at the end of September '41. We were in the 515th New Mexico Artillery." Another adds, "They're now called the New Mexico National Guard."

"We were in the Philippines when the Japs attacked the same day they attacked Pearl Harbor."

Russell turns toward the veteran speaking from behind him.

"Have you heard of the Bataan Death March?"

***

When Russell finally opens the door to the banquet hall, a wall of rock 'n roll hits him. His parents are there, his mother nervously toking on her cigarette. Only then does Russell feel the tears rolling down his cheeks. Trembling, he walks over to his father to do something he can't ever remember ever doing before. Russell embraces his father before kissing his cheek.

"I love you dad," he says.

Elsie embraces them both.

At the bar in the adjoining banquet room patrons hover around the television. Ambrose and Jenoa are watching a Bulletin News report. They hear the band start playing their next song.

Ambrose is aggravated by the music from the other room, especially after what he just saw on TV. The pulsating sound of the music is disrespectful. He tosses away his American Legion cap and storms into the banquet room, where he steps up onto the stage.

"What's Uncle Ambrose doing?" asks Russell.

Ambrose takes command of the microphone. The band stands quiet, agitated.

"Ladies and Gentlemen, I hate to disturb this celebration," Ambrose says, "But moments ago, in Los Angeles, Robert Kennedy was shot dead!"

A lady in the audience screams.

The teenagers look around dumbfounded, as Esther cries out, "Not again, not like his brother! It can't happen... Not again."

***

Late August 68

Peter opens the front door for his brother, Freddy, who drags himself inside, drops his duffle bag and plops down on the couch.

"School starts next month and I don't know if I can take any more of these two-day football practices," he says.

"At least I can see what's in store for me next year," says Peter.

"Wish I could do the morning practice and leave in the afternoon."

"Coach would kick you off the team."

"How is my football player?" Elsie calls from the kitchen. Getting no response, she walks to the living room where she finds Freddy with his eyes closed, snoozing.

She strolls over a thick, green lawn out to the new post box at the curb and pulls out several envelopes. She looks down the quiet street at the lawns and maturing trees, remembering when she and Julian bought the house. There were no lawns then, much less trees.

Shuffling through the bills and junk mail she finds a large envelope addressed to her son, Russell. She is startled by the return address: United States Induction Service.

Later, Elsie, Julian, Freddy and Peter wait for Russell to get home from work at the hardware store. No one is in a rush to eat. Elsie watches the clock.

"Where is that boy?"

"Start thinking of him as a man, *mi corazon.* Our boy is a man."

The '66 Ford Mustang finally pulls into the driveway.

"He's home!" says Peter, stating the obvious.

When Russell walks in, he sees his family ready to pounce on him. An ominous feeling is in his gut. "Who died?"

Elsie loses it and wraps her oldest into her arms. "Oh, my baby."

He looks to his dad. "What's wrong? Tell me."

Julian hands him the envelope, which he tears open. "The draft board has selected me for a physical," he says.

***

Halloween, October 1968

The Chevy Bel Air maneuvers into a parking place at the U.S. Army Recruitment Center. The car doors open with dread as all Arias family members exit. The lot is filled with other cars, each surrounded by people suffering emotional farewells. Russell trembles with a smile as he approaches his parents.

Julian fights emotion with small talk. "Take your last look at the old Chevy. After 13 years, I will be trading it in soon."

"We've had it a long time, pop." Russell says as he hugs his father.

"My baby," Elsie whispers.

Russell hugs her, pulling his dad in at the same time. Fred and Peter look on.

"We'll walk you inside," says Julian.

"No, pop. Let's make it easier. Once I'm inside, I'm inside."

"But, Russell, we want to see you off," Elsie says.

"Elsie, our young man is right."

Russell turns to his brothers.

"I'll keep all your friends updated," Fred says in his matter-of-fact manner as he shakes his brother's hand.

Peter wipes his blood-shot eyes.

Russell says, "Get that dust out of your eye and get over here."

Peter bear hugs his big brother. "I'll write you updates about dad and mom," he whispers.

"Thanks, man."

Elsie, Julian, Freddy and Peter watch as Russell picks up his bag and disappears through the building's swinging doors. Out of sight from the familia, Russell's tears run down his face. His jacket sleeve is soon soaked.

***

Three Months Later

The newly imported Italian crystal chandelier reflects a prism of color across the walls as it hangs over the dining room table. Fashionably dressed, a string of pearls around her neck and in high heels, Elsa is the first to sit at the family dinner table. She welcomes Jenoa, then her sons, all wearing neckties, to sit.

"Isn't it lovely to have the family together?" she says.

"*Moto beno*," Jenoa kisses his wife's cheek. He pulls chilled wine from the bucket of ice and goes through the procedure of pulling the cork and sniffing the bouquet before pouring four glasses. Elsa passes them to her waiting sons.

As he throws back his long brown hair, Victorio nervously glances at his older brother Palo who squirms in his chair. Relief overcomes them as the family butler and servant carries out a silver tray with roasted chicken and vegetables. Jenoa's smile is wide in anticipation.

"*Ah, fantastico*," Jenoa tells him.

"Fine eye appeal, Marcello," Elsa says.

"You do us good, Marcello," says Victorio.

The servant replies, "Grazi, familia de Domenici."

"I get hungrier just looking at it," says Palo.

Victorio asks, "And what's for dessert tonight, Marcello?"

Through his Italian accent, "Young sir, I will be serving cheesecake with pecan glazing. The pecans arrived fresh today from the Las Cruces farms."

"You will need the energy to carry all that hair around." Jenoa says, reaching over to flip Victorio's hair in disgust. "How many times do I have to tell you to cut it short?"

"Pop, I told you that it is the groovy thing now a days, especially for musicians."

"Look at your brother's hair. Clean cut, just like a real Domenici. Not like a girl."

"Girl?" He almost stands up. "Do we have to talk about my hair again?"

"Let's enjoy our Sunday dinner without talking about hair," says Elsa. "Unless it's mine."

Everyone smiles. Victorio nudges his brother. Palo immediately shakes him off, as if to say, 'Not yet.'

"So, my darling wife, you were invited to join that women's group? Have you decided to?"

"They are called the Junior League of Albuquerque. It's an honor. They have invited me to visit with their membership committee this week."

"If it will help business. I say do it."

"Do these women have daughters?" asked Vic.

"I am glad you asked that, boy. With the way you look with long hair, I wonder if women will even look at you."

Older brother Palo says, "Are you kidding, papa? Women like his hair."

As Jenoa shakes his head in disbelief, Elsa places her hand over his, causing him to relax. He breaks more bread onto his plate. Again, Victorio eyes his older brother. Palo glares back in resistance, but knows his brother is right.

"Papa, mama, I have news."

Jenoa reaches for the salad bowl. Elsa hands it to him.

"Yes, sweetheart," Elsa answers.

"Papa, mama I um...when I graduate next year I'm going into the Air Force. I signed up today in the ROTC."

Elsa drops her silverware and stands up. Jenoa seems frozen in his chair.

With shock on her face, she says, "Why would you make that decision without discussing it with us? There's a war on. We didn't send you to UNM so you'd go to the military."

She looks at her silent husband. "My God, say something!"

"Elsa, sit down." He reaches for his wife's hand and looks at his oldest son. "Your mother is right. We didn't know you were even thinking about joining."

"I have been leaving Air Force brochures around the house for months. Where do you think they came from?" Then adds, "With my college degree, I can enter into officer's training. I want to fly."

"Fly? Fly what? You have never shown any interest in airplanes. What brought this on?" asks his mother.

"Why are you guys so surprised? Why do you think I've been taking so many math and especially trigonometry and aeronautical courses?"

"But there's a war on," Elsa says. "This is no time to go into anything military." She pushes her plate of food aside.

Victorio's eyes widen as Marcello swings through the kitchen door carrying cheesecake and placing it in front of him.

Elsa immediately tells the family servant, "Please, please Marcello. Take it back. Suddenly, it's not the time."

Marcello says nothing. Victorio shows depression as their servant takes back the dessert.

Jenoa speaks. "You should have discussed this with us, your own parents."

"Why? I am 21—it's time I thought about my own future."

Through frightened eyes, Elsa looks at her suddenly mature son.

"Jenoa. They could send him to Vietnam like Elsie's boy."

***

May 10, 1969
16 degrees 15' 11" North 107 degrees 10' 29 East
Hill 937, Dong Ap Bia, Shay Valley, South Viet Nam

In a hooch, a sand bag built barracks at Base Camp, Private Russell Arias, Alpha Company, 3rd Battalion, 101st Airborne Division lays across his cot, upper bunk. His mind diverts to counting the time he's been in country. Three weeks, three days and seven hours he finally calculates.

His squad nervously waits for the order they have all been standing by for. Get ready to move out, with gear packed. It was the stereotypical U.S. Military syndrome called, "Hurry up and wait!"

He quickly pulls the radio close to his ear as he hears his current favorite song on RADIO AMERICA. A sense of comfort fills his soul when he takes

in a favorite on the Country charts. It's now being sung by a former Albuquerque boy, Glen Cambell. "...the Lights of Albuquerque shimmer in the
desert night..."

Suddenly the sergeant breaks into the hut, "Ready you sonsofbitches?
Let's move it, move out! Move it! Move it! Move it!"

Quickly Russell's fellow troops strap on their fifty-pound back packs. Before hustling out of the fan cooled hooch. They all pound the ground, double
timing to their waiting choppers.

"Move it! Move it!" the Sargent barks.

One, two, three, four, five, six, seven, eight, nine, ten choppers lift off
before turning towards their destination. In each are eight fully equipped,
armed to the teeth fighting men. In and around Russell, in their air cab, he
knows that he is surrounded by fellow draftees. He's taken up the habit that
he started when he came to this humid country. He lights up a cigarette.

Private Arias watches past the open sliding door. His view easily scans
downward to the green, squared off rice paddies below. The roaming hills in
the distance, their destination, gets closer and closer. The only sounds he can
hear is the whirling and swooping, whirling and swooping rotor blades above.
Sullen, but focused expressions cover his fellow platoon members' faces. All
don't bother to say a word.

Finally all birds start to lightly set down in waist high grass. And no
sooner do all ten choppers empty their cargos, they immediately lift off to
return to base to pickup other platoons.

The sarge says nothing. He only gives his arm signals to move forward.
Along with his fellow troops, Russell slogs and sloshes through the tall grass
and mud. The loudest sound that he now can hear is his own heart beating. A
jungle forest stretches out in front of them.

Then from the top of the hill, it suddenly starts happening. North Viet
Namese cannon fire opens up. Explosions blast a line straight in front of them.
A fellow private that he hasn't known even a week, gives off a quickly snuffed
out scream. Russell can see this soldier's body parts scatter in all directions
as it flies in the air before it smacks into the ground. Instinctively Russell
quickens his pace toward the cover at the base of the hill.

All Russell can think of is getting to the row of green jungle covering mere feet away. At that moment in time, his mind tells him what to expect over the next split second. His momentum pulls his boot off of a metal click. He knows that he is dead as his body lifts off the ground. Then all he can feel is a dull thud as his body must have hit the ground.

How long has he been lying there? He does not know when he opens his eyes to excruciating pain!

All Russell can think of is cry out, "Mama! Mama!"

Seemingly in no time, he can see the medic appear out of nowhere. Kneeling over Private Arias, he sticks a needle into Russell. And like a miracle, the pain fades, fades, fades.

The medic shakes his head to the approaching Chaplain before moving onto the next wounded soldier. Russell can see the Chaplain say a prayer over him. Then he knows. Nineteen year old, Private Russell Arias then simply closes his eyes.

***

Springtime
Mother's Day 1969

Riding in their brand, new four-door '69 Dodge, the Arias family pulls into their driveway after Sunday morning mass. Elsie, Julian, Fred and Peter exit. The bright sun and blossoming rose bushes color their home with red, pink and yellow. A mild breeze wafts their aroma in greeting.

Fred loosens his tie.

Peter does the same, saying, "I can't wait to take you to lunch, mom. I'm starving."

Elsie glances back at the army green vehicle parked at the curb just as two army uniforms get out. She watches the sergeants come up the front walk.

One of the uniforms says, "Excuse me. Are you the family of Private Russell Arias?"

Julian holds his wife tight. His gut wrenches as he realizes what this means.

With pride, Peter says, "Yes sir. We sure are."

Elsie turns pale. From her WWII experience, she knows. Her legs buckle. Julian and Freddy ease her down to the lawn.

"Mama!" cries Freddy. With naivety Peter approaches the sergeant who holds out a paper to them.

In a matter of fact voice, the sergeant says, "Family Arias, your country and President regret to inform you..."

***

Within the hour, the Domenici family car pulls into the Arias driveway. Elsa jumps out before the car comes to a stop and hurries to enter her lifelong friend's home without knocking. Jenoa and the boys follow. Minutes later, the car carrying Ambrose, Esther, Rose and Diane pulls up front of the house. Esther gets out to open the back door for her mother. She holds her mother's arm to support her slow steps up the front walk.

Rose cries out, "My *niño*, Russell, my *niño*, my *niño!*" Ambrose bites his lip as he holds the hand of his crying daughter.

They are met at the front door by Julian's brothers and sisters.

Watching from across the street while pruning her roses, a neighbor weeps openly for the brave boy she watched grow up. She remembers his beautiful smile, and how he helped her fix little things around the house. She watches the Arias' next door neighbor pull into her driveway and step from her car with a bag of groceries, and calls to her.

Grief rips the neighbor's face at the news. She puts the bag on the ground and rushes to her next-door neighbor's home.

"That dear, brave little boy," is all she can say about the fine young man she remembers so well.

Within the hour, young men with crying young women—friends of Russell, Fred and Peter—stand outside the overflowing Arias home. They make way for a man walking up the front walk carrying a book with laces hanging out. He wears black slacks and black shirt with a white collar. One of the boys opens the front door for him.

"This way, father."

Neighbors down the street come out to see what's going on this early Sunday afternoon. Neighbor to neighbor the word spreads. The fellow in the last house down the street is sweeping off his driveway when he hears the news.

He remembers the friendly, hardworking kid who came by several times every summer pushing his lawn mower, asking for a job. He always had a smile. The neighbor slams his broom to the ground. "Damn it!" He picks it up and slams it down again. "Damn it to hell!"

As he picks it up again, he sees his neighbors, one by one, lower their house flags to half-mast. With a lump in his throat, he finds himself doing something he hasn't done in a long time: wiping tears from his eyes.

***

Three Weeks Later

Clouds of desert dirt spit from two autos as they cut their way through the countryside. There is no road. Through mesquite, chamisa, cactus and snakes, temperatures hover between bearable and roasting. The Arias ranch has always been situated in the middle of God's obscure country. But now these vehicles rumble over dirt roads, flatlands and through gullies.

The Arias' white Dodge follows Russell's white '66 Mustang convertible deep into the family's ranch. Both slow to a stop. Julian climbs out of the Mustang, Fred gets out from behind the wheel of the Dodge, and Peter exits the passenger side.

Without a word, Julian points to the time carved gulley that parallels their path ahead. Both sons nod in acknowledgment as they watch their father get back in the Mustang. He guns the engine. More dirt spits from the rear tires as the Mustang goes full bore into the gulley. As planned, the screeching and crunching metal wedges between the thin sides of time-worn dirt. The roaring engine is turned off.

Julian pulls back the cloth convertible top then climbs over the windshield before opening the hood. Fred and Peter approach carrying handled cans out of the rear seats of the Ford. They open the Mustang trunk to pull out two more handled containers. The trunk is left open.

All three climb up to the sides of the gulley to look down onto their son's and brother's pride and joy. Still no words are needed to be said. The brightness of the overhead sun makes them all wipe their foreheads with their sleeves. Julian places on his sunglasses while his sons' gander around their graceful isolation.

As planned each grip a can. Julian pours his over the engine. Fred pours over the front seat. Peter pours his can over the rear seat and open trunk. Elsie wanted to give Russell's car to charity. She still thinks that it is what's being done. The men disagreed and feel what she doesn't know, won't hurt her.

This decision is sparked by another fact Julian decided Elsie didn't need to know: The Army informed him at the funeral that Private Russell Arias stepped on a land mine, which is why the mortician advised against opening his sealed military coffin. It contained only his right femur.

It was Peter who reminded his brother and father that Russell always admired Viking funerals. That is why the decision became simple. The sons bow to their father as he flicks a zippo lighter, dropping it into the Mustang. Flames explode ten feet higher than they stand. As the heat forces them back, the ground under their feet trembles and the gas tank explodes. None of them can hold back their tears.

Soon the smell of the burnt electrical and smoldering interior is all that remains as the flames die.

Julian says, "Nature will take care of the rest."

But still, he grips and then pockets the keys to his son's Mustang. Fred and Peter follow their dad back to the Dodge. Dust clouds bellow behind. None of them speak as their father drives through the rarely traveled isolation. Silence is easier as both sons lose their thoughts among the dried chamisa.

***

July 20, 1969

The Arias family remains close knit, despite months of grief. Every Sunday has been the same. Go to church, come home, eat a meal together, then stare at either black-and-white TV or the four walls. Smiles and laughs have become strange commodities. Tonight, however, is different. Excitement is growing here, as is likely in every American home.

As the sun goes down on a hot summer day, Elsie, Julian, Freddy and Peter gather around the television.

From her sofa chair Elsie says, "The last time I watched Walter Cronkite on TV with such intensity was when he reported President Kennedy's assassination."

Cronkite cuts away to strange beeps and squeals, which are the only sounds coming from the television. Intense focus is given to the square box in the corner of the Arias den.

Then they hear, "Ten forward, five down. Five forward, two down," followed by more beeps and squeals. No one can remember seeing Cronkite so intense. Then dead silence pulls them closer to the box. Finally, everyone in the world hears, "Houston, we are kicking up dust." More silence with occasional beeps and squeals before people all over the earth hear, "Houston. Tranquility Base here. The Eagle has landed."

Cronkite takes off his glasses, and smiles with pride. "Ladies and Gentlemen, America has safely landed on the moon."

Fred and Peter jump up to slap the ceiling with the palms of their hands. Julian pulls his wife into his arms. The first signs of happiness and pride in months fill the Arias household.

***

Mid-August 1969

It is five thirty in the morning when the father confronts his son at the top of the stairs. As he grows angrier, his thick Italian accent comes through.

"For the last time, cut your hair!" demands Jenoa.

Elsa stands in silence next to her husband as he tugs at his son's long brown hair. Vic pulls away.

"Ah, pop, you know I can't do that."

Vic picks up his duffle bag and starts walking down the stairs. His parents follow. At the bottom of the stairs, as if to inflame his father, he ties a sweat band around his forehead.

"And shave that dirt off your face." Victorio runs his hand over the peach fuzz he is trying to grow.

"And look at your clothes." The father points at his worn blue jeans and tie-dyed shirt, "This is not how a Domenici dresses. Why can you dress clean-cut like your brother?"

Victorio pulls the duffle bag strap over his shoulder, "Ah, pop, let's not go there again."

"Where are you going, baby?" asks Elsa.

"Mom, I've been telling you guys for weeks that Jeanie and I are going check out a rock 'n roll movie."

"When will you be back?"

"Several days before classes start."

Victorio reaches for the front door, stops and turns around. He steps over to his mom, hugs, then kisses both of her cheeks. He looks over to his angry father and throws his arms around him. He kisses both of his father's cheeks.

"I love you, pop."

Jenoa surrenders his anger.

Both parents follow their son out the front door and watch him toss his bag into the back of a waiting rainbow painted Volkswagen van. He climbs in and closes the door.

"Hi, baby." He kisses the girl behind the steering wheel.

Janis Joplin's throaty voice plays through the eight-track stereo. "Oh, Lord, won't you buy me a Mercedes Benz. All my friends drive Porsches..."

"Ready, sweetie pie?" she asks.

"Sure am."

"Groovy." She tosses back her long black curls, adjusts her baggy flowered dress, and turns on the ignition.

"Placitas, here we come," says Vic. "It's only twenty-three miles."

Elsa and Jenoa watch the van pull away and over the road between the rows of grapevines. With surrender in their eyes, they kiss and walk back inside.

Vic's girlfriend puts on her heart-shaped, rose colored glasses. Gravel spits from under the back tires. As the VW van exits the winery, Vic pulls out from the glove compartment a plastic baggy.

"All the top actors are there. I can't wait," she says.

Vic runs his fingers through the baggy.

"We go east through town," he explains while spreading it open. "Then north to Bernalillo, and east to Placitas." He pulls out a pre-rolled marijuana jay while pushing in the van's cigarette lighter, then places the jay between his lips, lights it, and inhales. Holding the smoke in, he hands the jay to his girlfriend. She places it between her lips. With eagerness, he lets the smoke out and shouts out, "Hollywood, here we come!"

His girlfriend exhales. From the eight-track stereo, they hear Janis Joplin singing, "...me and Bobby McGee..."

***

Less than thirty minutes later, the rainbow painted Volkswagen van passes a village sign that reads Placitas. Yellow signs with arrows nailed to various light and fence posts point the way to the movie set. Countless parked cars have found spots along both sides of the chamisa laden dirt road. The yellow van finds a vacant spot among them.

Victorio holds his lady's hand as they stroll up the road. They soon see trailer truck after trailer truck parked in rows as they move closer to the set.

One truck has its back-swing doors open revealing technical equipment like arch lighting and their stands. A crewman sits in front of what appears to be audio gear because he's listening to something through earphones. Each of the other trucks have their own signs, Costumes, Make Up, Dressing Rooms, Craft Services. Another truck is labeled Peter Fonda, and the next is Dennis Hopper.

Victorio's gal grips his arm tighter in excitement. He likes it. As they follow their instructions, they approach a van marked Casting. They check in and a production assistant gives them an eyeball inspection from head to toe. Next, they sign payroll, paperwork, are given their wardrobe and told to report to the makeup truck.

When they emerge, they are full-fledged flower children, with baggy bell bottom worn-out jeans. He wears another tied-dyed shirt. She does, too, but hers sports a bare midriff. Their hair has been fluffed to appear longer and fuller. Both follow instructions and report to the set.

They seem to be the last to arrive at what looks like a two-tier common house for this hippy commune. The set is filled with other actors who look more unwashed. A few kids run up and down in front of the camera. Their parents stand behind the camera and lights.

Victorio counts fifteen or sixteen actors and whispers to his lady. "I've never seen so many mother earths before."

Two production assistants—one male and one female—place their actors at specific spots on the set. After evaluating the first look, they decide to mix and match the couples. Victorio and his gal are split up. She is on the opposite side of the set from Victorio. Both show initial reluctance, but realize there is nothing they can do about it when she is placed on the upper level away from him.

Another round of actor adjustments is made. It is obvious that a couple of hippy actors are the principals because lighting levels are adjusted around them. Even though he doesn't know their names, Victorio thinks they look familiar. He's sure he must have seen the male on Star Trek recently or something.

Then comes an announcement: "All quiet on the set for the director."

All eyes watch a small fellow walk to the center of the room. Most of the actors adopt the familiar facial expression of recognition of their director. Some think back to the film "Giant" when they saw their director argue with Rock Hudson.

Director and actor Dennis Hopper addresses his cast. "Greetings, ladies and gentlemen. Welcome to the set of the film "Easy Rider." Each of you has been specifically cast for your looks. We hope today's shoot will be quick and easy, despite the large number of you."

After more adjustments and Hopper's long descriptive hand motions to a fellow behind the camera who nods his understanding, Hopper announces: "Everyone on the set talk to your neighbors as if you are visiting and discussing the crops you are raising. Talk about the rain. Talk about the babies that are running around here. Use normal expressions unless you tell a joke and you laugh. Later, I will want to hear those jokes when we break for lunch. Get ready. Quiet on the set."

A heart beat passes when the clapper is snapped in front of the camera. Dennis Hopper shouts, "Action!" The camera completes a pan of the set.

Soon enough he shouts, "Cut!" He asks the cameraman, "How was that?"

The cameraman smiles, nodding. "Good, but let's do another for security."

"Okay," Hopper agrees. They successfully repeat the shot. He tells his assistant, "Bring in Peter."

In short, Peter Fonda comes on set. He's led to a vacant spot directly next to Victorio. But despite being next to the famous actor's son, Victorio is more impressed with the beautiful actress who is also placed next to him. He watches Hopper approach. He can hear the direction he gives the actress, who apparently is to be receptive to advances from Fonda.

As Action is called and as the scene develops, Victorio watches her. He thinks it must be good being the son of a famous movie star. Soon he hears "Cut!"

Chapter Thirty-Three

September 1970

When Rose reaches First Street and Route 66 she finds workmen in hard hats wrapping up the day's labors. She has been dreading this trip. Until now, she has only heard heartbreaking reports.

And it is worse than she feared. Tears well up in her eyes as she realizes her lifelong memories have all been destroyed, piled now in heaps of rubble. Across the street, she finds a bench on which she sits to ponder her loss.

Through floating dust particles, she watches the workers leave their giant bulldozers. Chain link fencing surrounds three city blocks. Within them lie mountains of ruins and remnants of what used to be a noble temple to a glorious age. There was once a seemingly endless Parthenon of marbled arches surrounding lush green lawns and gardens of award-winning red roses that are now gone; all gone. There remains no hint of the three floors of the commanding hotel that held the gardens. The nightclub/restaurant once located within hosted the hottest swing bands of the 1930s. She recalls one night in particular when Benny Goodman and his orchestra performed.

Rose was 22 when she began working in the dining room as a famed Harvey Girl in 1922. Those were the days. This site was the preferred destination for the Atchison, Topeka and the Santa Fe railroad, a playground for some of its passengers.

And when she grew too old to waitress, the hotel management accepted her as a chef trainee. The rest is history. Her entire life has evolved around this place. She met her husband and father of her three children here. And, of course, she has been in the hotel business ever since. Now that her original location has ended, she realizes it is time for her to retire as well.

She decides to walk the length of the fenced property. The Harvey Girls Boarding House is gone. She remembers many a party they threw in that place. She met girls from all over the county. Most were friends for years, at least until they lost contact during the war.

Her memories become overbearing and increasingly painful. Reversing her steps toward an approaching yellow cab, she waves it down. The driver gets out and walks around to open the rear door for his passenger. Rose sits inside staring at a dangling sign atop a mountain of debris. She remembers it hung over the front entrance to the lobby. In bold lettering, it still states Alvarado Hotel.

She dabs her eyes and tells the driver to take her home.

***

June 1971

Two weeks ago, Interstate 25 was closed by antiwar protestors stopping the 70 mile-an-hour traffic on it. That is, until, state police wearing riot gear put an end to that. But not before a police shotgun went off and wounded a protestor. Since, pockets of antiwar sit-ins have happened all over town. Today brings a dry summer afternoon with blue skies. But antiwar emotions are still in the air.

As result, the friendly University of New Mexico campus has become the center of these protests. Antiwar sentiment has been increasing ever since. At first, sit-ins congregated along old Route 66 at Yale Park, lightly attended by the long hair, grungy hippy bunch. War news since has grown from bad to worse as more New Mexico boys are being killed—with no end in sight.

Currently, several thousand protestors are gathered at the center of campus. All roads to there are clogged with mainstream students and general city populace. Jimmy Hendrix's growling electric guitar music bounces off building walls that seduce people in closer.

"Excuse me while I kiss the sky..." which blends into his psychedelic rendition of the "Star Spangled Banner."

Elbow-to-elbow crowds merge around the stage where public address announcements are repeated over and over.

"Nixon, Get Out of Vietnam Today, Not Tomorrow, Nixon!"

Anger is fanned in the surrounding sea of humanity by shouting, on-stage antiwar militants. Raised fists emphasize hundreds of placards that read Get Out of Vietnam Nixon, Down with Nixon, and Make Love Not War. Simple signs just have a peace sign.

To the south and rear of the thousand-plus throng, is the Route 66 campus that borders Yale Park. Non-participating students toss frisbees that are caught by their shirtless long haired friends. Other frisbees are being retrieved by four-legged friends that are jumping high into the air. Students read while sitting on blankets laid on fresh, green grass. An errant frisbee falls in the laps of a pair of students. Shirtless Freddy Arias laughingly runs up to them.

"Sorry about that, folks. A little help, please."

The pair tosses it back. Freddy spins it toward his friend on the far side of the park.

Without warning from the opposite northside of the campus plaza, sounds of explosive pops echo off the building walls toward Rt. 66. Yale Park occupants divert their attention to the distraction before their focus is rudely redirected by lights blazing and sirens screeching. Police squad cars are surrounding the park.

From campus center, giant puffs of smoke move fast toward the stage as someone shouts through a microphone: "Tear Gas!"

From their elevated view, those on stage can see straight lines of the crowd squeeze closer. The sudden rush of humanity presses against the raised stage. Someone announces, "Don't panic, people."

Using a bull horn a voice commands people leave the area. "Everyone Disperse—NOW!"

The smoke mushrooms to finally extend over everyone as National Guard riot shields and fixed bayonets encompass the stage to force the crowd back. Choking people panic and drop their antiwar placards.

From the stage a coughing militant shouts, "Don't let the pigs beat you down. Stand up for your rights!"

Hearing those fighting words, angry students pick up smoking tear gas canisters and lob them back at the National Guard troops. Others join to throw back more canisters. As the crowd is forced back, people on stage start to abandon the speaker's platform. The thousand attendees scatter away faster and faster, stomping on their once angry placards. As smoke wafts further south, suffocating, crying, retreating people reach Route 66.

Along Route 66's Yale Park, frozen students watch approaching panicked crowds. Without thinking, Freddy gives extra wrist action to the frisbee to his friend Patrick who stands across the park. The frisbee flies farther than intended. The friend runs faster to catch it and pays scant attention to where he is headed—unintentionally, running into an approaching police officer. Both hit the ground. Hordes of panicking people are falling back out of nowhere. When he can get a clear view of his friend, Freddy sees several cops beating him with fists and batons.

He runs toward them yelling, "Stop! Stop!"

From the front lines, National Guard batons are swung with maximum force at people who cannot move fast enough, forcing them to the ground. No mercy is shown; no prisoners taken. With the exits clogged, the mob is forced to back away from the smoke onto Route 66 and off the University of New Mexico campus.

Freddy watches as the cops drag away his bloodied friend, tossing him in the back of a squad car, only to be diverted by throngs throwing rocks and bricks into nearby store-front windows. Freddy's friend screams for help, so Freddy picks up a fist sized boulder and bashes out the car's side window. After pushing away the glass, he unlocks the door and puts his friend's arm around his shoulder before pulling him out. He runs away as best he can.

A gang comes along and picks up the rock. With resentful fury, one of them tosses it into the squad car's windshield. Overwhelmed, a few police officers watch the angry hordes of people overturn their unit which soon explodes into flames.

Bleeding people fall to the ground, crying out for help. But no one nearby is available.

***

Peter turns on the family's black-and-white television for his new habit: the daily national 5 PM news. He starts with CBS and later switches to ABC and NBC. He purposely stays close to the volume knob in case mom walks by, so he can reduce the volume. She still cries every time she hears Vietnam. Cronkite's report is stopped in mid-stream.

"We interrupt this regularly scheduled program for a special local bulletin," says the announcer.

The screen shows a reporter with burning police cruiser in the background. He says, "I am outside the main entrance to the University of New Mexico campus, where bedlam beyond anything known in Albuquerque's history us taking place." Peter ups the volume. "An antiwar rally has exploded on campus. Reports are that Governor Bruce King has called for additional National Guard troops as rioters spread west and east on Central. Businesses report broken windows, looting and fires." The reporter puts his hand over his ear, saying "Apparently, there are many injuries. We are moving to the emergency room at St. Joseph's Hospital."

Another reporter appears. "...ambulances are pulling in here at a rapid rate. I've seen injured police and National Guardsmen. Reports are the same from nearby Presbyterian Hospital where civilian injuries are arriving..."

Elsie hears the report and walks into the room.

"Freddy had classes at UNM today." She sits to watch.

The original reporter returns. "I am asking the camera to pan down Central. As you can see, flames are shooting out of the Barn Restaurant. The adjoining book and music store are threatened. The flow is west toward downtown. Police are unable to let the fire trucks in because antiwar rioters outnumber them."

"Shouldn't Freddy be home by now?" Elsie wonders.

The reporter covers one ear again. "We are being ordered to move." He points to the camera to aim in another direction, toward a convoy of National Guard trucks pouring onto the campus. Thrown tear gas canisters bounce off the moving trucks.

"We've temporarily lost our signal," says the reporter. "This is just in from the mayor's office. A 10 PM curfew has been established for the entire city.

The governor has requested martial law status. Stay tuned for more breaking news. Now back to our regularly scheduled program."

Walter Cronkite's face returns.

***

Elsie watches the clock and her long-prepared dinner table. "It's after seven and they're still not home."

Peter knows that's unusual but says nothing, not wanting to worry his mom. They both almost jump out of their shoes when the phone rings. Elsie rushes to answer.

"Yes, it is," she listens. "I'll be there right away." A concentrated calm overtakes her. She now knows about her son. "Freddy's at Presbyterian," she says.

"Let's go."

"No. Stay here till your father comes home. Where are the car keys?"

"But mom, Presbyterian is right in the middle of all that antiwar stuff."

"I don't care—my boy needs me." She runs her hand over his face. "When you become a parent, you'll understand."

In no time, she's in the white Dodge, making her way down the street. Within minutes, another car pulls up in front of the house. Julian squeezes out the backseat.

"Thanks, Bob. This has been an adventure, guys." He waves to his car pool buddies as the car pulls away.

The first thing Julian notices is the empty garage with its wide-open door. With concern, he goes through the front door and sees the waiting dinner table.

"Anybody home?" He can hear the water running from the backyard. Through the den screen door, he sees Peter watering the lawn. "Hey," he shouts to his son.

"Dad! Your home!" Peter turns off the water.

"The base kept us. They didn't want to let too many people out at once. Plus, many streets were blocked off."

"Mom took off. Freddy is in the hospital. He got caught up in the riot."

"What?" Julian turns on the TV for news. "Your mom is brave to go by herself, especially in that battle zone." His forehead wrinkles with worry.

Peter says, "You should've seen her, pop. She didn't give it a second thought."

***

By the time she reaches the intersection of Route 66 and University Boulevard, the National Guard road block stops Elsie. She has driven with extra caution by smoking two cigarettes. It took over an hour for this, normally a fifteen-minute drive—backed-up traffic is being diverted again. But she's determined not to be turned back for the umpteenth time despite the approaching crowd of rioters. The hospital is only blocks away.

"What to do?" she wonders, lighting another cigarette.

She's jolted by reality. In front of her, the tall plate-glass window of the Cadillac dealership crashes down. The National Guard troopers that stopped her rush to the scene. They shoot tear gas into the midst of the surrounding rioters, scattering them.

The smoke blows back toward the intersection. As it wafts into the Dodge, Elsie makes a U-turn to get out of there fast. Wiping her stinging eyes, she realizes it's the first time she's tasted pungent tear gas.

Her desperate decision is to drive west on parallel Grand Street until she can find an opening to cross Route 66 to Presbyterian Hospital. But she is frustrated along the way either flashing police car lights or a National Guard truck blocking the way. Several blocks ahead she sees troop trucks blocking Interstate 25, closing her in. Obviously, they are trying to block rioters from reaching downtown. After a couple of aborted attempts, she pulls into an apartment parking lot and parks.

"Think, Elsie, think," she tells herself. When the sun dips behind the western horizon, she knows it's after 9 PM. At that very moment, night lights from the towering hospital one block away, flash on a few steps beyond the other side of the road block. "Maybe I can run across."

Without pausing, she's out of the car, walking fast. She sees a troop truck approach her crossing point with a trooper holding a fixed bayonet rifle. Sirens blare in the distance. The guard spots her and shouts, "Halt! Who goes there?"

Elsie raises her arms high.

"My name is Elsie Arias. I need to get to the hospital," she says.

The guard sees a middle-aged woman. "Halt. Go back. You cannot pass through here," he shouts.

"Please, sir, my son is in there." She points at the hospital.

"I'm sorry, ma'am. No one passes."

"Please! My son's there."

"No one passes. Move on," he shouts.

She complies by fading into the darkness. She looks at her watch; it is after curfew. Nevertheless, she is determined. She studies the situation by walking in the shadows. Half way down the block, she looks back and sees that the guard is talking to someone in a police car. With a deep breath, she decides to run across the street.

Luckily, the guard ignores her, knowing she really is harmless.

She's soon in the crowded Emergency Ward. Gurneys line the hallways. She looks beyond the injured to the armed police, looking for only one familiar face. After an hour going up and down several floors, her frustration almost turns to tears. She dares not inquire for her son at the nursing station since it is after curfew and there are police standing in the corridor. Finally, she notices a familiar figure sitting in the corner holding his bandaged head.

"Freddy? Freddy!"

He raises his head in her direction. "Mom?"

"Oh, baby," she says, embracing her middle boy. She examines the bandage around his head, only then noticing the blood stain. "Oh, my baby. What did they do to you?"

"I got five stitches. Where's dad?"

"Never mind. Let's get out of here."

With her arm around his waist, they retrace her steps. Outside, flames from burning store fronts light the night sky. Unbelievable relief hits her as they cross several streets to the waiting Dodge. Elsie's heart still pounds in her chest as the drive home proves comparatively easy.

As she pulls into the driveway, she is amazed that it's only two hours past curfew.

***

Two Days Later

Fifty-year-old oak trees populate the hills of Roosevelt Park. Its grass is covered with picnic blankets and coolers. Fathers throw balls to their sons. Mothers with girls lay out goodies from their baskets. Palo pulls up in his Thunderbird and parks under a tree.

From the north side of the park, he can hear the disturbing roars of a growing crowd. As they spread out from the campus less than a mile away, antiwar protesters carry placards onto the park. A knot grows in Palo's gut when he can see the approaching rabble. He trots across the street and anxiously rings the doorbell.

"Hurry, answer the damn thing," he tells himself. A petite brunette finally appears. "Hurry, hurry. Let's get out of here," he says.

"What happened to 'hello, sweetheart'?"

Palo opens the screen door himself, kissing her cheek.

"Hello, sweetheart." He pulls her hand. "Let's get out of here, now," he says, pointing to the forthcoming disturbance.

"Hold your horses, big guy. Let me get my keys and stuff."

Reluctantly, Palo enters his fiancée's house.

"We gotta get out of here, baby," he insists. "Cops are closing in. It doesn't look good."

"I have to change clothes and find my keys."

Palo rolls his eyes. "We gotta go." He watches her throw clothes around in her room.

She says, "I'm looking forward to the ball game. The Dukes are in town for ten games, you know."

"Nikky, I wish we had time to catch more games."

Unsuspecting, she says, "If your ROTC obligations didn't take so much time, we could, you know... well, you know how I feel about the military."

Activity from across the street pulls Palo's view back through the front window to the park. He can see picnicking families scampering away. Some leaving their food behind. He steps outside where hordes of protestors are taking over of the park.

He shouts, "Nikky, let's move. Now!"

"Hold your horses."

"We're not going to have any horses to hold if we don't move now! The cops are almost here."

Palo goes back inside. Nikky is putting keys in her purse. He pulls her outside. While she locks the deadbolt, Palo sees squad cars with lights flashing circle the park.

Sudden explosions of tear gas spread across the grass. Two protestors toss canisters back at the cops.

"Oh, my God, Palo, get us out of here!" Nikky cries.

"I think we should stay here behind your walls."

"Just get me out of here!"

They dash across the street to his car. He fumbles with the keys before opening the locked door. As he turns around, a panicked man with a boy runs into him. They all tumble onto the pavement. The father drags the crying boy away.

Nikky leaves the car to help her fiancé, and is knocked to the ground. A sweaty, long haired dude wearing a "Make Love Not War" t-shirt is on the ground next to her when a tear gas canister lands nearby. Climbing to his feet, the dude tosses it back at the approaching line of riot police before running away.

Nikky is slow to stand. A moment goes by before bloody-nosed Palo helps her up and pushes her into the T-Bird. Nearly breaking the key in the ignition, he pulls the steering wheel sharply left only to brake in a screeching stop. A sedan with lights flashing blocks him. A cop in full riot gear exits.

"Out of the car!" he orders.

Palo does what he is told. Nikky doesn't move. Palo looks in the car and sees she is having difficulty breathing.

The riot cop orders Nikky, "Get out of the car, now!"

"Officer, she can't. Can't you see she's hurt." Palo runs around the car to help her.

The cop is diverted by his squawking walky-talky. It causes him to notice several rioters on the other side of the park running toward an overturned police unit. He grinds his teeth as a rioter stuffs a rag in its gas tank, and lights it. Within seconds, the unit explodes into flame. After pulling out his baton, he sees the guy in front of him tending to a female in the car, and takes out his helplessness by swinging the baton across the guy's back.

Knocked to the pavement by lightning bolts of pain, Palo looks up to see the cop dragging Nikky onto the street, where he takes a swing at her with his baton.

Smoke blows across their path. The police officer coughs. "When I tell you to move, lady, you move!" He takes off on foot toward the park.

Palo spits up tear gas. He tries to stand but the world spins and he falls to the asphalt. He hears Nikky moaning. With his head spinning, all he can do is crawl toward her. From below the car, he sees more smoke rolling over the grass, and pulls himself up by the car's door. As the world settles some, he sweeps Nikky into his arms. Her mouth is bleeding.

"Ah, baby."

Palo knows he must get Nikky to the hospital, which is less than a mile away. So, with all hell exploding around them, he prepares to run the gauntlet. After placing Nikky back in the car, he decides to fight their way out of there. To circumvent the police car in front of him, he pulls onto Nikky's driveway and drives his Thunderbird across three neighbor's front yards, over the curb and back onto the street. He hears a loud pop before feeling the back of the T-Bird start to drag with a blowout. He hears himself shouting something he never thought he'd say: "Damn fucking Pigs."

Palo force limps the Thunderbird slowly across a couple of main streets to the hospital. A few blocks from his destination, the dead rubber is finally gone, which produces grinding metal sounds from the tire's rim on pavement.

Yet he continues to roll. Only a block away the wheel hub gives way. Without needing to look, Palo knows he's broken the axle.

Not caring, he leaves his prized auto in the middle of the street. He pulls Nikky into his arms and stumbles onto the pavement, determined to carry her the rest of the way.

She opens her eyes. "Palo, Palo."

"Don't worry, baby. I got you."

Sweat burns as it rolls into his facial scrapes. He is thankful for his ROTC training. That three-mile run every morning is paying off. The Emergency Ward opens to them as he carries her past crowded activity at the door.

"We're finally here, Nikky. We're here."

Hospital attendants guide him to a gurney. He walks alongside as it maneuvers around other injured people. But when the cut on his forehead bleeds into his eyes, dizziness stops him. He sits down just as everything goes black.

***

Elsa almost loses her composure as she moves through the frantic hospital corridors. She got the message at the winery during their Sunday wine tasting. The nursing station directs her to a curtained partition, where she slides the curtain open.

With great relief, she sees her son is on his feet. standing over a gurney where Nikky sleeps with an oxygen mask over her mouth. He is running his hand over her forehead.

Elsa embraces her well-built son who now towers over her.

"Oh, my baby," she says, touching his bandaged eye. "You look much better than I expected." She remembers her friend Elsie's story about her son. Stroking her soon to be daughter-in-law's hand, she asks, "How is Nikky?"

"She has a fractured rib from the cop's stick," Palo says. "The air was knocked out of her and the tear gas caused abrasions in her throat."

"Have you called her parents in Ohio?"

"Not yet."

"I will call them. It will be easier for them to hear the news from me."

"Have you called pop?"

She shakes her head. "I need to catch him at night when he's not around the family conducting business. I came running when I got your call. Besides, it's midnight in Florence."

Palo kisses Nikky's cheek. Then, he guides his mother outside of the closed, curtained quarters.

"Mom, I hate those bastards who did this to her and everything they stand for."

She holds his hand. "Palo, Palo."

"Nikky and I have been talking. I did not want to think about it, but with this afternoon's events..." He wraps his arm around her, "If I stay the course, I'll be headed to Nam."

Elsa's stomach tightens. "Your thoughts about this are well known. You want to talk about this now?"

"Mom, Nikky wants me to quit, too. But if I do, you know I still will be drafted and I'll still be sent there."

"Baby, we can talk this out when your dad gets home."

"I don't want to talk about it anymore. You won't think less of me if Nikky and I go to Canada, will you?"

***

Elsa and Palo maneuver around others in the emergency ward as they see their misery. Relief sweeps over them when they get out into fresh air. They cross from the shade of the hospital building into a wall of hundred-degree heat and onto the parking lot. Another ambulance pulls under the Emergency Ward portal.

"I want to shower and change clothes so I can get back here," Palo says. "I can't leave Nikky alone for long."

"Don't make any plans till your father gets back in a couple of days," Elsa says, spoting her car. "This decision that will impact many people."

***

217

Under the hospital portal, the ambulance driver opens the vehicle's rear doors. Elsie is helped to step out. She hovers over the gurney as it is lowered by two ambulance drivers. On the ground, one of them makes sure the oxygen mask is secure over their patient's face.

"Don't worry, I'm here, I'm here." Elsie says.

It seems like forever to Elsie but its only minutes until Julian hurries through the doors. Freddy and Peter follow their dad. Worry wracks their faces.

"I hate this place," Freddy tells Peter.

They find Elsie. Her eyes are full of tears as she loses herself in her husband's embrace.

"Mama died. Mama's gone. My mommy died," she cries.

Julian sheds tears as he holds his wife. "I'll take care of everything, *mi corazon.*"

Within 30 minutes, Peter sees his aunt Esther walk in with Ambrose and his teenage cousin Diane close behind. He approaches them.

Through bloodshot eyes, he says, "Grandma died."

Diane cries, melting into her daddy's embrace. Esther runs to Elsie, who is holding open the curtain to their mother's partition. A nurse stands over the body of Rose Lovato, making the usual preparations. As the curtain cubicle fills with relatives, she nurse moves back.

"Her heart simply gave out," Elsie says.

Julian, Ambrose, Diane, Freddy and Peter surround Rose as they watch Elsie and Esther place their hands over their mother's face.

"Mommy, I love you," says Esther.

"My mama." cries Elsie.

***

Within the hour, one by one, each family member leaves the cubicle. Ambrose steps out while embracing his trembling wife. Next is Julian holding his crying wife. As they move away, a debonair and tall, white-haired gentleman walks by the family and into the curtained cubicle.

Elsie asks the nurse, "Is that the doctor?"

With a question on her face, the nurse replies, "No, ma'am."

Esther forces her question, "Who is he?"

"He said he was your mother's fiancé."

Both daughters' jaws drop. Elsie rushes to push open the cubicle's curtain. The entire family can see the distinguished gentleman hovering over their mother, crying. They watch him place a ring on Rose's finger.

"Oh, my darling," he whispers.

***

A yellow cab pulls up to the Emergency Ward portal. In fresh clothes, Palo pays the cabby. He winces at his physical condition. The bruise around his eye is swelling, limiting his vision. But as he enters the hallway, he does a double take when he sees a couple of familiar faces.

"Hey, Peter! Freddy!" He senses their grief when he sees both have been crying.

Freddy sees Palo's black eye. "What the hell happened to you?"

"Same thing I heard happened to you a couple of days ago."

Freddy doesn't want to think about it. "Say no more."

With emotion straining his voice, Peter says, "Our grandmother died."

"Rose? Rose died?" Palo sees the brothers fight back tears while nodding. "No. No."

Peter says, "Heart attack."

Palo eyes well with tears. "Rose babysat me and Vic. She was my grandma, too! Oh, man, I'm so, so sorry. If there is anything I can do, just let me know. Vic and I would be honored to help in any way."

He shakes both brothers' hands. As he watches them leave, he remembers Rose. She truly was his grandma, too. It's funny at what he remembers: She taught him how to chop onions into the meat when making the greatest hamburgers.

He finds a pay phone.

Finally, an answer, "Mom, I'm back at the hospital. Afraid I have more bad news..."

Palo's chest churns at his mother's outburst.

Chapter Thirty-Four

One Year Later

Jenoa, Elsa, long-haired Victorio, and the military cut Palo and his wife, Nikky, nervously sit and wait in the family living room during the television network news. When Walter Cronkite breaks for television commercials, Palo quickly stands up and starts pacing back and forth.

"Waiting is driving me crazy," he says.

"Look at it this way," Victorio says. "The draft lottery already happened. That's old news, from eastern standard time. Its two hours old already."

"Remember brother, your turn is next year."

Elsa grips her husband's arm as Palo picks up his framed, newly minted college diploma from the fireplace mantle. He doesn't hide his nervous sarcasm.

"This Business Administration degree will be a great benefit in the jungles of Nam."

"Sit next to me, baby," says Nikky. "The news is coming back on." She pats the couch as Cronkite's graying temples contrast with the blue background.

"The United States Draft Board made its annual lottery draft this morning in Washington DC..."

They watch the news clip of a balding man turning a cage full of egg-styled containers.

Cronkite goes on, "...Three hundred and fifty-two birth dates were mixed by the director. He selected one hundred and twenty-six to be drafted into military service this, the tenth year of the U.S. involvement in southeast Asia..."

Elsa says, "It's always the old men sending the young men off to war."

Her husband adds, "It has been that way throughout history."

Cronkite continues, "...The first birth date was May 21, the one hundred and twenty sixth? November 12. In other news, Watergate conspirators were interrogated by a senate panel of..."

Jenoa turns off the TV.

Palo jumps to his feet. "What about the other hundred and twenty-four birthdays?"

Nikky says, "Let's get a newspaper." Palo grabs Nikky's hand and they rush out the front door.

The convenience store is their first choice. Before the car stops, Nikky is out the door. And before it's parked, she climbs back in, ripping the paper.

"Here it is," she says.

"Please let me look at it." Practically pulling the paper from her hand, he studies the bland print. "There it is: August 18. It's one hundred and twenty seventh. I missed it by the skin of my teeth! One by one, baby, our lives are saved by the luck of the draw!"

Nikky throws herself into her husband's arms. "We don't have to go to Canada!"

"It sounds moot now, baby, but I wouldn't, I couldn't have gone to Canada. Our family's reputation would have been devastated."

Relief floods through them.

***

Spring in the Jemez Mountains enhances the coming summer. Away from the city, temperatures mellow on sheer cliffs cut by the winds of time. The main road—the only one in and out—dips into a valley surrounded with Mother Nature's blossoming forests. A roadside sign reads: Jemez Springs, Population 1200.

As Fred maneuvers his Fiat Spyder convertible through the rustic town, his lady love rests her hand on the inside of his thigh. John Denver's `Rocky Mountain High' plays through the FM radio station. The breeze blows through their heads of shoulder length hair. Her hand moves to his shoulder to run her fingers through his curly hair. With the tip of her forefinger, she traces his long sideburn.

"Just think: less than an hour ago, we were in the concrete forest of downtown Albuquerque."

"Right now," he says, "I can't think of a better place to be with you, baby."

She kisses his cheek. The Fiat passes an old bar in the middle of town. To the left, they roll by one, two, three tourist rest stops with several recreational vehicles already camped out. Smoke from their fires blends into the picturesque surrounding trees.

Across the street from the General Store sits the white, block-long abbey that belongs to Franciscan Catholic nuns. A procession of six black and white habits leave it and walk single file along the main road, like a row of penguins.

Fred's lady friend stands up in the slow-moving car to watch the nuns.

"Baby, what would you say if I told you I once thought about becoming a nun?"

He studies how well she fills out her tight blue jeans and 'Make Love Not War' t-shirt. Her straight brown hair blows in the wind. But, for safety, he wants her to sit back down. He reaches between her legs to pull her back down.

"Patty, oh Patty, let me count the ways how I am happy that you didn't."

She laughs. "How would you like it if I grabbed between your legs?" Her left hand cups his crotch.

He smiles, says nothing, and keeps her hand where she placed it until the first stop light in town. When nuns cross the road in front of them, she pulls her hand away.

"What? Afraid they're going to slap your hand with a ruler?"

They both laugh.

As they drive to the far side of town, the afternoon sunshine turns to shadows. Once again, the road cuts through two mountainous cliffs. Linking the sides is an overpass. Fred drives under the bridge. To their left, they see a large mountain lake.

Patty says, "It looks like the mountain run-off is good this year." The Fiat hugs the road, blending one switch-back into the next.

She warns, "The turn off is coming up." Fred slows down. She points to a mail box. "Here. Turn here."

A dirt road appears between strands of small gauge barbed-wire fence. Fred slows the sports car to a crawl as he turns onto a road that cuts through the fresh, thick forest of pines and shrubbery.

"This is so beautiful. Smell that clean air." He takes in a deep breath.

Patty says, "Stop the car here."

Fred does so. He knows what Patty has planned as she brings her tee shirted breasts to his face. With her toothy grin, she slowly reaches for the locket around her neck. Her dainty hands are perfect for snapping it open to pull out two small fingertip sized tabs of blue paper. She carefully places one in the middle of her tongue then swallows. Then she says, "Open, baby." He does, and she puts the other in his mouth. "Keep on driving for a bit."

"Anything you want baby," he says. Patty holds her hand out to touch the branches in amazement as they slowly roll by.

"Dad talks about selling all of this, but doesn't. Mom won't let him."

Fred laughs as the LSD starts to kick in. The dirt road in front of him widens, then narrows, then widens again. "Of course." Soon both pull up to an idle log cabin. Fred looks up its red stone chimney as it telescopes into the sky. "That's the tallest man-made thing around here," he says under his breath.

Without opening her door, Patty jumps out of the convertible. She pulls out her key and instantaneously steps up onto the wooden porch. And as Fred gets out of the car, Patty starts laughing while unlocking the front door and entering. He pulls out his satchel and her three heavy bags from the back seat. The surrounding forest greenery suddenly brightens. So he drops the bags onto firm porch timbers. He searches for the front entrance. He explores around the cabin's long, telescoping side wall before back stepping to finally discovering the front entrance.

He shouts through the front door, "You never told me your parents owned a castle in these mountains..."

As he enters, his jaw gaps open before grinning widely. Through the bright sunlit shades of pink, yellow, orange then dark red interior lighting, he enjoys the view. With only shoes on and a blanket over her shoulder, she stands naked across the room. She murmurs, "I'm a bird. Do you want to hold my pretty feathers?"

He quickly shucks everything but his shoes. Patty darts out the back door laughing, flapping her blanket wings. He follows, of course. They run through the forest, buck naked to Mother Nature. He chases her deeper into the never-ending foliage. He figures she should know the way back. She taunts him deeper into the woods by waving her beautiful white feathered wings, weaving and ducking behind almost every tree. Her laugh has turned into a siren's call.

Finally, she tosses the blanket on an open space, cushioned by leaves and between two fallen tree logs. Only then does she decide to let him catch her.

***

April 25, 1972

The wind blasts full bore on this sunny, summer afternoon. Middle-aged Elsie and Elsa ride side by side in one of the winery's pickup delivery trucks through the west side of Albuquerque. As in the old days, Elsa is again behind the wheel. But this time the door panels read: Domenici Winery.

"The last time we made deliveries, we were teenagers," remembers Elsie.

Both laugh at the memory while perspiring from the heat in the closed, wind-protected cabin. Elsa reaches for the air conditioner switch.

"But this time we have cooling."

Both gaze through their windows as they cross the slow flowing Rio Grande on the Route 66 bridge.

Elsie says, "Take a right here to Tingley Beach. It's been a long time since I've seen it."

Soon they pass the abandoned, mile long ditch. A few ducks and geese waddle over the slimy pond.

"This is not what I remember," says Elsa.

Almost under her breath, Elsie says, "It used to be so beautiful. Now, look at it. It makes me sad." She shakes her head. "I remember being splashed by passing speed boats as I laid on the beach and watching gorgeous guys dive into the water. I could almost cry."

Elsa drives away and toward the zoo. "That was a life-time ago, Elsie."

"The polio scare of the early fifties did it in."

Elsa steers through the old, small streets near the zoo. "The city will bring it back to its heyday, some day."

"We should live so long?"

Soon enough, they see the zoo off in the distance. Elsie is silent as Elsa parks across the street. They share the same memories of what they see now and don't see. They watch as a tractor shovels the last piles of rubble into a truck.

"Right after the war they leveled the barracks," Elsie says. "They are only now getting around to building the new Albuquerque Fire Academy."

They see that the only thing remaining from the old camp is the old guard tower. Elsa starts up the truck and rolls a little further down the road, slightly past the zoo. They see more tractors doing their thing across the street from the zoo's entrance.

Elsie continues down memory lane. "Again, after the war, they renamed that old ball field to the Dukes Baseball Field. Since they built the new stadium by the university, they're leveling this one." They watch till the last dump truck drives away.

"People don't want to know what was here before," says Elsa.

"Should they?"

"Jenoa says he has no urge to come to the zoo. It's the only Albuquerque memory he does not want to relive."

They slowly drive by several side-by-side land graders that level the ground clean of any hint of what was there before. Finally, Elsa starts up the pickup and drives away.

"They say they are going to build a little league field and some tennis courts."

"Tennis?" Elsa steers the truck down 10th street, away from their memories. "I always wanted to play tennis."

Soon they pass Lead, then Coal as they approach the stop sign at Gold. Both know what Gold Street means to their trip down memory lane.

Elsa asks her friend, "Want to?"

"It's been so long and we're here. We might as well."

Elsa turns right onto Gold. They look left and right at the new buildings.

"Ever since Urban Renewal came through, more than half of the downtown has been rebuilt," Elsie tells Elsa as she continues past 6th Street, then 4th. "When Mama got bought out, she got more money than she ever had in her life." As they approach 2nd Street, "Now a hotel stands over our old house, and the entire block of 3rd Street for that matter."

Elsa slows the truck, practically coming to a stop in front of the old bakery, where the sign now reads, Bavaria on the Rio Grande.

"Since living in the far north valley, coming downtown has been impossible. This is the first time I've seen this place since I've been back. Can you believe that?"

Both people walk in and out of the building.

Elsie says, "And since I live in the heights, coming downtown has always seemed too far... At least they still serve."

"What did you expect? Although it definitely misses the old Santoni touch." Elsa goes silent while thinking, "Ah mama, no papa..."

They hear honking behind them.

"Want to get some coffee?"

Elsa pulls into the space to her right, and takes a deep breath.

"It's been almost thirty years," she says as they cross the street.

An exciting gentleman holds the door open for them. They acknowledge him with smiles. They stand in the entrance and marvel at the upgrades of the half-full dining room.

"They knocked back the bakery walls and extended the dining area," says Elsie.

"Isn't it lighter in here?" She grabs Elsie's arm while sniffing. "Does it or does it not smell the same?"

Elsie opens her eyes wider. "My God, yes. It's like memory flashbacks galore."

They chose a table by the window.

"Do you remember who we served every morning at this table?" asks Elsa. Elsie shakes her head. "Don't you remember Mr. Stromberg?"

Instant recollection floods Elsie's face, "I sure do. I also remember my old principal, Mr. Baca. Elsa you've got quite a memory."

"Whatever happened to that sweet old man, Mr. Stromberg?" asks Elsa.

Elsie says, "He and his family opened a successful chain of men's clothes stores around town."

A young waitress approaches their table.

"A coffee and pastry would be nice."

"Me, too."

The waitress leaves pastry menus while going to get things for her new customers.

"She must be as old as we were when we came back from Los Angeles," says Elsa.

They watch a couple of blonde men with kitchen aprons walk down the steps. One has long hair, the other is balding. Each carries a clipboard. They disappear behind the swinging doors of the kitchen.

"This dining room does seem bigger," says Elsie.

"It's because they took out the glass display cases."

"Oh yeah."

The waitress brings the tray of coffee to the table.

"Here you go, ladies." She places cups on the table. "Have you selected a dessert?"

"I do not see any Italian sweets," says Elsa.

"We are a German bakery. We have lovely strudels, especially cherry."

"German?" says Elsa.

Elsie asks, "How long have you been open as a German bakery?"

"It seems like forever. Papa and mama came here after the war. Saved up and bought this bakery. Me and my brothers were raised in this place."

Elsie reads the name on the waitress's badge, and says, "Theresa, you see a couple of older ladies in front of you. When we were your age, we were waitresses here."

"Really?"

"It was Santoni's Italian Bakery then."

"It's a pleasure to meet you ladies." As if remembering something, she asks, "Santoni's Bakery?" She pulls over and empty chair. "May I join you?" They nod. "I remember some old Santoni's menus around here somewhere."

"I'm Elsie Arias, but I was Elsie Lovato back then."

"I'm the former Elsa Santoni. My papa and mama were the owners."

"Your folks must have sold the place to my papa and mama."

The blonde man walks back in. "Theresa?" he says.

"Vaughn," she says. "Vaughn, come here."

He takes off his apron. "We have an order back there," he summons.

Theresa says, "Ladies, this is my big brother Vaughn." She explains who these ladies are.

A doubting and strange expression overcomes his face. As Theresa leaves the chair, big brother Vaughn fills in.

"It is a pleasure to meet you," he says. "Papa mentioned the Italian bakery. They kept the name Santoni's for several years until the German stigma wore off, when they named it Bavaria on the Rio Grande.

"Apparently, we worked here before you were born," Elsa says.

"Me, my older brother, and Theresa were born and raised in this place," says Vaughn.

Vaughn's attention gets redirected by the balding man. "Excuse me ladies, my older sibling calls."

Vaughn exchanges are few words with him after leaving the table.

"Greetings ladies, my name is Gustav," he says. "I am one of the owners of Bavaria on the Rio Grande."

"Please join us. I am Elsie this is Elsa."

Elsa says, "We just learned that your folks bought this place from my folks back when."

"So you are a Santoni?"

"Papa and mama escaped *Il Dulce* here before the war. This was a tortilla factory when we took it over."

"We worked our way through high school here," adds Elsie. "During the war, Elsa's papa and mama, God rest their souls, lived upstairs and worked downstairs."

Theresa pulls up another chair. "Upstairs is the office now. But me and Gustav were brought up in the cramped space up there. When I came along, they moved us all into the house."

"Do you still have your parents?" asks Elsa.

"They are alive and well and in Sun City, Arizona."

Vaughn joins them again.

Gustav laughs, "For many years, we had an Italian name that served German."

Everyone at the table laughs just as a customer walks through the door. The three operators of the Bavaria on the Rio Grande move to their stations.

"Did you hear that, Elsie?" As the front door closes, the bells chime again. "That's the same bell we had."

"Despite how much things change around here, others stay the same." Both look around. "It appears that your pop found a good buyer for Santoni's."

"Yes, he did. Yes he did."

Elsie glances at her watch. "We better get going."

***

Elsa drives the pickup onto the New Mexico State Fair Grounds. She parks as close to Tingley Coliseum as she can. As they walk toward the building Elsie says, "Look around. Gals are outnumbering guys at least four to one."

Elsa turns in her ticket. "That's why Jenoa didn't want to come. It's a show for us."

"Julian didn't want to pay a ten dollar a ticket for him."

"They didn't complain about paying twenty for each of us to see Liberace in Vegas."

Elsie replies, "Go figure."

"Men," comments Elsa.

Both ladies cannot hold back their disappointment when they see where their seats are located. They are behind a steel beam off the top row of the auditorium, located on the far opposite side of the stage.

"This place was built for ten thousand rodeo fans, not the King," says Elsie.

"I have been looking forward to this since we got the tickets." They sit behind the steel beam. "These crappy seats aren't going to ruin this."

"I told you about the last time I saw him."

"A million times, darling. A million times," says Elsa.

The lights in the auditorium go out as the stage lights go up. Applause grows. The orchestra starts the King's famous grand overture. Lights start flashing. He walks on to stage center. Deafening female screams echo off the walls. His white jumpsuit reflects an array of spotlight colors; his tall collar is tucked under his long jet-black hair.

Elsie and Elsa can't help themselves. They stand up as the King sings his slow, romantic ballad, Love Me Tender.

"Albuquerque, it's great to be back," he says after the song. "But...I don't know if I will be able to sing tonight." Sighs of disappointment. "Today I ate some of your chili. Wow, that's hot stuff!" The auditorium fills with laughter. Suddenly, the orchestra goes into the high energy of Jailhouse Rock.

Sitting again, the girls' feet start dancing. They smile.

His next song, One Night with You causes female swoons mixed with cheers. Elsie and Elsa cautiously leave their seats for vacant closer ones.

After several more songs, and while he sings, It's Now or Never, the ladies are seated a quarter of the auditorium closer.

"I can hardly hear him," says Elsa.

"Whatever excuse you need, I'm with you." They laugh like school girls as they move to closer seats.

When he starts, Are You Lonesome Tonight, the lights go out except for a single spotlight on him—which goes out at the end of it. The lights go back on as he throws his handkerchief into the front row of outstretched hands. The women go crazy with screams as he walks off stage.

After the intermission, the ladies find empty seats half-way to the stage.

The sax player kicks into the famous lick that eases the King into Return to Sender followed by You Look Like an Angel, The Chapel, and The Ghetto, and Elsie and Elsa find themselves only a quarter of the auditorium away from the stage.

"He's so handsome," says Elsa.

"He's not only gotten older, he's gotten better."

As he dangles another handkerchief, Elsa watches as Elsie reach out.

Elsa says, "That is why Julian didn't want to come."

Both laugh.

"And I'm glad he didn't."

He sings, Burning Love.

The ladies cannot see anyone sitting down. They continue hand-over-hand down the railing, closer and closer. Energy in the room is building.

"Ladies and Gentlemen, my last song is from back when I first met you all." The drummer brushes strokes, piano keys tinkle, and the guitar adds familiar licks. He sings, Heartbreak Hotel.

Elsie and Elsa find themselves on the railing directly to the side stage. As he ends his show, he walks side to side of the stage taking bows before walking off. The auditorium fills with deafening screams and applause. Both ladies bang their hands together wildly, fighting hard to hold back screams. The energy brings him back onto stage to a wilder response.

The orchestra kicks into the encore song when his body starts shaking to All Shook Up. The audience screams. The orchestra continues playing when he finishes. He waves goodbye, walking from side to side onstage and takes his final bow.

Elsie and Elsa hang over a railing overlooking the back stage. They watch him step from back stage down into a black limousine. As the limo rolls away, the place is filled with screams. Finally, a voice over the intercom vibrates off the cavernous walls: "Elvis has left the building."

***

ELSIE AND ELSA

August 9, 1974

Fred drops his keys, pocket protector with pens, and a slide rule on the coffee table.

"Patty, I'm home," he calls out but no one answers. He assumes she is at her mother's house, where she spends a lot of time lately when he is at work.

He sees it's after five and knows Cronkite is still on. Switching on the new color TV, he flops down on the couch. When he props his feet on the coffee table, he kicks off one of Patty's magazines. He glances at its cover to see a pregnant lady.

Cronkite reports as Fred views the back lawn of the White House.

"President and Betty Ford escorted Mr. and Mrs. Nixon to the helicopter to demonstrate the American peaceful exchange of power." Nixon waves goodbye as the helicopter door closes behind him. Moments later, footage of Air Force One is shown taking off. "Nixon took one last loop around Washington DC in route back home to California. Hours later, as Air Force One flew over New Mexico, the resigned President became citizen Nixon."

Fred mutters, "Good riddance."

Cronkite's final message: "And that's the way it is..."

***

The doors to the University of New Mexico's Popejoy Hall open wide for intermission. Throngs of theater goers flood into the tile and marble expanse of its lobby.

"I love it. Love it," says one lady.

A teenage girl says to her mother, "Groovy."

An older couple nod in approval. "The costumes are perfect," she says.

A young man sings to the lady at his side, "Camelot, Camelot..."

Two couples hurry out. Elsie and Elsa are followed out by Jenoa and Julian.

"Your Victorio is cute as the Spanish Knight of the Round Table," Elsie says.

"And Peter looks darling in those tights dancing around in the chorus. He's prominent."

Elsie beams with pride, "He's been rehearsing that solo for weeks."

Elsa adds, "That goatee makes him look so mature."

Elsie's smile turns to a frown. "Now that I don't like, he's only fifteen."

Julian rolls his eyes.

"Soon he'll be a grown man?" says Elsa.

Her friend responds, "I don't have to like my baby growing up, do I?"

"Victorio is already working on his next show. He's going to play Jesus in Jesus Christ Superstar," she says. "But, I know what you mean. He wants to go off to New York and try getting on Broadway." Elsa frowns.

Julian gestures to Jenoa by bringing two `V' pointed fingers to his lips, then pointing toward Elsie. Jenoa does the same to Julian.

"I need a cigarette," says Elsie.

Julian looks at Jenoa with a smiling validation.

"Me, too," says Elsa. "Let's step outside." The men follow.

"The Albuquerque Civic Light Opera always does good shows," says Elsie.

"And it looks like we're going to be seeing more of them," says Elsa.

Chapter Thirty-Five

The Next Summer

Greenery from hundred-year oak and pine trees define this north Rio Grande valley upscale neighborhood. A white banner stretches over the front entrance sign: WELCOME TO DOMENICI WINERY TEN YEAR ANNIVERSARY.

Valet attendants guide each automobile, quickly diminishing parking spaces. Arriving patrons stroll through the luxuriant vineyards and enjoy the Venetian statue fountain that pours into gathering ponds.

In the far corner of the estate, a small makeshift amphitheater holds rows of padded folding chairs. The stage features a white grand piano with an open top. A stage hand makes final adjustments to the light and sound equipment.

The line of tables are staffed by attendants who pour endless Domenici wine varieties into glass goblets for its guests, who sniff, then savor their selection of white through red.

As he greets his patrons in a three-piece suit, Palo keeps an eye on his servers. A smiling patron with an entourage of suits approaches while carrying a glass of white. Palo gulps at who the guest is.

"Congratulations on your event, Mr. Domenici. It is one of the top events on the city's social calendar this year."

Palo, can't help but show admiration for this guest. He fights to maintain his composure. "My family appreciates you joining us tonight, Mr. Senator. I know all of the Domenici's support your campaign."

"Thank you for your confidence," says the smiling Senatorial candidate.

"Please call me Palo. We appreciate your support of our vineyard opening, Mr. Senator. Oh, pardon me. I realize you are only running for the Senate. But I believe it is a foregone conclusion that you will win."

"Call me Jack," says the guest. We are grateful to have your family's support as well."

"New Mexico Senator Jack Harrison Schmitt," says Palo. "That sounds great for someone who was the second to last man to walk on the moon."

"We are impressed that your family has built the largest winery in our city, especially in such a brief time. We are looking forward to your show."

As the entourage walks away, Palo feels a tap on his shoulder. "Aunty Elsie! I am happy you could make it." He embraces her.

"We couldn't miss this big night." She says.

Julian is with Elsie, cradling the newest addition to the Arias family.

"Uncle Julian, I am happy to see you!"

Palo smiles into the baby's tiny face. "Hello, baby Arias."

"Congratulations to the new General Manager of Domenici Wineries," says Julian, grasping Palo's shoulder. "We're proud of you."

"Coming from you, that means a lot because you've been here since the beginning." Palo sees their son Freddy. "Good to see again, buddy. Hello, Patty. How's the new mommy?"

"Sleepy," she says, taking his hand, "Thank you for inviting us."

"I saw Esther and Ambrose a few minutes ago." Palo says to Elsie as he glances around. We've arranged special seats up front for you," he adds. "Peter's backstage calling the shots for us."

Julian smiles at his wife. "I still wonder where my youngest kid ever got the show biz bug."

Palo nods. "I am happy to have him managing the show. My hands are full out here."

Elsie asks, "Young man, where are your folks?"

"They're still up in the house getting ready."

A server approaches. "Mr. Domenici, Mr. Domenici?"

As the baby starts to struggle, Elsie hands the bundle to her daughter-in-law, then embraces Palo. "Well, Mr. Domenici we'll take our seats."

"Taste some of our wines," Palo says, stepping away to respond to his employee.

Patty pushes the stroller away as her husband walks behind. Elsie follows. As Julian walks behind his wife, he fondles her posterior. Elsie smiles.

***

Overlooking the forthcoming spectacle from their bedroom balcony a couple of acres away, Elsa and Jenoa Domenici again study their heaven on earth. They display love for each other through glances. They raise their crystal goblets. She clinks her white Chardonnay to his red Merlot.

Jenoa wraps his arm around his wife's girlish figure. He whispers, "*A bella, bella mi senorina.*"

Without warning, he slams his empty goblet to the floor. She follows suit with hers.

***

Darkness causes the patrons to find and settle into their seats. A solitary spotlight focuses on the centered white grand piano, purposely leaving its keyboard in the shadows.

Behind the staging area, seventeen-year-old Peter Arias oversees all of the activity. Wearing dress slacks, white shirt and undone tie, he speaks into his hand-held, walkie talky.

"Audience manager, please tell Palo Domenici it's time to come backstage. Spotlight, hold that setting. To all, five minutes to show time."

He notices his star performer, young Victorio Domenici, mentally focusing on his approaching concert. His fingers are outstretched as he mentally practices. Next to him is his wardrobe manager, Victorio's sister-in-law, Nikky, who adjusts his white tux, jacket, and tie. She brushes his styled brown hair over his shoulders.

Again, through the walkie talky: "Spotlight, throw that red light on the piano keys." directs Peter.

He can hear the audience simmering down in anticipation as Palo approaches. From the darkness far behind stage, Peter sees the audience's empty two front and center chairs.

"Tell your parents we are ready for them," he tells Palo as he hands him a slip of paper.

Palo nods as he turns toward the house studying the intro notes along the way. As he is about to turn the front door knob, it is opened by Jenoa and Elsa.

"Mommi, poppi, we're ready."

Jenoa nods and leads Elsa out, arm in arm. Nikky joins her husband Palo and immediately adjusts his suit and hairstyle. He kisses his adoring wife and pats her beginning baby bump.

Peter tells his crew: "Spotlight, here we go. As rehearsed, throw the light around the audience, then focus it on Mr. & Mrs. Domenici and follow them to their seats."

As the white beam focuses on the couple, the audience stands in waves to applaud the approaching couple. Jenoa and Elsa walk to their seats. As applause grows louder, Elsa's arm tightens around her husband's. They reach their seats, next to the applauding Elsie and Julian, Esther and Ambrose. Jenoa joins the applause with the audience and directs focus to the stage. As they sit, Elsa grabs her friend Elsie's hand.

Backstage, Peter watches Palo give a last second rehearsal to his crib note introduction. He taps Palo's shoulder. "Ready?"

Palo nods.

"Spotlight, kill the spot. Turn on full stage lights." As the stage floods with bright light, he tells Palo, "You're on."

Palo flashes a smile and walks on stage toward the center microphone to loud applause. Peter looks for his star performer still standing far off. He calmly approaches him.

"Okay, buddy, let's do it to it."

He guides Victorio to the side stage.

"Ladies and Gentlemen, my name is Palo Domenici, General Manager of Domenici Wineries." He pauses for applause to die down. "On behalf of my family, we welcome you to this benefit for the UNM Children's Hospital. We are also celebrating the sale of the first bottle from Albuquerque's Domenici

Winery." He bows to his mom and dad as applause rises and falls. "We hope you enjoyed your wine this evening—because our show is about to start!"

Elsa takes Elsie's arm into hers. "Thank you for being here."

Elsie pats her friend's hand. "Of course we'd be here. There is no place else on earth to be tonight," she says. She pulls out her golden chain necklace with the gold-plated rivet, the memento from their Rosey the Riviter days.

With a matching smile, Elsa displays her gold necklace and rivet.

A softer spotlight covers Palo head to foot. "As I look among you, I see family, friends and business associates. Thank you for coming." Palo applauds them.

"We know who our attraction is tonight. I've known him all my life, since the days back in Tuscany, Italy." Palo looks over his smiling audience. "I remember when dad first had all that grass out there planted. He got mad at my brother and me when we wasted no time wrestling over it, tearing up some of it." He watches his dad nod. "After tonight's performance, my brother is leaving Albuquerque for a national tour and to celebrate his debut recording. We are so proud of him. So, for the next hour or so, please welcome to the Domenici Winery stage, my baby brother, Victorio Domenici!"

As Victorio steps onto stage, Palo greets him with a brotherly bear hug before stepping off stage. Standing, the audience breaks into the biggest round of applause of the night, so far. Victorio moves to stage center, and bows.

"Ladies and Gentlemen, thank you for coming to my family's winery this evening. As you look around, please know this winery is the culmination of a dream brought here from Tuscany, Italy. My father Jenoa met my mother Elsa here in Albuquerque. He actually worked these fields as an Italian prisoner of war before he was sent to work in my grandparent's Italian bakery on Gold Street downtown." His smile grows wider.

"And now he is a brand new American citizen!" The audience applauds again. "I now dedicate my first selection to him."

He steps around to the piano.

From behind the stage, Peter whispers into his walkie talky. "Stand by... as he sits, kill the stage lights." They go out. "Now put one spotlight on his hands when he places them on the keys."

Victorio's fingers dance across the keys from one end of the keyboard to the other. He does it again, building more flare. He suddenly goes into a soft transition of a familiar melody: The Star-Spangled Banner.

Jenoa is on his feet with his hand over his heart. The audience follows suit, and continues applauding approval of the opening selection. Within a few measures, the recently sworn in American citizen, Jenoa Domenici, wipes a tear away with his sleeve. He again puts his hand over his heart. Elsa does likewise. So then do Julian and Elsie, Esther and Ambrose, followed by their offspring. Audience members do the same. So, during this warm summer evening under the clear star-lit sky, they all stand with hands over their hearts.

***

August 1976

Fredrick Arias sits in an outer office waiting for a job interview. He thumbs through a technical magazine. He wipes his hand over his bristly crew cut, barbered only yesterday. He picks at his threadbare suit and tie. Patty carefully ironed his white shirt this morning.

This will be his tenth job interview since graduating from computer school several months ago.

Pop got his first job interview where he works at Kirtland Base, but they had a six month waiting list for openings. He tried the city, county, and three banks. All he learned was how old and set in their ways and provincial their systems are. They all seemed insulted when he mentioned how they could modernize and increase their profit for less capital investment.

But now he and Patty are excited. This is the first time he's been called for a follow up interview.

The door beside him opens. A young, bearded man stands in the door-way—different than the guy who interviewed him before.

"Mr. Arias?"

"Yes, sir."

"Please come in. And kill the sir. Just call me Bill."

Bill signals for Fred to sit at the chair in front of his desk. Let me read this resume again," he says.

Fred watches him lean back into his chair and prop his legs on top of his desk. He becomes self-conscious about his suit. It seems like a futile effort when compared to Bill, who wears blue jeans torn at the knee, with tennis shoes with no socks. Fred wipes his hand over his clean-shaven face as he can see the blonde beard this guy has.

"It's very impressive, Fred, very."

"Thank you, sir."

"There you go again with the sir."

"Thank you, Bill."

"My partner Paul interviewed you before. He said you have the technical expertise we are looking for. I want to see if you can fit into this company's psychology, the way our company thinks."

"Ask me questions," is all Fred can think to say.

"We are a very young software company. We think the way things are, our customers need to move into the next generation..."

"I agree," Fred says. "The established school of thought is that the status quo changes every ten years. But I think practices should be implemented when new technical innovations are proven reliable. Which can be every two, five or even ten years."

Bill looks interested.

"Could interest you, Fred, that this company is doing just that..."

Fred sits up straighter.

"There is an invention—call it an innovation—about to hit the market. Have you heard of the Micro Instrumentation and Telemetry Systems' Altair 8800?"

"Yes, I just read about the Altair 8800 in Popular Electronics."

"Henry Edward Roberts, whom I call Ed, has devised a box of switches the size of a small suitcase, if you can imagine that. He has condensed a room full of equipment into a computer that will fit on your desktop."

"That kind of innovation is what excites me."

"Like Edison's light bulb, which was invented in Menlo Park, New Jersey, this private desk top computer, for a lack of a better description was invented here in Albuquerque. It's the reason my partner and I moved here from back East to start this company."

Fred says, "He told me you guys quit Harvard to come here to develop the software to run it."

Bill studies Fred again, then picks up his resume. "I see that you have a wife and baby?"

Fred nods with a smile. "And a new one on the way."

"Congratulations. However, you see, Fred we were just rejected for local bank funding."

"Fools. You will make them regret that someday."

"Possibly, but…reluctantly, this has caused us to accept out of state funding which will require moving the company."

Fred heart sinks.

"So how would your wife feel about Seattle, Washington?"

"You're talking about leaving New Mexico?"

"Yes."

"Our parents would not like it. But Patty and I would love a chance to escape."

Bill looks again at Fred's resume. "We're definitely moving to Seattle and we have to hit the street running up there. Until we get up to speed there, how would your Patty feel about receiving New Mexico pay up in Seattle? We'd throw in company stock options in the meantime."

"Sir? Uh, Bill? Are you offering me the job?"

"If your Patty agrees, I am."

Fred stands and offers his hand across the desk. "Well, Bill, we accept."

"Call me tomorrow for details."

In seconds, Fred is out the door and dancing a jig. He can't wait to tell Patty. The only problem is how their parents will take it.

As the office door into hallway closes, he reads the name of the company that gave him his first computer job out of college: Microsoft.

Chapter Thirty-Six

The following October

Despite it being almost 5 AM on this chilly Autumn morning, grasses on the field are summertime green. Thousands of eager people in thick winter coats and caps are here on the north edge of town.

After moving all over town for years, the first festival held on this over-sized field is welcomed by all. Hundreds of multicolored hot air balloons, some waving their national flags, prepare for launch.

Early arrivals watch crews pulling giant canvas sacks and gondolas from trucks. Others already have balloons rolled out flat onto the grass while making sure their creases are straight as they connect their gondolas. As observers go further the sound becomes deafening. Propane gas burners drive hot air into balloon envelopes, their light revealing a rainbow of color against the dawn sky. The onslaught of thousands of fans watch erect balloons bobble in zero wind as crews work to keep their gondolas tethered to the ground until they hear word pass down through the crews.

"It's a go for launch!"

As soon as the sun peaks over the eastern Sandia Mountains, fully erect balloons are released from their tethers, their crews waving goodbye to fans.

Two excited men walk with their ladies. Jenoa and Julian, Elsa and Elsie try to control their wide-eyed enthusiasm as balloons around them go up and away. They wave to the crews, even though they don't know them.

"I can't wait," says Elsa.

"I've been looking forward to this ever since the kids bought these tickets for my birthday," says Elsie.

"Julian," says Elsa, "You know it's too late to change your mind. Elsie asked me to join her when you said no way. You know that, don't you?"

Julian nods.

They continue walking until they find the one they are looking for.

Elsa points to a balloon that is almost fully inflated. "There it is! There it is!" she cries.

All four stop to watch. The crew aims its gas burner directly into the balloon's envelope thereby blowing hot air into it. The ladies' mouths are open as their balloon bobbles to full attention. The crew tethers the gondola to the ground. Only then do the four notice the roadrunner emblazoned across the envelope. The men reflect their amazement as the rising sun blazes yellow and orange colors through them.

A crew member helps the ladies over as he drops wicker steps in front of the gondola. Without hesitancy, the two life-time gal pals quickly approach The Roadrunner. One by one, they are helped up the steps and into the gondola.

They and the pilot introduce themselves.

He asks, "Are you aeronauts ready for flight?"

Elsa shouts for all to hear, "We are ready for launch!"

The pilot nods. The crew releases the tethers. The balloon slowly lifts up and away. The pilot attaches a roll of cloth to the front of the gondola. Soon, old glory's red, white and blue rolls out and lightly flaps in the breeze.

The ladies wave to the men below and watch as they become tiny in the distance. Both look wide-eyed at the beauty of the landscape below.

Julian grins as Jenoa pulls a bottle from his vest. They know the tradition. Upon completion of their virgin ride, as their wives set foot on the ground, they will be sprayed with champagne. Both men laugh.

Elsie and Elsa are amazed at how silent it is to float in the air. They take in the mountains to the east, the desert to west, planes landing and taking off from the airport and base to the south. As they float above the Rio Grande, the elevation gives them brief views of Santa Fe.

"Elsie, did you ever think we'd be doing this when we met back in high school?"

Elsie shakes her head. "Not until the kids got me these tickets a couple of months ago."

The ladies put their arms around each other as they watch the toy-sized population below start another day, old glory rippling in the breeze.